Last Seen

by

Jo A. Hiestand

The McLaren Mysteries

Last Seen

Cover Art by *Angela Anderson*

The Wild Rose Press, Inc.
PO Box 708
Adams Basin, NY 14410-0708
Visit us at www.thewildrosepress.com

Publishing History: previously published by
L&L Dreamspell, 2011 as *Swan Song*
First Mainstream Mystery Edition, 2015
Print ISBN 978-1-5092-0169-3
Digital ISBN 978-1-5092-0170-9

The McLaren Mysteries
Published in the United States of America

The footsteps moved faster this time, the crunch of gravel firm and headed toward McLaren.

He kept the booth between them, creeping as quickly as he could to the opposite wall as he corkscrewed around. The figure evidently didn't hear, his light and gaze on the ground. When the light suddenly snapped off and only the rumble of thunder sounded, McLaren froze. Should he remain there or move? What was the person doing?

Despite the warmth of the night, perspiration soaked McLaren's shirt. His pulse throbbed in his throat. He considered tiptoeing around the booth's corner and jumping the man, but if he mistook the man's position, coming face-on, and the man saw him…

The gravel shifted and the steps turned the way they'd come. McLaren stepped back as the light played into the lot. When the figure cleared the booth, McLaren lunged forward.

His fingers reached for the man's clothing as he found himself falling. The torches crashed to the ground, and McLaren and his adversary were plunged into darkness. Arms and legs thrashed as both men fought for control. McLaren grabbed a wrist but felt it turn and slip from his grasp. His palm pushed against the ground to keep him upright, but he crumpled as a shoe kicked his side. He fell in a rush of pain and blackness.

Dedications

To Paul,
in gratitude for keeping Dena's ordeal real
and McLaren's reactions believable
~*~
To David,
in thankfulness for your comment
about McLaren's personality,
and for prompting me to steer him back to his old self.
I still don't know how he wandered.
~*~
To Chris,
in appreciation for helping me think through
the pages of mess
and finding a way out of the morass

Characters

Kent Harrison: Music teacher and folk singer
Sheri Harrison: Kent's ex-wife, tour guide at Tutbury
    Castle
Fay Larkin: Kent's fiancée
Clark MacKay: Curator at Tutbury Castle
Ellen Fairfield: Curator at Rawlton Hall
Aaron Unsworth: Kent's neighbor, president of local
    Kent Harrison fan club
Fraser Unsworth: Aaron's teenaged son
Dave Morley: Kent's singing partner, clerk in a music
    shop
Ron Pennell: Herbalist
Trevor Pennell: History teacher
Lorene Guard: Kent's student at school
Booth Wragg: Lorene's boyfriend

~*~

Michael McLaren: former police detective,
    Staffordshire Constabulary
Jamie Kydd: friend and police detective, Derbyshire
    Constabulary
Dena Ellison: McLaren's girlfriend
Gwen Hulme: McLaren's sister
Jerry Hulme: Gwen's husband
Cheryl Kerrigan: Home Office forensic pathologist
Charlie Harvester: McLaren's former colleague,
    Staffordshire Constabulary

Chapter One

A wave of July heat rose from the flattened grass underfoot, smelling of dry vegetation and parched earth. An odor common to every part of Tutbury Castle that day. Dena breathed deeply, reveling in the scent. For a moment she imagined she was in Portugal's Algarve region with McLaren, visiting the nature reserve and strolling along the sunbaked beach. That wonderful, all-too-brief holiday…

"So, where was the body found? Actually here at the castle?"

The question jerked Dena back to the present, and she blinked.

Dena's friend Gwen Hulme picked up the hem of her cotton blouse, damp from perspiration, and waved it slightly. Her hand went to her neck and she grabbed a handful of her hair, holding it out so the breeze could cool her skin. She pushed her sunglasses farther up her nose and looked into the crowd. "God, it's hot. This crowd is awful. No air can circulate in this space with all these people. They should've had a set number of tickets to sell to keep the attendance down. Where's Jerry? I thought he was with us." She seemed already to have lost interest in the original topic.

Dena stared at the fragment of tower to their left, a remnant of the castle's glory days, uncertain if the swinging man was really there or her imagination had rigged the sight. "Jerry? I think he left us. Or we lost him. Whatever it was, I last saw him at that herbal booth. I didn't know he went in for natural health stuff."

"I think that was merely something he passed on his way to something else. He most likely is getting a beer. Or ale. Or whatever he can find. He'll probably have to settle for some drink brewed in bygone Times."

"Would you like anything, Gwen? We don't have to be back home at any set time, do we?" Even though she was dying to talk to Michael, to get him interested in investigating again... She avoided Gwen's glance, suddenly feeling foolish for her phone message to McLaren. It was best to leave her feelings on the subject unsaid. Trying to get McLaren interested in another cold murder case would probably produce more animosity than enthusiasm. Still, that cold case last month had pried him out of his protective shell—started him back on the path to becoming human again. "I suppose we could fan out to look for him, but in this crowd, it's probably hopeless. Maybe he'll meet us at the car." She let the blade of grass flutter to the ground.

Gwen released her blouse and waved to the man approaching through the dispersing crowd. "Call off the bloodhounds, Dena. Here he is."

"I don't think he found his beer. He still looks thirsty."

Gwen snorted. "I've concluded it's something he was born with. Jerry! We were about to start a search for you."

The brown-haired man alternately looked at his watch and some men dressed in armor clanking past. "What? Sorry. I was longer than I thought I'd be. You two ready to go?"

"I guess so. Unless you want to see the jousting."

He shook his head, glancing ahead to the profusion of booths. "Not particularly. It's probably a re-mix of yesterday. I enjoyed it then, but I don't need to see it again."

"Just asking. We may as well take in everything we want to as long as we're here."

"Two days is enough for me. We've hit all the main events."

Dena dabbed at the perspiration on her throat and tried to appear unscathed. Despite the heat, her short skirt and scoop-necked blouse looked crisp. "I'm about Renaissanced-out, to tell you the truth. This reenactment is fine, but I don't mind going now."

"History is great," Gwen said, "but if I have too much at once I get muddled. Mary, Queen of Scots is about all I know of the place. And even that is confined to knowing snatches of her imprisonment and that bloke in her household who died. Hanged, I think."

At the mention of the long-ago murder, Dena glanced at the north tower, standing sentinel-like beyond the castle's gatehouse. It felt solid enough; the main hall and towers were solid enough, but what images presented themselves on moonlit nights? She could believe the tower had harbored a body back then. The place held that sort of feeling—at least for her. Stone ruins, turrets, legends of ghosts. Who knew how many murders and deaths had occurred within Tutbury Castle's stone walls? Hundreds probably, considering the place's long life. She crouched, plucked a piece of grass, and wrapped it around her index finger.

She vaguely remembered that tale of Mary, Queen

of Scots, housed here for part of her long imprisonment. It had been nothing more than schoolbook. It took on soul-shaking reality when they'd heard the stories that morning in the castle's courtyard. Of course, all castles seemed to have their own White Ladies or Keepers or Phantom Drummer Boys, but there was something about this place, especially at dusk, that you couldn't laugh off as mere tourist clap.

Her gaze shifted again to the jagged edge of the tower and she squinted at the dark slit higher up the tower's length. What horrors had Mary suffered when she found one of her priests hanging outside that window swaying like a chunk of meat in the wind? She closed her eyes but the image stayed in her mind.

Jerry nodded and mumbled that once you saw one sword fight, the others were pretty much the same.

"Well, I'm ready. Unless either of you'd like a beer or early lunch or something."

"I'm fine," Gwen said. "You want any more photos of the tower, Jerry? The sky's so nice behind it, all those clouds."

"The tower?" He looked around, startled.

"That one." She nodded toward the one nearest the car park. A flag fluttered from its top.

"Isn't that where that musician was found murdered?" He squinted at the edifice, as though a body might be swaying from the rigging.

Gwen shrugged, looking confused and curious at once. "I can't recall. Do you know, Dena?"

"Yes." Her tone slid from her earlier determination to one of pain, and her voice quavered slightly. "This is why I want Michael to investigate the death. That man died in my village. I knew him."

Chapter Two

Mist lay thick among the trees, as though caged or entangled in branches and grasses. McLaren cursed the vegetation and the early hour, and walked deeper into the wood. Seconds later he saw the boulder. And the depression where the body had lain.

McLaren angled his mobile phone closer to his mouth. "Thanks for holding on, Jamie. I'm back."

Jamie Kydd, his mate in and out of the police force, yawned into McLaren's ear. "So you can locate a rock. Smashing. Is that why you rang me up at this ungodly hour?"

"I want a bit of information about the scene. As long as I'm here, I may as well go over it properly. It'll save time. What do you remember about it?" He stood a moment, imagining the scene as it was one year ago. Snippets of television news items flashed in his mind's eye, crowding into Jamie's narrative. "White male, forty-five years old, local music teacher."

"Last seen wearing jeans and a short-sleeved shirt."

"At the Minstrels Court, right?"

"Yeah. He was last seen carrying a guitar case—"

"I'd heard it was a cello case."

Jamie sighed and went on without comment. "A few witnesses said he was carrying a dark rucksack."

"Must've been mistaken. That wasn't at the crime scene."

"Unless the murderer pinched it. Witnesses saw him drive off in a late model Land Rover."

"Not a new Range Rover? Are you sure?"

"He was last seen talking to the castle's curator," Jamie said more loudly, as if volume alone would correct his friend's misinformation.

McLaren refrained from saying the newscast had ID'd the person as a young female fan.

"But that was never verified about the curator. It could've possibly been his fiancée."

The possibilities echoed in his head. Last seen…last seen…last seen in the forest near Kirkfield. Dead.

"Is that what you wanted?" Jamie's voice shoved the voices from McLaren's mind.

"Yeah. Fine."

"Have fun frolicking in the dewdrops. I'm going back to sleep." He rang off through McLaren's thanks.

Crouched over, McLaren examined the ground as though he were once more a police constable carrying out a crime scene search, his fingertips probing among the leaf litter, vegetation, and fallen twigs covering the forest floor. He pulled up grass and tossed aside branches. At the base of the boulder he shone his torch. Even in the dawn light its bright beam threw dense, dark shadows across the ground, stretching the blackness until it blended with the gloom beyond the stone. Again he prodded the grass to yield something significant, but nothing surrendered to his persistence. He stood up, his back and hands sore, and stretched and flexed his fingers. Snapping off the torch, he wandered a few steps from the boulder. He stood, viewing the scene from a different angle.

The car path—hardly more than two ruts of bare soil hardly visible in the enthusiastic short grass of the verge—widened on its eastward journey as it approached the village, angling uphill before disappearing among the cliff faces and trees. But here, at the western end of Kirkfield, it had dwindled into a single-lane footpath nearly choked with Queen Anne's lace and thistles. It merged with the forest floor on the far side of the boulder. As though the rock were a popular destination.

But why had the body been here? Why hundreds of yards from the victim's house? Had he met someone here? Perhaps, but unlikely. The medical report stated the victim had been moved and placed here. So again: why here?

How long McLaren stood there, he didn't know. He found himself at times both an onlooker and participant in the processing of the scene, a stranger viewing as from treetop level and as police detective. Lights flashed—police work lamps, camera strobes, torch beams, car headlights, ambulance lights. Sounds familiar and mesmerizing echoed in his ears—police sirens, car doors slamming, twigs snapping, spoken orders, irreverent jokes. The sights and sounds pulled him into the scene with the intensity of a police investigation. He felt nothing, saw and heard nothing but the shimmering scene before him. Was that his partner's voice or his nemesis Harvester's?

The mist lifted slightly, bringing a defining shape to the blur of dark forms deeper within the damp grayness. Clumps of greenery—wavy hair-grass and toad rush—poked out of the haze, waist high and sun bleached to a deathly paleness, the rigid stems and fuzzy seed heads dotted with dew and rustling softly in the morning breeze. A birch eased out of the obscurity as a woodpecker tattooed its presence from a dead tree. The percussion jerked McLaren from the trance. He lifted his trembling hand to his forehead, suddenly aware of the sweat and his racing heart. As the police lights faded under the sunlight cresting an oak bough, the body sank back into the shadows; the white work suits receded into the mist. McLaren shook off the ghosts clinging from his former career and walked back to his car.

****

The drive back from Kirkfield was a pleasant break in the drenching heat, the wind rushing through the car window fanned his sweaty face.

Back home, the heat returned with a vengeance. A breeze wandered through the front room's open window, managed to stir the edge of the curtain as it passed, but did little to eliminate the stuffiness of the room. He raked his fingers through his hair, pulling the damp locks upward so the breeze could cool his scalp. Nothing he did made much difference.

Surrendering to the heat, he took a sip of coffee as he replayed the message left yesterday on his answering machine. Dena's voice was enthusiastic. Underscored with a bit of pleading. Nice touch. At least she knew enough not to add flattery.

He dropped onto the couch, kicked off his shoes and brought his legs up to the coffee table. The sun beckoned him to lay back and nap, forget his tired body for a while. But the mantel clock struck the half hour and prodded him to get on with his day. Napping was no way to earn a living—either as a mender of dry stone walls or as an inquisitive citizen.

He encompassed the mug in his large hands, not for the warmth, but the heat penetrated his stiff muscles. Work on the top course of a stone wall in Bamford had strained his hands and back. Strained his patience, too. Restlessness like he hadn't known for months settled on him like the weight of a boulder. Had stone wall work ceased to absorb him? Did the lure of police work, even as remote as asking unofficial questions, now beckon?

He drained the last of his coffee, put down the mug and punched the Play button again and listened to the message a third time. Perhaps it had been best that he'd been out early in Kirkfield. If he had taken the call yesterday he might have snapped at her, alienating her just as they were getting back together. Replaying the message like this had given him time to think.

The sound of talking, laughter, and music came up first, then Dena's excited words pushed the noise into the background. Her tone wobbled a bit as her mobile phone cut out briefly; then her voice rushed to him, enthusiastic and strong. "Michael, I'm here at Tutbury Castle, in Staffordshire, with your sister and Jerry. We're taking in the Minstrels Court festivity…"

He paused the playback, letting his mind catch up to the tumult of words. The Minstrels Court. An eight-day event styled in the medieval mode, featuring all the fun and frolic of 15th century living. Heavy on the music. Tutbury Castle added the authentic and dramatic backdrop.

He hit the Play button and Dena's voice sang to him. "…if you remember the death of that singer last year. Yes, I know you weren't in the job then, but I thought… Well, I thought you'd be intrigued by the case, being as it's a musician and an unsolved death."

Despite his reservations, McLaren leaned forward and concentrated on Dena's words. The background noise swelled and he frowned, exasperated that some of her words were obliterated. After several seconds her voice came through again.

"…last July. I guess I feel close to this…well, *upset*, actually, because he lived in Kirkfield, too. I'll ask a few people if they remember anything about his last appearance here and talk to you about this later. Love."

The message clicked off with an annoying beep, rousing McLaren from his mental image of Dena taking notes from an armor-clad jouster on horseback. He raked his fingers through his short-cropped blond hair—ancestral genes from the Scandinavian branch—sat back in the couch and sighed. Of course he had quit the police by then, but he still recalled the case from what few facts he could glean from the sensational speculation coloring the account. But he wasn't getting involved in another investigation. He was thirty-seven years old; he was off the job.

He grabbed the mug, wandered into the kitchen, poured another cup of coffee, and walked to the window looking into the back garden. The mist had lifted hours ago; the film of moisture on the stone wall marking the boundary of his land had evaporated in the suffocating heat. It would only worsen, McLaren thought, as he gazed heavenward, for the sun had already cleared the top of the willow and consumed the sky with its brilliance. The cloudless expanse of blue would offer no relief from the summer temperature, nor would there be much respite in the shade if the thermometer climbed much more.

A breath of wind, hot and dry from its wandering across the parched fields, nudged the stalks of foxglove planted along the front of the stone wall. A ripple of purple, lilac, and pink. Foxglove. Fairy Cap. Fairy Bells. Fairy Thimbles. Numerous whimsical names for a beautiful, deadly plant. Hadn't that man, the one whom Dena is urging me to investigate, died from a plant poisoning? Had it been foxglove?

So what if it had been, he reminded himself, swallowing a mouthful of coffee. He wasn't a ruddy copper any more. What did he care? What could he accomplish when the lads from CID tried and failed?

The flowers waved at him, as if beckoning. Did they know about the man's death? Did they know about poison? It would be so easy with that plant, for all parts of it were toxic. Easy to think the flowers would look nice in a fresh salad. He stared at the mass of color, bent at an angle and revealing the wall. For some reason, he was putting off his work. And he had plenty to do. Finish the Bamford job; a patch this side of Castleton, trailing up the steep Winnats mountain pass; a repair of the top course outside Elton; a new section to construct at a farm near Hartington.

But stonework couldn't satisfy him today. He was impatient, unable to concentrate, though he didn't know why. Normally he loved the solitude of stonework, sweating out his thoughts and problems with the backbreaking labor. He had grown used to hour after hour under the sun, rain and wind, sweating or chilled as the day dictated; his skin shone with the tan of the outdoors laborer, his hazel eyes threw back the golden glints of the sun. He had the physique for the work, too—tall and slim-hipped, with shoulders as hard and developed as some of the rocks he shifted. But he had no wish to apply his muscle to the stones today. He exhaled sharply, his gaze still on the wall in his garden. Was it due to Dena's message? Was that why he'd been in the wood early this morning looking at the site where the body had been found, instead of on the wind-swept hill in Castleton?

He set down his coffee, wandered into the front room, and grabbed his guitar, a Martin 12-string. He sat, pulled the flat pick from its resting spot, interlaced between the sixth and fifth course of strings, and clamped the pick between his teeth. The strings vibrated from the disturbance and set up sympathetic echoes from their neighbors. Angling the curved side of the guitar across his right thigh, he slowly thumped each string as he tuned. High E's tuned in unison to the low E's, octave D's second fretted to the high E, B's third fretted to the D. The steel string squawked while McLaren turned the polished chrome machine head, tightening the string and bending over the sound hole to hear the faint overtones dancing in the air. Halfway through he stopped, his finger resting on the B string. A phrase stirred in his mind. "Kent Harrison might have ingested some poisonous plant and, given time, might have died of it, but he died of strangulation."

McLaren's right hand slid onto his lap. If Kent Harrison was being poisoned, why strangle him? Because the killer couldn't wait for the poison to take effect? Because some event happened or was about to happen that required Harrison to die sooner? Or were two people wanting Kent Harrison's demise?

Chapter Three

"At least, I didn't know him well," Dena explained, her voice softer as she recalled the murder. "But anyone who dies like that…" She wrinkled her face.

"You actually knew Kent Harrison, Dena?" Gwen's question soared above the background noise of conversations, cheers, drums and bagpipes.

Jerry snapped his fingers. "Kent Harrison. Sure! That minstrel fellow. The folk singer. Right. The folkies dubbed him 'Cygnus' and some other names due to that song he sang. Oh, you know." He cut off the last phrase, clearly exasperated. "That swan song. A takeoff on 'The Bird Song'." He sighed as Gwen suddenly nodded. "The swan song that has those back and forth verses from the male and female swans."

"Cob and pen," Gwen corrected.

"Male and female…cob and pen. Whatever. Kent and some girl—Fay Larkin, I think—recorded it as a duet. The song was a huge hit. The bloke was famous."

"Too bad such a talent died. And you knew him, Dena?"

"Not well," Dena said. "Not as a friend. Just knew *of* him, saw him around the village. You know." She gave a shrug.

"Even so." Gwen grimaced.

"Bad enough," Jerry agreed. He eyed the beer in a passerby's hand and ran the tip of his tongue over his dry lips. "Is that why you want Mike to investigate? He knew the bloke also?"

"I don't think he knew Kent. At least…" Dena screwed up her mouth, trying to connect the two men. "They both like music, obviously, but I'm not completely sure."

Gwen looked thoughtful. "They could have met at a festival or at a pub, you're thinking?" She had been to enough folk festivals and open mic nights at pubs to know the music world was small—at least the world of traditional folk. Even if group members didn't flow from one band to another, they knew each other. Knew *of* each other: voice range, instrument played, musicianship, temperament. Qualities important in determining employment in a band. Qualities that placed you in "backup" or "lead".

"I just thought that shared love might draw Michael into the case."

"Well, whether you're exasperated or hopeful, if you're praying this case will set him firmly and finally among his family and friends again, I'll pray with you." Gwen grabbed Dena's hand and squeezed her fingers.

They had left the archery field and its blasts of heat. The field had been set up in front of the South Range, a section that housed the great hall and the former royal apartments when John of Gaunt had poured his wealth into the castle in the mid 1300s. Now, on the other side of the great hall's doorway, they strolled through the avenue of booths, striped fabric tents housing all manner of medieval wares. Scents of spices, dried herbs and fried meat pies, and cries of vendors hawking their wares, crowded the air. And music. A snatch of "When Morning is Breaking"—the old Welsh air "*Pan Gyryd Yr Heulwen*"—drifted to them.

The field flowers drooping, as fast fades the light, give warning foreboding, the sadness of night...

The song jarred something in Dena's mind. "The police think Kent was killed that night, when he had returned from the Minstrels Court." She stopped, the music, the castle's festival, and the date suddenly shaking her confidence. "If Michael looked into the death... He needs something mentally stimulating to bring him back permanently to us."

"But he's no longer a cop. He reminds me every time I even bring up a topic related to his days on the Force. Jerry and I have seen his house recently. His commendations are packed away, along with his ambition. There are empty places on the walls of his back room, which seem to me to state that fact, even if Mike forgot to mention it. As good as the mental work might be for him, are you sure you want to yank him out of his contentment and open up a case that neither Kent's family nor friends are anxious to re-examine?"

Dena glanced at Jerry to see if she would get moral support from him, but he was talking to a leather crafter. She lowered her voice and addressed Gwen. "It's my belief that Michael isn't content mending walls, that despite his pasted-on smile, he aches with his whole being to be back in the job. You may sense something different, being his sister and maybe knowing him better, but that's what I feel." She gazed at the row of colorful tents, wishing McLaren were that easy to put into a category. She turned back to the original subject. "At least the castle's curator and a few people at the performance stage recall Kent packing up his guitar and walking to his car that night. No one in my village recalls him arriving home, though. Of course, it could easily be an instance of familiarity. You know…you always see and hear the car so you don't notice it unless it's out of the ordinary."

"And that's where Mike comes into the picture." Jerry slipped a small package wrapped in brown paper into his back pocket as he rejoined them. "You think he'll be able to solve this where the police failed." He sniffed as though the suggestion itself stank. Or was too ludicrous to dignify words. "First, you've got to tear him away from his stones and tools. Then you've got to make him listen to you. Seriously listen, I mean. Third, you've got to interest him. I don't know which is the hardest. Any part of this is nearly impossible." He batted at a fly buzzing around his head.

"That other woman did it last month," Gwen reminded him. "The woman who was the victim's friend—"

"Yeah, she did. She got him to investigate. And look what happened."

"He solved the case!"

"He nearly *died*." Jerry looked around for the beer vendor as he pulled at the limp neckline of his T-shirt. "Or is your memory selective and you've forgotten the attack?"

"I remember. Don't rub it in." Gwen sniffed, her tone sharp as the look she threw him. "But I also remember how Mike shed his near hermit-like existence." She bit her bottom lip as her fingers pulled at her earlobe. "Go ahead, Dena. Mention the case to Mike. Bring in the music aspect, if that will lure him into investigating it."

Dena smiled and said she'd left a phone message for him last night.

"Fingers crossed it'll work, then." Gwen broke off as they came to the section of food booths.

Each booth was dramatically decorated in vivid colors, long pennants and brightly painted signs. Vendors in a variety of medieval dress—tunics, doublets, tights, bell-sleeved gowns, feathered caps mimicking the hues of peacock feathers and sunsets— called out their wares to everyone and no one in particular.

Gwen hesitated at an herbalist's booth while Jerry dawdled at one selling jewelry opposite. "Earth Child Herbs. Ron Pennell, Herbalist," she murmured, squinting to read the sign. Large and metallic, the pale blue rectangle caught the late morning sun's rays and threw them back onto the south tower's rock face. Bouquets of wild flowers were tied to the tent's corners, the satin ribbons flapping in the breeze. "Did you talk to everyone you wanted to so you can tell Mike some things?" Gwen said, her eyes still on the sign.

"I need some basic facts of the case, what some of the more involved people have to say about it."

"Well, all I can say is good luck. God knows we all want Mike back with us—mentally, physically, and emotionally."

"I talked to the vendors who were here last time. So, I've done all I can do, I guess."

"You spoke to the man in this booth, I assume."

"Oh, no." She glanced at the man standing behind the display table. "Someone else was here when I came by. *Carpe diem*, I guess." Dena walked up to the man, who appeared to be a confusion of cape-like sleeves and belts, and introduced herself. The man's smile faltered and turned into a frank stare. "This may seem like a strange question," she said, "but I was wondering if you were here at the Minstrels Court last year."

"I come every year." The speaker's voice, melodious and smooth, matched his smooth hair. "Did you purchase something last year that you don't see displayed? Can I help you find a particular item? Lavender sachet, lemon pomander, or perhaps mint vinegar? I use only natural ingredients in all my products." He picked up a brochure and held it so Dena could read it. The cover sported a large illuminated initial and watercolors of various flowers. "I claim no medical cures. On the contrary, I discourage the use of my products for anything more serious than first aid. But in cooking or massage therapy, my herbs and spices are perfectly safe and lawful."

"It sounds interesting, cooking with these flowers. But no, I'm sorry. Nothing like that. It's about someone you might have known. Or at least seen."

"Someone who was here last year?" The man returned the brochure to the stack on the table and set a bottle on them. The wind caught the papers' edges and ruffled them slightly. "Another vendor here?"

"No. A musician."

The man blinked. "Why? Did he buy something from me and he's claiming something was wrong with the product?" He leaned forward and a bit to his right, looking for the man in the midway's jostling crowd.

"I have a friend who's interested in talking to anyone who might have known him."

"Past tense." His eyebrow rose. "Why? What happened? If he died due to something here at the

Minstrels Court, you should contact the police. I don't know anything about anyone dying. Nothing like that happened here."

"I didn't say it happened here. I just want to know if you knew of the man. His name was Kent Harrison."

The man shook his head and smoothed the palm of his hand on his tunic. "I don't know a thing about this Kent Harrison's sickness. If there was a problem with my product, he should have come back to me. I stand behind everything I make and sell. Now, if you've nothing else to say…" He turned toward a teenaged girl who was holding a bag of strewing herbs.

Eyeing Gwen, who was immersed in a bookseller's wares a few tents down, Jerry walked up to Dena. "Any luck?"

"Yes. Bad."

"Hard cheese."

"You talk to anyone, or just do a bit of shopping?"

"This is your idea, Dena. I want to stay on Mike's good side." He flashed a grin. "And my previous purchase is something for Christmas, so don't say anything to Gwen." He pushed the box deeper into his pocket and patted it.

"I'm as silent as the grave."

Chapter Four

"That's a grave assumption, Mike. Two people plotting Kent Harrison's death." Jamie Kydd hoped he could be heard against the background noise of the lunchtime crowd. Even with the air conditioning unit chugging its heart out, the canteen felt oppressive in the day's heat. Jamie grabbed his jacket, rolled down the sleeves of his shirt, and pushed his chair back to the table. He fought the impulse to talk more loudly into the mobile phone's mouthpiece and instead walked out of the room. On the other side of the closed door he glanced the length of the corridor and, seeing no one, lowered his voice.

The quieter tone suited Jamie, complementing strangers' mental match with his slight physique. Yet his body harbored hardened, toned muscles that seemed to surprise those getting into scrapes with him. He nudged a lock of his light brown hair back into place, a common action lately as he fought to obscure his slowly emerging scalp. Satisfied, he leaned against the wall. "Any idea who these two people might be?"

"I'm not saying it's true, Jamie, just that it could be. If I've ever heard of any instance where two people could have been instrumental in someone's death, this is it. It screams it." He took a breath before muttering, "*Smells* of it, actually. Of all the bloody cases of hatred and murder and unjust—Well, I owe it to the victim to solve this. It's the decent thing to do. He needs his murder solved."

"Kent does, or you do?" He paused for McLaren's answer, then added, "I realize what you must be feeling over the injustice for the victim."

McLaren went on as if Jamie hadn't spoken. "Don't you agree this case's got the whiff of the fishmonger about it?"

"I *know* what it sounds like, Mike. Carbohydrate andromedotoxin in his system, and strangulation thrown in for good measure. But *two* people?" Skepticism seeped into his tone.

"What else could it point to? Two people, two methods of murder. You have to admit that's odd."

"I'll give you odd, but nothing else. The case has been investigated, Mike."

"I'll give you investigated," McLaren said, mimicking Jamie's tone, "but it's not closed, is it?"

"You know it's not or you wouldn't have rung me up. And on my lunch hour, yet."

"You must've finished. I don't hear the clatter and chatter of those happy diners."

"I've moved out to the corridor. I couldn't very well talk where dozens of coppers can overhear my conversation."

The hallway stretched a dozen yards in each direction, its cream-painted walls and brown-and-white lino floor throwing back Jamie's soft voice. No footsteps marked a potential eavesdropper; no noise bounced back to him other than his own words. He frowned, thinking once again how impersonal the place seemed, how it could do with an interior designer to bring some warmth, maybe make the work environment a bit more cheery.

McLaren uttered a soft oath. "They probably wouldn't pay attention even if they did hear you above the din. They're too busy gobbling down egg and cress sandwiches or sausage rolls, if I remember my happy lunch hours properly. What's the special today?"

"Why'd you ring me up before you've eaten? You're always in a foul mood when you're peckish."

"Am not. Anyway, you've changed the subject. I just want someone who's in charge of the case to consider the possibility that two people might be involved with Kent Harrison's murder. There *is* someone in charge of the case, isn't there?"

"Not officially. It's classified Cold. And don't ask me to make inquiries. Any new information poking through this morass would automatically scream for attention. Someone would be on it like a dog on a bone."

"Or a cop on a robber," McLaren added, the comparison not too far off the mark.

"Sorry, Mike, but if I make any waves, no matter how minute…"

A groan bored into Jamie's ear. He could imagine his friend about to throw the phone across the room. "If you're counting to ten, stop. I've nothing to do with this—policy or investigation. Save yourself an ulcer and attend to one of your walls."

"Well, if I turn up anything, can I at least tell you about it?"

"You can tell me anything, you know that."

"I'm not talking about true confessions or humorous episodes of my love life. I'm serious, Jamie."

"I know you are. That's what concerns me. But

fine. Nose around, ask questions." His voice dropped to a whisper. "Hold on. A possible ear." He paused, pressing the mouthpiece of his mobile phone against his stomach as two constables walked up to him. Nodding to them, he waited until they entered the canteen and the door closed before continuing. "Sorry. All clear."

"Who was it? Your Super?"

"Little pitchers. But I still didn't want them to hear."

"Ta."

"But really, Mike, I'm not convinced this is such a smashing idea. If you ask the wrong person and he gets mad... Well... Last month's run-in was bad enough. You might have been seriously injured or might have died from the assault."

"You believe it's going to happen again if I take on this cold case."

"There's always a danger of that."

"Because I'm not in the job any more?"

"That's not got a thing to do with it. But you do seem deaf to advice, even to your own counsel that might normally warn you to avoid investigations. Even if you don't admit it, it's true. Look how you rushed to the defense of your friend a year ago, when Harvester was investigating the pub burglary."

"What's wrong with righting another wrong? If I can help one overlooked victim, bring some relief to the family..."

Jamie let the silence build as he glanced at the in-house poster on the opposite wall—a close-up photo of wrists handcuffed together. The caption read Accessories Are 'in' This Season. Farther down the wall another poster showed a police car—the two tones lit, its back seat door open—proclaiming Preferred Seating. Jamie left the contemplation of the posters and spoke into his mobile. "You can do anything you want, Mike, but just so your tunnel vision doesn't land you in hospital. I'd hate to use my time off to visit you there."

"There won't be a repeat performance from last month. At least, if there is, the victim/aggressor roles will be reversed. Now, save your breath. I'm grateful that you care, but I'll just ask a few questions to see if there's anything that the original investigation missed. People sometimes talk after the spotlight's shut off."

"I'm a copper, you don't have to tell me." Jamie glanced at his watch. "Time for my delightful repast is over, Mike. Gotta go."

"Glad we could have lunch together."

"Food would have been a nice addition, but I won't wish for the impossible. One quick last question to satisfy my curiosity. Why now? Did the case fascinate you, does the one-year anniversary mean something, or is some relative of Kent Harrison's twisting your arm? And if so," Jamie added as he heard McLaren's deep breath, "why haven't they gone to the police? Why seek you out? I know you well enough to realize you're not hung up on fame or publicity, so your name in the newspaper's not your goal." A hesitation on the other end of the phone line gave Jamie the answer. "Oh. Dena."

"I haven't promised her anything."

"But you're interested, or you wouldn't even be doing preliminary work."

"Like I said, Jamie, I owe it to the victim. If two people did want him dead, that's a lot of hatred. I need to see what caused it and to bring him some justice.

That's it, pure and simple."

"Admirable." Jamie paused. He wouldn't say he was worried once more about McLaren investigating a case on his own. "Who will you talk to first?" The canteen door opened, letting out a blast of talk. "Sorry. Who?"

"Where the smart cop always begins. With the spouse."

"Not the girlfriend?"

"At last! We're talking motive."

Chapter Five

"I know your motive is admirable." Jerry stopped his car opposite Dena's house. It blended in with the others on the lane, a two-storey stone cottage embraced by its neighbors—being one of several in the row of houses—and emphatic flowering window boxes. A previous owner's difference of opinion had topped Dena's house with a darker colored roof, giving it an air of rebellion and individuality in the dreary sea of otherwise light gray slate. The string of residences was the last vestige of the village's southern end; beyond it sprawled the farmland, meadows, and wood. The northern end melted into the village proper, merging into the High Street, along which shops huddled cheek-by-jowl. The High Street, in turn, curled about to the A515 west of Parwich, losing its village flavor when it disappeared in the tangle of roads that converged in Buxton. But all that lay to the west and beyond the slight rise of the hills. Jerry's attention was on Dena.

She extracted her keys from the clutter in her handbag. "But will Michael believe it, admirable as the motive may be? You know how he gets, Jerry."

"Isn't that like asking the Trojans to accept the gift of another horse? Okay, okay," he added, as Dena frowned, "bad joke. But opening a cold case, and especially having an ex-police detective open it, is not my idea of a good time had by all. So you prod Mike into investigating it. Super. But he may not be successful if he starts poking about. What if he fails? Have you thought about that?"

Dena's voice was nearly a whisper. "He may sink back into his depression, overcome by failing at something he used to excel in."

"At the critical time, too. Just as he's making overtures to shake it. And if he slips back, he may never get out. Do you want to be responsible for that?"

She left Jerry and Gwen in a whirlwind of emotions, anger being the major one—anger that he thought her senseless or stupid. Anger that he had no idea of the depth of her love for McLaren. Fearful that Jerry might be right about getting McLaren interested in the cold case. Worried that he wouldn't be interested in the cold case and slip back into his apathy. Now, thirty minutes later, she merely felt wretched and impatient with McLaren, Jerry, and Life in general.

She set down her teacup and walked into her back room. Apple green, red and white, the room held a mix of new and antique pieces. A white wicker rocker and green, red, and white plaid sofa framed the large fireplace. Photographs of landscapes and wild birds grabbed the wall space between the white-framed windows. Though highly polished, her grandmother's desk carried the scars from a long, useful life. Her great grandmother's cream pitcher, sporting a blue-and-cream checkerboard design, served as a pencil holder.

Dena sat at her desk and turned on the computer. A minute later she was reading an online newspaper article of Kent Harrison's death.

Tuesday, 12 July. The pastoral calm shattered late Monday when the body of Kent Harrison, 45, was discovered in the wood bordering the village of Kirkfield, Derbyshire. Harrison, an apparent murder victim, had been missing since late Sunday evening when he left Tutbury Castle where he had been performing in the Minstrels Court festivity. Fellow musician and sometimes-singing partner Dave Morley said he had been trying to contact Harrison since 23.00 hours Sunday. "He had told me just before we parted Sunday night to ring him up a bit later," Morley said. "We were going to talk about our performance for Monday. When I couldn't get him on the phone, I got worried. I drove over Monday night, walked to the wood, and that's when I found his body." Although police refuse to comment at this point, it looks as though Harrison had been strangled. His guitar, wallet, money, and keys hadn't been touched. Police are unsure of a motive, but urge anyone who may know anything about Harrison or his death to contact them. Morley, a shop clerk at Joyful Sound Music, said Harrison's passing is a great loss to the music world. Harrison taught sixth form classes in music at Grange Hall Performing Arts College in Ashbourne.

Dena leaned back in her chair, staring at the computer monitor. The article blurred. She was no detective, but Dave Morley's statement didn't make sense. Why hadn't he and Kent Harrison talked right then, before they parted Sunday night? Why ring up later and confer over the phone? And if Dave had been so worried about Kent, why wait twenty-four hours before driving over to look for him? The wood outside the village seemed an odd place to search.

She logged on to another website. The article read nearly the same as the previous newspaper account but gave a more personal slant by adding that Kent Harrison had been a well-known folk musician on the brink of national stardom. His recording of "The Swans' Song" had sold out of its original press run and had reached the number three spot on one radio station. Yet, despite the fame and fans, Kent Harrison remained true to his teaching career and looked forward to his students…

"Blah blah blah," Dena muttered, glancing over the remainder of the article. A photo, probably courtesy of his website or from his manager, accompanied the article. It showed him on stage, smiling, his left hand gripping the neck of his guitar, his right arm raised to greet the crowd. She studied his face—radiant with joy, his brown eyes slightly obscured at the outer corners by folds of skin. His brown hair appeared too dark to be natural, but it could have been the angle at which the photographer took the picture. Still, Kent looked younger than his forty-five years, more like an overgrown university student than a teacher of students.

She checked one more website, read essentially the same thing—with the inclusion that Kent Harrison was recently divorced—and logged off, thinking it amazing how the media abbreviated a person's life.

As she turned off the computer, she glanced at the clock. Mid-afternoon. Plenty of time. If she was going to pry McLaren from his stone wall work she had best get the proper lure. And what better one, she thought as she grabbed her handbag and keys from the kitchen table, than her prime suspect? The venetian blinds banged against the back door window as she left to talk to Dave Morley.

Chapter Six

McLaren slammed down the phone receiver, impatient to get started. His notepad held what information Jamie had time to relate:

1-Kent Harrison had been found Monday at 22:30 hours by the boulder 117 yards into the wood bordering Kirkfield.

2-Sporadic singing partner Dave Morley had the dubious distinction of locating the body, deliberately beginning his search outside Kent's house and then fanning out into the field and forest. He knew that "if I didn't find him at his house, I could probably find him by the boulder."

So the wood wasn't such an illogical spot to search as the investigating officers had first supposed. They believed Dave had tried contacting Kent as often as he claimed, for a check of his phone records confirmed this. But as to whether Dave had dumped Kent's body earlier, after killing him Sunday night, or merely located the body…well, that they couldn't prove.

3-Kent's car sat in his driveway, testifying that he had arrived home. Or someone had driven him home. A meticulous search of Dave's car confirmed Kent had been a passenger at some time. Suspicion may have been in the officers' minds, but finding Kent's hair, shed skin cells, and fingerprints didn't automatically damn Dave. As he pointed out, and as the officers believed, Dave and Kent often rode in each other's cars; it saved the cost of petrol when they sang at the same venues.

4-The lab techs extracted a small amount of DNA from Kent's car that couldn't be matched to any known person involved in the case. The few strands of head hair had been tagged and stored for that hopeful day when they'd come up with a match. But it, too, might have been transferred in a completely innocent manner. How many strands of hair, skin cells and fabric particles does the average person carry away from someone else, only to shed the foreign hair elsewhere? Still, the hair needed saving.

Jamie promised in a stealthy whisper that he'd email McLaren one or two photos of the area where the body had been found. For, as he had murmured, barely audible, "Red Riding Hood's wolf lurks."

McLaren hung up, comprehending the danger Jamie faced if he were discovered scanning and emailing the photos, yet appreciative beyond words that he had his friend's help. Some coppers did have big ears, as Jamie had alluded to, and loved nothing better than to gossip or report rule breakers.

He picked up the phone's receiver again but held it, staring at it. He found himself thinking of Charlie Harvester, another detective at the Staffordshire Constabulary. A nasty piece of work. A copper whose hatred of McLaren snaked back to their police training days.

He leaned back, shut his eyes and, as he massaged his forehead, envisioned a snatch of the letter he'd composed when he quit.

The anxious beeps of the phone seemed to slip into

the bleat of Harvester's incessant accusations. Shaking away the images and surreal echoes, McLaren cleared the phone and punched in the number of Cheryl Kerrigan, the Home Office forensic pathologist who worked on the Kent Harrison case.

She answered his call on the second ring and McLaren found himself again swamped in a rush of memories and mental images from his police days. He could also remember her—small and delicate, her dark eyes staring with a frankness and inquisitiveness that ate into his soul. Her long, dark hair was always swept into a bun to be out of the way as she worked, or maybe in a ponytail, revealing a pair of dangly earrings she loved to wear. She'd be wearing a white lab coat over gray or blue trousers, two of her favorite colors. Her smile most always consumed her face. He swallowed before responding to the "Hello?" asked on the other end of the line, momentarily wondering if he were doing the right thing. "Hi, Cheryl. It's Mike McLaren."

A slight intake of breath preceded her stammered "Mc...McLaren? *Mike?* God, of all people! How are you?"

"Hi, Cheryl," he repeated, suddenly embarrassed and reticent about renewing the colleague association after so much time had elapsed. His fingers toyed with the handful of ceramic and wooden beads strung on a leather thong around his neck. He seemed to resort to this talisman-like action when he was anxious. The larger, center bead was grooved like the ridges of corduroy, and he rolled it beneath his index finger and thumb. "I'm fine. How about you? Still in the job?"

She laughed, a river of silver coursing through McLaren's veins. "Does the sun rise in the east? Do badgers like peanuts? Of course I'm still a pathologist. Why? You need something?"

McLaren heard the pause, sensed the unasked question in her voice. He answered it. "No, I'm not back on the Force. I'm building and repairing stone walls in Derbyshire."

"Derbyshire! Really? Why there?" Again, he felt that she didn't state the obvious, that he had put miles between himself and the scene of his anger.

"My childhood home in Somerley. The village I was reared in. I thought it was better than…well, safer to leave Staffordshire."

"Safer for you, or safer for Harvester? Never mind, don't answer that! It's none of my business, Mike. But knowing you, it's safer for Harvester. God, what a sorry excuse for a human being he is. Anyway," she said, the warmth coming back to her voice, "you didn't call to chat about old times. As I said, do you need something?"

"I'm not sure now that I should have rung you up."

"Am I that forbidding? I haven't changed any."

"No, not forbidding. Just that…well, the favor."

"That shouldn't bother you. I assume it's a postmortem report or you wouldn't be talking to me."

"Yeah. It's from a cold case."

"What's the case? I assume I worked on it or you'd be ringing up someone else."

"Kent Harrison. A year ago this month. No one was charged with his murder."

"Harrison. Yes, I remember. A popular teacher and a talented singer. His claim to fame was a song about a swan, wasn't it?"

"Yes."

33

"He was found near Kirkfield, wasn't he?"

"Yes. Dumped in the wood."

"That one made me mad, too, Mike."

"If you've got a minute, I need to know something about that case. Jamie Kydd told me you'd done the postmortem." He knew he was repeating himself, but it was harder than he had imagined talking to her. Not only due to the length of time since he'd last seen her and had worked with her, but also because the conversation sharpened his image of Charlie Harvester. He took a deep breath and rushed ahead. "I need to know the particulars surrounding his death. Approximate time, cause."

A pause greeted his request. He heard Cheryl clear her throat, then her measured response. "You know this is highly irregular, Mike."

He felt his cheeks flood with heat. "Yes."

"Giving information to any unauthorized person, former police detective or not, could seriously prejudice any later criminal proceedings if the case comes to trial."

"Highly unprofessional, too. I know. It's just that…" How could he phrase it so she would understand his urgency? "If Kent Harrison's killer is ever to be caught, something needs to be done. A manila folder sitting in a filing cabinet never put anyone behind bars."

She put him out of his misery. "Just a minute." A soft thud as she put down the phone's receiver preceded a high-pitched squeak of a metal filing cabinet drawer being opened. Then came several bangs while she shifted the drawer farther out, a few scrapes while the metal ends of hanging file folder rasped across the support bar, a mumbled "Hell" as something fell to the floor. Moments later, she fumbled for the receiver. "Sorry. I dropped the damned thing."

"If this is a bad time—"

"Not at all. Hold on while I find...yes, here it is." There was another rustle of paper. "Right. Now I recall it. Kent Harrison died of strangulation. Garroted by a thin wire."

"Could you determine what type?"

"I can't put a manufacturer's name to it, but I'd say from a musical instrument, like a banjo or guitar or even a piano. It had to have been flexible and strong. Some sort of metal."

"So, no nylon string, then."

"I very much doubt it. Don't musicians have a choice of various string types?"

McLaren nodded, thinking through the scenario. "Steel, silk wrapped steel, bronze, nickel, titanium, chrome. Various gauges."

"Any of those are stronger than a nylon string. Of course, the wire could be from jewelry making or from any number of industrial or home uses."

McLaren sighed, shaking his head. "Not so easy, determining where the wire came from."

"Or its previous use. Have any jewelry designers or cable television installers on your list of suspects?"

"Wish I did."

"Well, it's food for thought, anyway. But the odd thing I found during the postmortem examination was the contents of his stomach. He had ingested a large quantity of hydrangea flower buds. All of the flower parts are poisonous, of course, but the buds more so."

McLaren made a sound between a whistle and a

cough. Cheryl ignored it and went on.

"Symptoms are vomiting and severe pain in the abdomen while the material is in the stomach. No traces of vomitus showed up on swabs I took from his mouth, nose and throat, however."

"So at that time he hadn't yet consumed a large enough quantity of hydrangea buds."

"No."

"How long would it take for the vomiting and abdominal pain to appear?" He paused in his note taking.

"Varies by person. We all digest food at different rates. But it took a while. As it passes on to the small bowel, the symptoms of cyanide poisoning occur between within one half hour to two hours."

"Dizziness, blushing, slowed breathing…"

"…seizures, weakness, and coma. Death would be from respiratory and heart failure. But of course Mr. Harrison didn't die of cyanogenic glycoside. He died of strangulation. Though he was rendered semi conscious first by a blow to the head. Probably so he wouldn't struggle. A slight indentation to the skull, on the right side just above and behind the ear, suggests a rock as the weapon."

"But not hit hard enough to kill him."

"Not at all. More like he saw stars."

McLaren made a note to ask Jamie if any vomitus was found either in the wood, Dave Morley's car, or Kent's house. That would at least give him an idea how long Kent had been eating the flower buds. He tapped the top of his pen on the notepad as he thought. "Thanks, Cheryl. I owe you one. Maybe a drink some evening?" He hesitated, wondering if he should offer something more expensive, like dinner out.

Another rustle of paper and a few sharp taps told him that Cheryl was returning the report to the file folder and straightening up her desk. "That would be nice, Mike. Then we could really catch up. And, uh, Mike?"

"Yes?"

"Do *me* a favor, would you?"

"Yes?"

"Don't mention where you got this information. If my name comes out…well, it could be…you know."

The end of your career, he thought, as Charlie Harvester's grinning face flashed across his mind's eye. "Don't worry, Cheryl. No one will ever hear your name from me."

"Thanks, Mike. I-I'm glad I could help." She rang off, repeating that a chat and drink would be nice.

While he'd been talking to Cheryl the photos of the crime scene came through on his email. He clicked on each attachment, studying the photos in turn and relating the information he had to the images on his computer screen.

The first photo showed the general crime scene—the boulder, the body lying beside it, the end of the trail as it blended into the soil of the forest. More photos detailing specific areas followed the broad view: small soil depressions that might or might not have been made by shoes, a bare spot in the leaf litter, a few discarded beer cans and cigarette ends, a fresh vertical scrape that had removed lichen along one section of the boulder, a broken dog collar.

Pictures of the body revealed Kent Harrison lying facedown on the forest floor, his head near the base of the boulder. McLaren wondered briefly if Kent had struck his head on the boulder when he fell, accounting for the head injury Cheryl had discovered during the post-mortem. He discarded the thought just as quickly. Kent's face or head would have shown signs of scraping along the stone. Most likely there would be lichen in his hair, and Kent's skin cells on the stone. Kent's arms, straight and angled from his torso, implied he hadn't tried to brace his fall. His fingernails held no remnants of another person's skin or clothing fibers, forest soil, or fragments of plant material. They weren't broken, either, so none of that suggested Kent had struggled with his assailant.

The neck held the classic V-shape that resulted in strangulation, when the garrote is fairly low on the throat and pulled up higher at the back of the neck. No blood matted his hair, which seemed to underscore the minor quality of the head wound that Cheryl had mentioned.

He got up and rubbed his scalp. His eyes and head hurt from the overload of information. He walked into the kitchen and was surprised to see the morning had advanced. A rectangle of sunlight lay across the worktop and spilled onto the floor. He put the kettle on to boil, dropped a teabag into his cup, and walked to the window. The fields stretched uphill, broken occasionally by clumps of trees and stripes of stonewalls. In the west, toward Chinley Head and New Mills, cumulus clouds sped before the wind, their shadows racing over everything in their path.

The kettle flipped off with a snap, startling him. He poured the water into the cup and, as it steeped, got the milk from the fridge. He considered phoning his sister while he waited, but thought better of it. He hadn't the time or patience to listen to Gwen's chatter.

He took his cup into his office and set it on the desk as he sat down. But it sat untasted as he considered the crime scene. If it had been during the winter Kent's clothing would have indicated a day or night assault, but due to the summer heat he hadn't worn a jacket. Even at night. He was clothed in jeans, a cotton shirt, and trainers. No rips, holes, or blood on his clothes suggested he'd been involved in a fight. The soil embedded in the soles of his shoes was consistent with that of the forest. All in all, McLaren thought, a nice collection of photographs that didn't tell him anything astonishing.

He printed them, studied them again, but saw nothing that might aid his investigation. Still, he put them into his slowly growing file folder.

He emailed Jamie back, asking about the vomitus. Jamie replied that there had been none—either in the wood leading up to the stone, in the vicinity of the stone, in Kent's car or house, or on the earthen track leading to the wood. Or in Dave Morley's car. And the lab technicians would have surely found traces when they searched Dave's car for Kent's DNA. Which told McLaren that the quantity of hydrangea in Kent's stomach hadn't been enough to induce sickness. Maybe whoever had been poisoning Kent had just begun. Or, he mentally added as he grabbed his keys from the kitchen worktop, perhaps Kent had been on the verge of being sick but had been strangled before the hydrangea poisoning killed him.

McLaren hit the lull in Monday afternoon traffic that occurs between the lunch crowd gathering and the end-of-workday homeward rush. Jamie had given him the ex-wife's name, and McLaren had found her address in the phone book. It was no secret that Sheri Harrison and Kent had been married—their names had been linked frequently in all the media reports at the time—so McLaren wasn't betraying Jamie's confidence. Besides, the staff at Tutbury Castle knew both parties, Sheri still being employed there. McLaren allowed himself to whistle as he turned his red Peugeot 207 onto the A515 out of Buxton, heading toward the castle. He had phoned ahead; she was working until five o'clock.

He lowered his car windows. He rarely used the air conditioning system, enjoying the fresh air fanning his face. When he had been in the job he had lived in that mechanically created coolness and thought nothing of it. But his year outdoors, working under too hot, too cold, frosty, and rainy conditions, had reminded him how much he loved the natural world. Now he kept his windows open most of the year and relished the changes of all the seasons. The sun beat down on his right arm lying along the window opening and he sang along, full throated and joyful, with his folk group's rendition of 'The Carman's Whistle.'

Traffic thinned out in the stretch south of Buxton and he had a chance to glance at the countryside. It was flatter, more open land here in the White Peak area than that which comprised the Dark Peak District on the northern side of Buxton. The Dark Peak. Bog moss, peat and tough grasses coated the millstone grit at the heart of this wild, dark land—a windswept, cloud-draped panorama. Rolling hills covered in farmed fields and sheep replaced the Dark Peak's rocky crags, steep slopes, and forests. Sounds, too, were different in the White Peak and the southern dales. Field and hedgerow loving birds such as robins and larks, brought the pastures and gardens alive with song, a descant to the motors of farm machinery. Mix with that the fragrance of mowed grass and banks of evening primrose, and he could be out for a stroll as compared to serious, gear wearing climbs in the Dark wilderness.

Two songs later he passed the village of Ashbourne and soon turned onto the A515. Traffic was heavier here, closer to Derby and Uttoxeter. Directional signs pointed toward Sudbury Prison and Sudbury Hall. McLaren thought, not for the first time, how incongruous that looked—one a prison for Category D male prisoners, and the other the epitome of seventeenth century elegance. He snorted heavily as he drove past the sign announcing the prison. What a laugh. Six hundred sixty-five inmates escaping from the prison in the past ten years. They get bored with the facility's education and evening classes? Training in bricklaying, farming, and gardening he could see as useful. But Enhanced Thinking Skills and Cognitive Skills Booster classes were beyond a joke. Fancy, meaningless names for a therapy whereby the inmates reflect upon their displeasing behaviors and consider possible future actions. In other words, mimicking psychology and probationary terms to pull the wool over the cops' eyes. Throw in a listener scheme for prisoners at risk from suicide or self-harm, and an anti-bullying committee... McLaren shook his head, wondering what had happened to non-coddling police work.

The road angled eastward. The River Dove, the

boundary marking Derbyshire and Staffordshire, looped and rambled along his right side, out of sight yet constant. Several miles on, he hit Staffordshire and turned off at the first major road. Tutbury's famous castle, picturesque in its ruins, topped the hill one hundred feet above the town.

The car park wasn't full as it would be after work tonight, or during the weekend. Still, in the midst of the summer long holiday, school-aged children, parents, and tourists made a good showing. McLaren found a parking spot near the embankment.

But he remained in his car while he punched Jamie's number into his mobile. A question had nagged him during the drive, and he needed it answered.

Jamie answered with a wary "Hello?" then asked McLaren's location.

"At the castle. I've got a question."

"I figured you didn't ring me up to tell me you were buying me lunch. What gives?"

"Just making sure before I talk to people. Dave Morley never had a confirmable alibi, right?"

"Lived alone, didn't have a girlfriend, didn't order in Chinese, and wasn't seen by anyone. Is that what you want?"

"I want to get this sorted out correctly. I make a fool of myself without sticking my foot into something everyone else knows. Is that right about the non-existent alibi?"

Jamie's voice dropped slightly. "Nothing was ever proven, and the lads in blue talked to everyone they could think of. Not only to eliminate Dave as a suspect but also to gather information."

"It's times like this that a live-in girlfriend would

be beneficial."

"Even if he had one, Mike, the lass might lie to protect him."

"Sure, but I can dream of interviewing a completely honest person, can't I?"

"CCTV can be less stressful and holds up in court."

McLaren ignored the jest. "Did he have anything from the crime scene on him? I'm thinking soil that could be matched, or traces of a particular plant."

"That's been looked at, Mike. No red flag fluttered at the time, so he wasn't under the radar. Personally, I think he's clean, but you can form your own opinion."

"Maybe the soil or plants weren't different from that at his house. Maybe he lucked out."

"Whatever. Gotta go."

"Sure." He thanked Jamie and rang off as he got out of his car.

The castle's south tower, tan and glowing now in the afternoon sun, claimed that portion of sky. But it was the north tower, a lone fragment of stone that was long associated with Mary, Queen of Scots' imprisonment. Her apartments had been in a black-and-white building, no longer extant, stretching between the tower and the South Range. How many hundred yards was that, he wondered as he bought a ticket from the seller at the little shack. Hardly the prison he had envisioned in primary school. Some jail! Shaking his head, he walked up the slightly sloping path to the entrance, his boots crunching on the hard-packed gravel.

Once again, the castle cast its spell on him. As he approached the gatehouse with its twin columns and narrow, tall doorway, he tried to imagine the castle's approaching 950 years, stretching from its construction begun in 1068 to its present renaissance as a living piece of history. He never really could do; there were too many monarchs and sieges in that time span. He was content to focus on the snippets of history he knew—Henry VIII visited in 1511, Mary imprisoned four times between 1569 and 1585, and the brief consideration in the early 1830s to use the castle as a prison.

He crossed the center court, a grassy expanse now holding vendor booths and archery contests. The land and the castle stones had baked under the July sun all day and now threw it back in oven-like blasts of heat. McLaren eyed the beer vendor, longing for a long gulp of cold liquid, but walked on. Beneath his boots the grass bent and broke, as brittle as old parchment, as tan as the beer he wanted. He came upon the main stage holding the musicians and singers. The heat throbbed here, funneled along the south wall of the castle and the vendors' booths. A faint breeze threaded through this corridor, scented with human sweat, perfume, and heat. The area to the right of the castle entrance was reserved for the tumblers, jugglers, and acrobats. All very authentic, all part of the exuberant Minstrels Court.

He found Sheri Harrison in the castle's tearoom, a ground-floor restaurant acquisitioned from the rooms making up the main building. A brunette with faint streaks of gray in her hair, Sheri wore the air of exhaustion that comes with too much work and meeting continuous deadlines. She looked up as he approached her table, her eyes inquisitive behind round, metal spectacles. Her openness faded somewhat when he introduced himself, but she offered him a chair.

"Would you like tea?" She reached for the small ceramic pot beside her teacup. "I think there's enough left for one more cup. If you want to get a cup from the counter…" She shifted in her chair to see the stack of cups and saucers. "Or I could get you a coffee." She hesitated and peered at him from over her glasses.

"I appreciate the offer," McLaren said, aware that she waited for his order, "but I'll pass. I'm rather too hot for tea. No offense."

"Of course not."

"Thank you for seeing me. I realize you don't know where my questions will lead, that you're no doubt considering if it's a good idea to talk to me. I can't answer that for you. But your cooperation is greatly appreciated."

She nodded slightly, perhaps acknowledging the truth of his statements, and showed a faint smile. "Were you walking around for a while outside, taking in the festivities?"

"Why? Do I look that hot?"

"Not too awfully. It's just that your face is red enough for it. Walking up from the car park and across the courtyard has most people panting in this heat, including me. I get here ten minutes early of a morning so my coloring returns to normal." She suggested lemonade or other cold beverage. "Guaranteed to cool you down."

"Thanks just the same. I'm fine." McLaren looked around the room.

Pale green walls set off the honey-colored window blinds, casting an aura of comfort through the area. A combination tearoom and souvenir shop, it held a quality selection from both quarters. People contemplated picture postcards, books, mugs, maps, CDs, DVDs, small toys and games, and tea towels. They sat at tables or queued for tea, peering at the menu board or the food selections in the glass display counter. Conversations and the clink of metal cutlery against china, the ring of the cash registers and the restaurant door latching shut blended into the hum of background noise as McLaren gave a quick look at Mary, Queen of Scots. The painting's artist caught her—magnificent in her dress—arriving in 1585 for her fourth period of incarceration in the castle. Poor Mary. Each time she had left Tutbury she probably had thought she had escaped its horror. What must she have felt on learning she was to return? He gave the painting one last glance before he turned in his chair to face Sheri—the picture of cool and crisp in her wrinkle-free linen skirt and cotton blouse. Unlike me, he thought, wiping his fingers across the right side of his neck to mop up the sweat. Maybe I should have a lemonade. "So you're fine with talking about Kent, then."

"Certainly. It's not a topic I relish. Kent and I had a nasty parting, but I don't mind answering some questions. Provided they're not too personal." She looked at him, expressionless but for the hint of challenge in her eyes.

"I appreciate your honesty and I accept your condition. When was your divorce, if you don't mind telling me?"

"Why? Is there some magic number, like after eight months, four days, and seventeen hours you no longer hate each others' guts and wouldn't dream of making life rough for the other?"

"Was that true in your or Kent's case, then?"

"Now you're talking motive, Mr. McLaren."

He snorted. "Of course! Don't tell me that surprises you. I'm sure the police thought the same during their initial investigation. I don't know that motive necessarily always dies with time."

She nodded her head slightly. "I don't know if my ill feeling...well, you can call it hatred, for that's not too strong a word...toward Kent would have eased much even years from then."

"Has it eased any, now that he's dead?"

"Somewhat. Not much. I don't know. I haven't actually considered my current feelings. I've tried to bury them now that Kent..." She tapped the spoon against the lip of the cup and set it on the saucer. Leaning back in her chair, she looked as though she had all the time in the world; her workday had ended, and she was too comfortable—and tired—to move just yet. She said rather slowly, "It's best that way, you know. You can't live long with so much hatred inside you. It's not healthy. It eats away at your being; it saps your energy and your will to do anything else. I know I wasted a lot of hours planning vengeful, spiteful things. Like I had suddenly inhabited a different body, had become a different person, and that's all I could think about or had the desire to do, avenge myself on Kent because he had hurt me. And I don't mean with his girlfriend, Fay. She came along after we decided we weren't working out. No. There was another reason for our split." She lifted her eyes from the cup to find McLaren looking at her. "Sorry. Bad habit of mine, feeling sorry for myself. Well, it's water under the dam and I've got the rest of my life to forget Kent Harrison."

"These vengeful, spiteful things you were

planning. What did you do?"

"Oh, I never carried any of that out, Mr. McLaren! It was more a cheap, therapeutic exercise than anything physical."

"Fifty ways to kill your lover, eh? With apologies to Paul Simon."

"I probably came up with fifty-one, but in my case I changed the word to 'punish' because I didn't kill him."

McLaren let the silence fall between them as he considered her statement. He didn't know her, but he believed, given enough motive and anger, anyone could kill. The question was if Sheri Harrison was that sort of person, and if she was lying.

"How did you two meet?" He eyed her, curious beyond the mere words of the inquiry. He could see why any man might be attracted to her, but he was interested about Kent meeting her. "And when?" he added quickly as Sheri shifted in her chair.

"It's fairly boring." She picked up the teaspoon.

"Perhaps, but 'boring' doesn't bother me."

"Here at the castle. During one of the events."

"Minstrels Court?"

"No. Earlier in the year than that. Just a weekend of period music. I liked his music, went over to watch, became intrigued by him, and..." She shrugged and gave a half smile. "We dated, fell in love, got married a year later. Here at the castle. It seemed romantic at the time."

"And you made your home...where?"

"In Kirkfield. In the same house he lived in before we met. My place was too small. A flat in Swadlincote. So even though Kirkfield was slightly farther from my work at the castle, his house suited us better. So I moved in right before our wedding. Moved out right before our divorce. I now live in Ashbourne."

"You were working at the castle before and during your marriage. Where did Kent work during that period?"

"At the same place when he died."

"*Murdered*, Mrs. Harrison. Kent was murdered."

He emphasized the word so strongly that Sheri jerked her head. "Yes. Of course. When he was…" She frowned slightly, as though fishing for a word McLaren would like, reluctant to use his offering. "When he was…killed. He still worked at the school in Ashbourne."

"Did you always live in Swadlincote?"

"Seems like it, though my parents and I lived in London until my first birthday. Then Dad got his job in Swadlincote and we moved here. My folks still live there, by the way. Dad's itching to retire. He has two more years until he can."

"What does he do?"

"Computer work. Repair and website hosting. Mum works from their home as a website designer."

"What did you and Kent do for fun? Holidays, clubs, hobbies," he suggested when she looked blank.

"At first it was music. That's what had brought us together."

"Early stuff, like the type he sang?"

"Certainly. We'd go to folk clubs, too. Some of the songs he sang actually fit that category, and when he popularized some of them, they easily fit the folk vein. We'd make the rounds every so often. You know, The Malt Shovel on Tuesdays, The Harried Fox on Fridays.

But it wasn't cast in stone."

"Not *every* Tuesday for the Malt Shovel, then." Actually, the idea's not abhorrent. And if you change it to performance instead of attendance, that would be nice for my group. A steady engagement where there's a loyal fan base, good pub grub to keep the audience there. And close to home so you don't spend half your free evening driving to and fro. A local following helps push you over the top with popularity, too. They get attached to a song, tell someone else about it... Nothing wrong with a reliable performance schedule.

"No," Sheri replied, pulling him from his mental plans. "Nothing like a weekly or monthly social outing. We had other interests, although the music was important. Kent and his occasional male singing partner—"

"He sang regularly with someone other than the woman with whom he recorded 'The Swans' Song,' I assume."

"What? Oh, yes. That recording was with Fay Larkin. They weren't an act, not like Kent and the other bloke. I think Fay just came into the picture to make that recording, since he needed a female voice. Dave Morley was his usual partner when they chose to sing together. They got together every month, or month and a half, for a boys' night out at a pub to talk over an upcoming venue or recording session. I'd either stay home, or pop over to a girl friend's or my parents' for the evening."

"No clubs on your own?"

"No. I like to read during my time off. Or garden or go out with friends. I don't like organizations, church groups or fitness centers. Nothing structured like that.

But we did have friends over about once a month for dinner. Or we were asked to their homes."

"Any particular friends? Did you see them on a fairly regular basis?"

"You want names?" Without waiting for his answer, she opened her handbag, took out a small notepad and pen, and wrote down names and phone numbers. She handed it to McLaren. "We're a dull bunch."

"Keeps you out of trouble that way. Thanks." He glanced at the paper, folded it, and put it into his shirt pocket. "Sounds like your lives were full. What drove you apart?"

Sheri sighed and pulled in her bottom lip. Dropping the pad and pen into her bag, she said, "What drives people apart? You eventually have different goals for your lives, your interests change until you're just two people sharing a house and who merely nod to each other while heading for different appointments."

"No person got in the way, then. No long hours at work." This echoes Dena and me, he thought. Wasn't that her main complaint before he broke off from her last year? He was never home, and when he was, he still carried his job with him, mentally and emotionally. It'd been hard to separate the loves of police work and Dena. Both consumed him, but the first was his livelihood. Even if Dena had realized that, she couldn't accept the backseat in which he'd placed her. And it sounded as if Kent had done the identical thing with Sheri, except he'd chosen music instead of the Force. Either way, the result was the same—instead of two couples, there were four separate people.

"No," Sheri said, her voice slightly bitter. "No

other woman or even a hint of an affair came between us. Kent became more and more involved in his music so I compensated for the hours alone by working longer at the castle. And going on weekend trips with a friend."

"Who's the friend? Where did you go?"

"Nothing lurid, Mr. McLaren. A girlfriend. Her name's on the list. First one. Her husband is often in Munich for his job, so Judy has quite a few weekends free. We go bird watching.."

"So these people on your list are the ones you and Kent socialized with as a couple, for the most part."

"Yes."

"And since your divorce…you said you're still employed here at the castle."

"Yes. Full time tour guide and some time event planner."

McLaren glanced out the window. One of the castle towers caught the sunlight, tinted to gold, and he thought it would be an interesting place to work. "Which do you like best, the guiding or the planning?"

Sheri shook her head, her eyes clouding for a moment. "Hard to answer. I like the tour guide position because I like teaching and seeing the interest in people's faces. I love history, which plays into being a guide, of course, but it also is an essential part of event planning. I get a great satisfaction from a well-staged and attended event."

"How long after you moved out of your house was your divorce granted?"

"A year. I felt as though I was aging a month for each day I stayed married to Kent. It's still a shock to realize I'm only thirty-six. I feel twice that." She glanced at McLaren, looking as though she challenged him to say something consoling, like she didn't even look thirty-six, then she pressed her lips together and shifted her gaze.

As the silence fell between them, Sheri again stirred her tea. Playing for time, McLaren wondered, or hoping he'd leave?

"I had an alibi for the time of his death, you know." Her words, soft as they were spoken, broke the silence.

"Tenth of July. Where were you?"

"Nowhere suspicious. It's fairly common knowledge. I was working late. Here, at the castle."

"Others saw you and vouched for you, I take it."

"My boss, Clark MacKay. We were together. Until about eleven o'clock."

"Rather late to be working." The suspicion crept into his voice again.

"Yes. But we were putting the final touches on an upcoming event."

"On a mental roll."

"Yes. There were a myriad of small, last minute details to finish and we needed to get it completed."

"What was the event?"

"Tudor Days. We held it later that month. I'm talking about last year, you understand."

"I'm aware we're talking about last year, Mrs. Harrison. He was *murdered* last year." His eyes narrowed slightly, wondering if she was nervous or perhaps thought him an idiot.

Sheri nodded, her cheeks slightly reddened. "Yes. Sorry. It's just that...talking about days and years... Well, I didn't want you—"

"I'm right with you. Your alibi is tenth of July, a

year ago. You were working late."

She rushed on, as though trying to gloss over her verbal *faux pas*. "Yes. Our first Tudor Days was the previous year, in fact."

"Two years ago." He smiled, showing he could do the mental math.

"We had spent several years saying 'what if' and 'why can't we' and other procrastinating phrases until I suppose we tired of the excuses and rolled up our sleeves three years ago and planned the thing. I'm awfully glad we did. It was a huge success so we held it again last year. Even though last year's was only the second time for Tudor Days, we felt we really had a winner."

"Attendance was that good, then."

"Oh yes! We had nothing but rave reviews. From everyone, the media, the booth vendors, the performers, and the public."

"Congratulations."

"Thank you. We focused on the castle's history during the reigns of the Tudors, had cooking demonstrations, food, art, music and contests pertinent to that era."

Kids would probably love it, he thought. Who didn't like dressing up, playing at Knights of the Round Table, sword fighting? And if the vendors were smart, they'd have kid-sized and kid-themed items for parents to buy… He glanced at the items in the gift shop. A plastic sword and shield would fulfill many a child's dream. "You mentioned music. Did Kent perform at that event?"

"Yes. I believe he did." She tilted her head slightly. Light from the overhead fixture reflected off her spectacles, masking her eyes from his view. Then, as quickly as they had slipped into obscurity, they stared back at him as she again shifted her head. She blinked several times, perplexed. "Why do you want to know about what happened during Tudor Days? You think someone there trailed him home and killed him? Isn't that rather far-fetched, targeting your victim like that? I thought that was just movie drama."

"You also mentioned food. I assume you had demonstrations and booths."

The sudden switch in topics seemed to catch her by surprise. Her eyes widened and she blinked before she replied. "Pardon? Oh, certainly. That's standard in most of these fairs and reenactments."

"I know this is an absurd question, but did you know if Kent ate anything at one of the booths?"

"Oh. You're trying to figure out how that poisonous plant got into him. Well, it wasn't me, Mr. McLaren. I didn't brew up hemlock tea and make him drink it. He wouldn't have eaten anything I'd have given him, anyway, which I wouldn't have done. That would have necessitated me getting within communicating and seeing range. Neither of which I had a desire to do. So you'll have to look for your poisoner somewhere else."

"You were divorced by then, or planning to be?"

"Divorced. Cleanly separated. Nice and legal."

"And that was…"

"One week to the day before he wound up dead. If I'd known that was going to happen, I would have saved my time, energy, and money and not hired my lawyer. Life's funny, isn't it?"

Chapter Seven

Dena thought she could have saved some time and energy, and certainly petrol money, if she and Dave Morley had talked by phone. But she wanted to judge his demeanor, see the facial expressions behind his words. After all, Michael always talked about 'reading' people. The phone masked communication nearly as well as email did. If you didn't have voice inflections or couldn't read body language something as mundane as 'Everything's just fine' could be interpreted either as sarcastic or elated.

Joyful Sound Music was a modest sized shop in Buxton. While not situated on the High Street or the Crescent—two of the more traveled spots—it was still in a location that brought a respectable amount of trade. Dena parked her MG opposite the store, applied a fresh coat of lipstick to her dry lips, and combed her hair while she mentally rehearsed what she would ask Dave Morley. Smoothing a non-existent wrinkle from her blue trousers, she took a deep breath, then walked into the shop.

Unlike the stony, traditional front of the building that seemed to muscle room for itself between the bookstore on its left and the bakery on its right, the interior was light, airy, and open. One wall held guitars, banjos, mandolins, and lutes, while across the aisle woodwind and brass instruments waited to be bought.

Large glass-front cases of accessories squeezed in between racks of sheet music and shelves of concertinas and tin whistles. Leather-cushioned stools dotted the interior, inviting the customer to sit and try out an instrument.

Dave Morley turned from dusting a 5-string banjo, saw a potential customer in Dena, and laid down the dust rag. He smoothed his thinning hair and gave her a hesitant smile before asking if he could be of assistance.

"I hope so." Dena fought a sudden surge of panic. Maybe this wasn't such a good idea. She had no credentials like McLaren did; she had no authority like a police officer; she wasn't even a friend or family member of Kent Harrison's. Why would Dave Morley talk to her?

"I hope I can, too," Dave returned, coming up to her. He was tall and thin, with a receding hairline that visually added more years to him than was warranted. He had musician's fingers—long and thin, good for playing a stringed instrument. Or a piano. Dena remembered some of the nearly impossible note reaches she'd attempted. Her hands had been too small, barely stretching an octave, so she had resorted to a quick roll of the chord. Glancing once more at his fingers, Dena thought how strong they probably were. Just chording alone developed muscles.

"Do you wish to see an instrument?" Dave broke her reverie. He rolled down the long sleeves of his pinstriped shirt and flicked a piece of lint from the cuff, giving her an optimistic smile. He leaned forward slightly, implying he was on the balls of his feet and ready to spring into action at her first word. "Or are you interested in an accessory or sheet music?"

"Actually, I'd like to speak to David Morley. Are you he?" She glanced at his nametag.

"Yes. Did someone recommend you to me?"

"I have a few questions, if you have a minute or two." She should have phrased that better. He thinks this is about music. She started to explain further, but he said, "That's why I'm here. Ask anything you'd like."

"I'd like to ask you about Kent Harrison, about the night he died. You knew him, I understand."

Dave's dark eyes seemed to soften. He jammed his fists into his slacks pockets. "Why are you asking about Kent a year after his death? Did Sheri send you?"

Dena blinked, startled at the question. "I'm sorry—Sheri?"

"She must have done. She or Fay. Who was it?" A muscle in his forearm twitched.

"I assure you, Mr. Morley, neither of those two people sent me. I don't even know them."

"Then why are you here?" His brows lowered, as if he were mentally sizing up her authority and interest in him. He nodded slightly, evidently satisfied of the answer. "Newspaper. That's it. You're a reporter."

Dena opened her mouth to protest, but Dave rushed on.

"Sure. One year anniversary of the murder. Only, there's no planned vigil or prayer gathering at the castle. None that I know of, at least. And I think I would've been told, seeing as how Kent and I were singing partners." He stopped so abruptly that it was several seconds before Dena could think of something to say.

"You're under the wrong assumption, Mr. Morley.

I'm not a reporter."

"You're not a cop, either."

"No." She was tempted to say that her boyfriend had been, but that wouldn't add any weight to her basis for being here. "I was at the Minstrels Court festival at Tutbury Castle today. It reminded me of Kent's last performance there and I want to see it solved. You see, I have a friend..." She paused, unsure if this were the best approach.

Dave sighed, visibly bored. "I've got work to do. Can you get on with it?"

"My friend..." She swallowed, blushing as she spoke. But Dave remained mute, his lips pressed together, staring at her. She took a deep breath and continued. "I think he could look into Kent's death and find out who killed him."

"Your friend can do this even though Derbyshire's Finest failed. Who is he...Superman? Maybe Marvin the Mentalist?"

"I should think you'd want Kent's killer caught. You were his friend."

"Right on both accounts, luv. But you could be telling me anything. I don't know you from Adam. Well..." He paused, his eyes taking in her well-proportioned figure and trendy hairstyle. Her understated clothes spoke of Money. "*Eve*. Like I said a minute ago, Sheri could have put you up to this. I've never seen you before."

"I'm not accusing you of Kent's murder."

"I should bloody well hope not."

"I just have a question."

"Like what?"

"Why you waited twenty-four hours to look for

Kent. If you and he were such genial mates, I'd have thought you would've looked for him much sooner."

"You would, eh? Well, I have news for you. I did look for him. "

Dena opened her mouth, then thought better of her response, and merely looked at Dave.

"I spent hours driving around, going to pubs and places I knew he frequented. I was worried sick. I couldn't sleep, so I tried to find him."

"But you said in the newspaper interview—"

"I know what I said. I was scared I'd be accused of kidnapping or murder. I-I needed this job and I didn't want to lose it by rotting in the nick. I know some folks are accused of crimes they didn't commit and they end up behind bars for years, trying to prove their innocence. I had no alibi for that evening and that's all I could think of. I was scared. I lied to the police."

An embarrassed quiet settled over them and Dena tried to think of something to say.

The shop door opened and a woman and teenaged girl entered, the girl chattering about the merits of a used Goya versus new Martin, Cordoba or Ramirez classical guitars.

Dave ran his tongue over his lips and coughed. "Sorry. I have a customer. If you'll excuse me…" His hand went to the knot of his necktie. He pulled it tighter and straightened the tie. "I'm sorry if I'm a disappointment to you, but Kent was actually the god. I just played second fiddle." He stepped aside to allow Dena to precede him to the front of the shop. Dena felt his eyes on her as she exited—the bell attached to the door jangled. She peeked around in time to see him smile toward the mother and daughter.

****

The bell's sound seemed to follow her into the street, multiplying into a dozen gonging tongues, deafening and whispering simultaneously. Trying to shake the clatter, she turned to her right and hurried up the street. Shoppers and workers crowded the pavement, slowing her escape. But she pushed through the sea of bodies, concentrating on the snippets of conversation and traffic noises. Dave's hiss and the bell's clamor seeped into the surrounding sounds. At the top of The Slopes she stopped. She had shaken off the din. And the embarrassment.

But she hadn't shaken off the memory of the sound of hand bells. Hand bells and mockery.

She sat on a nearby bench. It had been...what? Twenty years ago? Yes. She nodded, the group of teenagers and the church hall once more standing before her, dredged up from some recess in her memory. They had been practicing their music for the village wakes. The week long celebration would begin the following day, opened by a village luminary who had blazed into fame through the music world. And therefore not only created excitement in the teenaged bell ringers but also added to the pressure to perform perfectly. They were on edge. Dena's concentration had faltered during a passage; she hadn't put down her hand bells to use the choir chimes. Consequently, the melody dipped into and out of prominence and eventually produced more foul ups. Normally Dena would have shrugged off the mistake, making a humorous excuse. But the jests and name-calling hurt more than usual, cut deeper and stayed longer. Remained with her even now, twenty years later. Nerves may have produced the initial verbal storm, but personal gripes and animosities flamed the exasperation into hatred. And the hostility turned into sharp-tongued gossip, following Dena for the rest of the year.

A woman's mobile phone chimed as she passed, and the adolescent recollection faded. Dena got up slowly, glancing around to see if anyone stared at her, guessed her inner turmoil. But the human rush concentrated on its own wants and problems, having no time or desire to notice a solitary figure sitting idle. She returned to her car, questions resonating inside her head. The questions rang with the voices of McLaren, Gwen, Jamie Kydd, and Dave Morley. And, most upsetting, herself. Approaching the music shop, she glanced at its front, half expecting to see Dave Morley leering at her. Or at least standing in the doorway to bar her entrance. But the shop front harbored no one.

Somewhat placated, she slid into the car's driver's seat, questions in her mind as persistent as the noise in the street. Was Dave Morley apparently telling the truth now? Perhaps more to the point, why is he so certain Sheri Harrison prompted my appearance? Does that mean she knows who's behind Kent's death?

Chapter Eight

Does that mean Sheri was happy about Kent's death? McLaren wondered. Or merely making an observation about coincidence? He left the castle car park, shaking his head, swearing he'd had enough of women, cold cases, and poking his nose into other people's lives.

When he got home he showered and changed clothes. He pitched the perspiration-soaked shirt into the linen bin, glad to be cool and dry once again, and downed a large glass of water in deep gulps. The wet leather cord of his necklace left damp impressions on his T-shirt.

McLaren made a cheese and tomato sandwich and took a bite from it as he carried it into the front room. Still chewing, he put the plate on the coffee table and got out his guitar. He sat on the couch, his back to the front window, and strummed a few chords, deciding on a song. The first verse of 'The Swans' Song' poured from him in an emotional rendering, as though he were singing it at Kent Harrison's funeral. Startled, he paused, his pulse racing. Then, realizing it was his subconscious reaction to the day's questioning, he went on, singing the entire song.

Ah, says the swan a-swimming on the lake;
I'll tell you why my heart did break.
Once I courted a love so fair

And when he left I did despair.
—

Ah, says the cob with his feathers white;
I loved a lass in the pale moonlight.
She proved untrue and from me fled
And since that day I bow my head.
—

Howdy dowdy diddle dum day
Howdy dowdy diddle dum day
Howdy dowdy diddle dum day
Hey li lee a-riddle dum dum.
—

Ah, says the pen on the wide millrace;
I knew a cob with a handsome face.
His words of love, they did deceive,
Now night and day I sit and grieve.
—

Ah, says the cob a-sitting on a stone;
I had a love but now I'm alone.
I brought her gifts by night and day
But she from me did fly away.
—

Ah, says the pen on the grassy bank;
I'll tell you of a cruel prank.
He I loved, he did me woo;
Alas for me, he proved untrue.
—

Ah, says the cob with a saddened air;
Once I courted a lady fair.
She proved false, from me did turn,
But for my love I still do yearn.
—

Ah, says the pen with a mournful cry;

I loved a cob with a roving eye.
With words of love he filled my heart;
When he did leave it broke apart.

As the last chord of the song hung in the air, McLaren thought about himself and Dena. The past year they had been much like that swan couple, but Dena had done more of the grieving. At least demonstrative, he corrected, setting the guitar on the floor and leaning its neck against the edge of the sofa. And if he were truthful, he'd admit he was just as lonely. And hurt. He slowly shook his head, lowering it as his shameful behavior toward her welled up inside him. He would never treat her like that again. Her or anyone else he loved. It was a sin against God and a slap of her face.

He glanced at the partially eaten sandwich, wondering why he had thought himself hungry, and grabbed his guitar again. After a quick tuning, he sang 'Some Rival Has Stolen My True Love Away.' The words hit him with a fierceness that he couldn't contain, especially the last lines of the final verse.

But it's I'll be as constant as a true turtle dove,
For I never will, at no time, prove false to my love.

He should take that as his motto. He laid the guitar on the sofa. Tattoo it on my cheek so I'll see it when I shave; chisel it on the side of the stone wall. Better than his flippant phrases that his group heard all the time. He left the sandwich on the table and went into the kitchen.

He passed the next half hour phoning the Harrisons' friends, making notations and tick marks next to the individual names on Sheri's list. Everyone, in varying frequencies, had been to their home for dinner, had joined them in other social activities, had seen their marriage deteriorate over several years and finally fall apart, and had felt sympathy for them. Some had taken sides, some had abandoned the friendship, some had offered philosophy and shoulders. No one, however, harbored any suspicion that Sheri Harrison had killed Kent Harrison. She wasn't that sort of person—even if she did end up hating Kent's guts. Besides, hadn't Sheri been working late that night? So, you see, she couldn't have been in two places at once.

So much for opportunity, McLaren thought, even if motive is still rife. Besides, would *all* these people lie? They might if they were Sheri's friends.

McLaren was pouring himself a cup of tea when the doorbell rang. As he walked into the front room, he glanced out of the large window. Dena's red sports car sat in the driveway. Smiling, he put the cup on the side table, opened the door, and pulled her toward him.

"I was hoping you'd drop by," he mumbled, his lips against her cheek, and thought how soft her skin was. "It's been a while."

Dena gave him a swift kiss and struggled out of his embrace. "Just two days."

"Seemed more like two weeks. You're not working at the sanctuary today?" He followed her to the sofa but remained standing while she seated herself. The turquoise color of her blouse complemented the coppery strands in her brunette hair. "Want some tea? Coffee? Wine?"

"Nothing, thanks. I just dropped by for a minute."

"Then let's make the most of that minute." He took the seat next to her and waited for her to find the words.

"You got the message I left on your ansafone, I guess." She raised her gaze to his eyes, looking doe-eyed and hopeful at once.

"Yes." He left it hanging there and watched her top teeth bite into her lower lip. Her fingers twisted the ring on her finger while she tried to bring up a smile. Pathetic. He needed to put her out of her misery. He sighed heavily and leaned back. "I couldn't quite figure it out so I played it a few times." He glanced out the window and fastened his gaze on her car. "It still made no sense, so I erased it." He waited for the cry. It came right on time.

"You erased it! Why didn't you ring me up if you didn't understand what I was saying? I go to all this trouble to—"

McLaren spoke slowly, as though addressing the car. "I really couldn't see anything interesting in what I could make out. Besides, I've been working on a stone wall job up in Hathersage." He turned, eyeing her flushed face. "All I could make out is that you have some murder case gone cold, right? At Tutbury Castle. Well, if the body was found elsewhere…"

"It's that murder that happened last year. Kent Harrison. He was performing at the Minstrels Court. I thought you could give it a try, if you're not too busy." She rushed on with her explanation. "It had everyone baffled at the time. Do you recall the facts?"

"I reread the newspaper account. Is the castle curator making noises about the death? Is that why you want me to look into it?"

"No. Not that I know of. I just thought that since it's been a year, and since the police don't seem to be making any headway, and since—"

"Since I cleared up another little cold case last month, you thought I might as well strike while I'm hot and clear this one up, too. Right?" He smiled as she glared at him.

"Not at all. It's a matter of justice, that's all. You care about justice."

"Without saying the obvious that everyone should, I'll comment that I just got out of that previous case by the skin of my teeth. Harvester and some other not too friendly coppers weren't half pleased with me popping up again. You want me to go through all that a second time, maybe get stopped for something that will stick, something other than a suspicion of driving under the influence?" A surge of heat hit his cheeks and he was painfully aware that his heart rate had increased. Talking about Charlie Harvester, his former coworker and current nemesis, did that. "Do they allow prisoners to get mail these days? We'll have to look up when my visiting days are." He leaned back, the red in his cheeks starting to fade, and looked at Dena.

"I won't dignify that remark with a response, Michael. I'll assume you're joking. But honestly, I did think you'd be interested in the Harrison case. Besides being a bit of a mystery, the chap was a musician."

"So I'm supposed to feel this overwhelming brotherly love for a fellow guitarist?"

"Well, that's part of it, sure. But he touched so many people in his life. Positively, I mean."

"The Great Influence? He was such a smashing teacher?"

"Yes, I think he was. And more than that, Michael. He was a human being who didn't deserve to be killed. He was too young and his killer got away. It's indecent that it happened to him. To *anyone*."

"So you call me in to fix everything."

Dena pursed up her lips in a half pout. There was a small whine to her voice. "I thought you could. That you might be interested. That you might want to help his family and friends see some justice done."

"That's what the police are for, Dena. I'm through with the Constabulary, remember?"

A silence fell between them, thick as the skin he'd grown to ward off prisoners' insults and threats, the mockery of the public, the chastisement of his bosses and judges. A year ago, he'd thought a year ago when he had left the job and taken up the work of repairing and building dry stone walls that he could forget all that. But the voices sounded remarkably loud at times, the words as sharp now as the day they had been hurled at him. They hadn't faded with time, nor lain forgotten. They woke him some nights, wouldn't let him fall asleep other nights—whirling in his mind with the clarity of the judge's gavel emphasizing a verdict. He was surprised they still had the power to hurt.

A motorcycle roared past his house in an eddy of dust and nodding roadside grasses, ascending the hill on its way to Castleton, perhaps. The noise startled him back to the present and he became aware of Dena again. He stared at her, as though he were annoyed, then grinned. "You look miserable. Relax, sweets. I've already talked to a few people who are connected with the case."

"A few people... You spoke with them today?"

"Not before breakfast." He dodged the thrown pillow.

"You... Making me think you..." She took a deep breath, her emotions too swift to express. "You ought to be—"

"I'm sure I should. I thought you'd be glad your phone message was so persuasive."

"Maybe I should have been a lawyer. What do you think?" She stood, picked up the pillow, and set it back on the sofa.

"I think I like you just how you are." He grabbed her wrist and pulled her against his chest. "It might ruin my reputation if it became known I was kissing the other side."

"How do you know I'd be a defense lawyer?"

"Because that's who you are. Defender of the downtrodden, voice of the helpless."

"Latecomer is the more accurate term." She allowed him a kiss before she picked up her handbag and car key. "I'll be late if I don't leave now."

"Where you off to, then? Should I be jealous?"

"Just tea with a friend. A *girl* friend," she said as McLaren's eyebrow rose. She stood in the open doorway, looking undecided about something, then laid her right hand on his chest. "Thank you for doing this, Michael. It means a lot."

"A lot to whom? To you, I know it does. But to the family?" He shrugged, his right hand on top of hers, dwarfing it with its size.

"They've been conspicuous by their absence, haven't they?"

"Maybe they've been hounding the police. Just because it's not in the newspaper…" He shrugged again, not particularly caring why the family wasn't staging one of the yearly vigils that recently have become popular. Anniversaries of missing people and murder victims usually were lead stories in television news spots.

"Kent Harrison's friends might be glad of your solving the case, even if the family has moved away. Just because they're not pounding on doors doesn't mean they won't welcome your investigation, Michael."

He kissed her once more before she left, answered her exuberant declaration of love, and watched her car snake down the road until he could no longer see it.

He remained in the doorway for several minutes, aware of her scent on his clothing and in the air, feeling the heat and pressure of her fingers imprinted on his palm, hearing her whispered words in his mind. A lamb bleated on the hill behind his house and he walked inside, leaving the shadows to darken and lengthen in the approaching twilight.

****

Actually, she hadn't really lied. Dena glanced at the rearview mirror. McLaren was fast becoming a dot in the thickening light. Her car rounded the bend in the road, obliterating the last of him from her view. She did have to meet Mary, but not as soon as she'd told him. She needed to do this first. Now, not tomorrow. She needed to talk to one or two more people so she could hand him some more information. But why, she challenged herself. He said he'd already begun. Why was she still playing at detective? Was she harming his chance of success if she inadvertently angered someone?

Like Dave Morley, the music shop clerk...

She frowned, suddenly wondering if she should just forget this wild idea and head into Buxton to meet Mary. But the chance to share one of McLaren's passions whispered at her, lured her on. It would bring

71

them closer. It'd show him she supported whatever he did and that she wanted to be part of his life.

Or does it? Does it show, perhaps, that she has no faith in his ability, that she thought he needed help, no matter how amateurish and inept it might be? After all, if she was so bent on supporting him in whatever line of work he did, why wasn't she hauling rocks for his stone wall work? Why wasn't she bringing him lunch on some mountaintop? Why was she poking her nose into a murder case, of all places! *Because I like it.*

The reason rushed at her with all the fascination and sparkle of a fireworks explosion, with the inescapable lure of wrapped Christmas gifts discovered in her parents' bedroom closet. Because it was fun and she liked solving the puzzle. Because, it gave them something to discuss. She drowned the nagging voice with a dose of American bluegrass music, punching the Play button on the car's tape deck console. The Lynn Morris Band underscored her mental discussion by singing 'no one has to tell me what love is.' Dena nodded and applied her attention to the road.

The MG hesitated momentarily as it started up a hill and Dena changed down into third gear. The motor rushed ahead with a growl as the tires bit into the asphalt and as she crested the hill she glanced at the cottages and farms spread below, the green earth sectioned off in gray, stony lines, the clumps of trees darker green and thickest along the brook. Her hair caught the wind, streaming behind her as the car descended in a clatter of groaning engine and excited birds flushed from road-hugging bushes. She headed south, toward Ashbourne, wanting to talk to Kent Harrison's colleague. Maybe the teacher would remember something occurring at school that would have a bearing on the case.

She made good time on the A515 and soon after turning off the main road she arrived at Trevor Pennell's house, a semi-detached of brick with U-shaped orange terra cotta roof tiles. She parked in front of the house but let the motor idle. Was this really a good idea? She had no authority—she wasn't a police detective. Not even a former one, which would lend a bit more weight to back up her inquiry.

She had just talked herself into leaving when her mobile rang. Without looking at the caller ID, she flipped it open. Gwen's voice gushed over the line.

"Dena, hello. It's Gwen. Have you talked to Mike yet? About the case, I mean. Explained it to him?"

"No."

"No? I thought you were going to. I thought you were going to his house after we dropped you. Change your mind?"

"No, I didn't. I didn't have to tell him."

"What?" There was a pause, and Dena envisioned Gwen shaking her head, perhaps mouthing something to Jerry, like 'She's round the twist.' "I think I came in the middle of this, Dena. Back up and tell me what's going on."

"He's already begun the investigation. I didn't have to say anything."

"Already begun?"

"You heard me. He's talked to some people already. I didn't need to plead or cajole or bribe."

"You forgot lure, but it's probably just as well."

"I may need to lure, though."

"Why? What's going on?"

"I'm about to talk to one of the people associated with the case."

"What!" Gwen's concern exploded over the phone. "You're going to talk… Dena, leave this to Mike. He's had experience. He's a pro. You might get—"

"More information than he does?" she interrupted, purposely misreading Gwen's statement. "Get him jealous?"

"Might get into trouble," Gwen finished, her voice taking on an edge of worry. "Who are you talking to? You want me or Jerry to go with you? Safety in numbers, dear girl. Where is this person? I can meet you—"

"Too late for that, Gwen. I talked to a few before I met Michael. It was just to get some information in case I had to use it as lure."

"But if you didn't need the lure… You said you were about to talk to someone else. Why, if Mike's already interested?"

Trevor Pennell opened the front door of his house and let his dog out. Dena lowered her voice and angled her lips closer to the phone. "Look, Gwen, I've got to go. I'll tell you all about this tomorrow. Promise." She rang off and called to Trevor before she heard Gwen's squeak of protest.

Trevor looked to be in his mid-fifties, with dark hair and eyes. He remained on the front steps, watching his dog, and asked what she wanted.

"Mr. Pennell?" Dena's voice came out slightly breathy from her sprint up the walkway.

"Yes. And you are…"

"Dena Ellison."

"May I help you with something?"

"If you have a minute or two, I'd like to ask you about Kent Harrison. You and he were colleagues, I believe. You teach at Grange Hall Performing Arts College."

Trevor's eyes darkened and he tilted his head slightly, as though a different view would clear up the confusion. "I'm sorry, but I don't know why you wish to talk about Kent. He's not at the school any more."

A euphemism if I ever heard one, Dena thought. "You were a friend of his, correct? As opposed to someone you just nodded to in the halls, I mean."

"Yes." He hesitated, as if thinking of consequences if he spoke to her. "Where's this leading?"

"I'm with a group of people who think his case should be reopened."

"That's a difficult procedure. I'm in favor of it, if that's what you came to find out. Have you a petition you wish me to sign?" He glanced at her purse as though expecting her to produce a clipboard and pen.

"Not at the moment. Right now I'd just like to know how well you knew him."

"What does the degree of our friendship have to do with anything?"

"If you knew him well, I hope you'll give me names of other friends to whom I could talk, that's all."

Trevor nodded, his hand scratching his chin. He called his dog before he answered. "Logical, yes. Of course I'd like it to be solved. A year is a bloody long time to live with something like this. His friends are still upset over it, as am I, and we'd like his killer arrested. I wasn't very close to him, but we had the camaraderie of academia and the shared love of teaching. It's a damned shame such a talent is gone."

"In the year since his death, have you thought of anyone who might've killed him?"

"Motive is sometimes difficult to divine. There are always people who let envy or greed rule them. It could be that."

"Dave Morley, you mean?"

"I'm not naming names. But jealousy could point the finger in Kent's instance, since he was so talented. I guess there's always the spurned spouse. Don't those people seek revenge?" He patted the dog and frowned. "Although, I don't believe that applies here. I still like envy. Well, good luck to you."

She thanked him for giving her something to consider, got into her car and started the engine. Envy certainly could be a deciding factor. Or desperation if the killer could do nothing to appease his envy. She didn't put the MG in gear right away, but sat looking at the countryside. Due east of Ashbourne lay the A517, and not many miles along the road Rawlton Hall perched on top of its craggy hill. Rawlton Hall, whose curator Ellen Fairfield had been so eager to lure Kent to her events. Maybe Ellen knew about envy. She'd been envious that the castle claimed Kent as its own. She swung her MG onto the A517 and thirty minutes later stood in Rawlton's massive hall, talking to Ellen.

****

The Hall probably would still be recognizable to monarchs and visitors who had visited in its heyday, for nothing much had changed except perhaps the gardens. The main structure spoke of late Medieval, built in the early 1300s when Edward II reigned. Two hundred years later, a magnificent great hall of Tudor design had been added, its movable carved screen and large stone fireplace among the Hall's architectural gems. Dena stood beside one of the tapestries decorating the northern wall.

"This is magnificent." Dena gazed at the woven tableau depicting a courting couple in Tudor dress. They sat in a garden of red roses. Two swans drifted lazily on a lake. "Is this Tudor or an earlier period? I'm not up on my historical eras, I'm afraid."

"Tudor." Ellen watched Dena.

"I'm a Yorkist myself." She smiled.

The curator said nothing and the hall fell into silence except for the chatter of a magpie in the back garden.

Obviously not a people person, Dena thought. Better suited to office work. "I appreciate your time," she said, hoping to break the ice. "I realize you're terribly busy, so I shan't keep you too long." She explained that she and her friend were delving into Kent Harrison's death.

"I left him alive and well." Ellen's blue eyes flashed, as though resenting the intrusion into her workday and the topic in general.

Probably puts her in the Bored Rich Girl category, Dena thought, aware of the woman's frank assessment of her clothing and makeup. A woman in her early thirties, of minimal build, average height, and substantial voice, Ellen wore a dark blue skirt and pale yellow blouse—neither of the garments exceptionally well tailored or of the current fashion. But the style suited the woman. Simple lines, straightforward colors and fabric. Utilitarian, Dena thought, taking in Ellen's short bobbed hairstyle. Nothing complicated. Just something to wear that will get her through her day. No doubt a mirror of her personality. And she was probably wondering how to get rid of Dena without appearing involved with Kent.

"Why would I kill him if I wanted him to sing at the Hall?" Ellen shoved her silver bangle bracelet up her forearm. "Shouldn't you, or your friend, be looking for someone who hated him?"

"And that's not you?"

The woman drew in a deep breath, seeming to inflate her petite stature. "I didn't hate him. I was envious of his talent and I was jealous that Clark MacKay corralled him into appearing exclusively at the castle. I admit that. But I wasn't enraged to the point of killing him if I couldn't have him. That's absurd. My type of envy didn't lead to murder. I was working on an event for the Hall, and Kent wouldn't have been able to resist participating in it. He would have come." She uttered the last sentence almost as a challenge. Dena noticed Ellen's flushed cheeks. But a suggestion of sadness tinted her tone, seeming to yearn for Kent's appearance.

"You said you left him alive and well." Dena rushed on, not wanting to be trapped in Ellen's sentimentality. "When was that? Sunday night as Kent was finishing his last set? Sunday afternoon?"

"I don't have to answer that. You're not a cop and you're not here on Kent's behalf."

"I realize you don't have to speak to me, Ms. Fairfield, but I thought you might be able to shed some light on his death. Perhaps you overheard something that night or maybe you know of an argument he had that—"

"Look." Ellen pointed her right index finger at

Dena. "I had an alibi for the time he went missing, all right? That satisfy you so you'll stop looking at me as his killer?"

"I'm not looking at you as the killer or as anything particular, Ms. Fairfield. I just want to know if you were aware of any quarrel that may have got out of hand. Then the police would have a line on his killer. Don't you owe it to Kent to help bring this person to justice?"

"Kent was a super human being and an incredible singer, and I'm sorry for his death. But you're wasting your time with me. I wasn't at Tutbury that night. I was working here at the Hall. I'm out of the picture as far as Kent's murder goes. I wasn't there and I don't know about any personal problem Kent had. He didn't confide in me, and I didn't see him that day. I'm not involved in any of this. It's the Castle's and Ashbourne's problem."

"But surely, as a simple matter of justice and as a courtesy to Kent, wouldn't you want his killer caught? Won't you sleep better, knowing you helped bring justice to Kent?"

"I just told you." Ellen exhaled deeply and thrust her hands into her skirt pockets. "I don't want any part of this. I'm not mixed up in it, either directly or from any knowledge. I was elsewhere that night, and since I have neither clairvoyance nor clairaudience ability I don't know what went on or who killed him. I'm sorry he's dead. A talent like he had is a staggering loss to the musical world. But it's over. It was over a year ago. Let the past stay past. Don't dredge up things that might only hurt the living. I'm not interested in helping you or the cops or your friend, and I sleep just fine. I've nothing preying on my conscience, as you just implied. I don't know a thing about any of it. Plain enough?"

Plain as a pikestaff, Dena thought as the Jacobean carved staircase creaked with each step of her exit and the massive wooden door whooshed closed behind her.

Once more in her car she gazed at the Hall. The oriel windows threw back the sunlight and reflected the glories of the summer garden. Rawlton really was a perfect setting for any period-type event. She envisioned Kent in medieval dress sitting under the willow. A gardener pushing a cart filled with sacks of fertilizer and gardening tools strolled past, breaking the spell. She started the engine and drove toward Ashbourne. She had turned onto the A515, heading back north, when an explanation whispered at her. The idea broke through the bluegrass group's rendition of 'Ain't Necessarily So.' Ellen stressed her type of envy wouldn't lead to murder. But had she another type? Had she tried to affiance herself to Kent and failed? Revenge was also a powerful motive for murder.

Chapter Nine

"I'm afraid I have nothing to tell you, Mr. McLaren. Nothing new that I haven't told the police last year, that is." Aaron Unsworth leaned against the front wall of his house, his figure in shadow, the tip of his lit cigarette a glowing beacon in the dusk. His arms were folded across his chest, revealing his muscular biceps, strengthened and toughened from lifting large, steel pots and pans in the restaurant where he worked. The smooth skin mirrored Aaron's head, hairless and tanned from days off in the sun. He flicked the column of ash off the end of the cigarette before taking another puff. "You used to be one of them, right? A police officer, I mean."

McLaren nodded. Where was this heading? He repeated the phrase that was fast becoming an automatic reply. "You're under no obligation to answer any of my questions, you know. I'm investigating on my own."

"I understand." Aaron finished his cigarette in one long puff, then dropped it. It rolled several inches along the front step before stopping beside his feet. With the toe of his shoe he smashed it against the concrete in a slow rocking movement, crushing the life from it. A garden gate clanged closed somewhere on the street, breaking the brief silence. "A question occurs to me, if you won't mind answering it."

"If I can."

"Certainly. Then you understand any constraints on my answers."

"You may refuse your answers on any grounds, Mr. Unsworth. I'm not going to hand you over to a constable. What would you like to know?"

"Are you here because a family member employed you?"

Of all the questions Aaron could have asked, this was one of the few McLaren hadn't anticipated. His eyebrows lifted slightly. Why does who hired him make a difference, McLaren wondered. Was he engaged to one of them? Linked by business? He considered the various answers he could give, from frivolous to evasive, but a glance at Aaron's serious expression decided him. "Could we go inside? This is hardly a conversation for the whole world."

Aaron nodded, turned, and opened the front door, allowing McLaren to enter first.

The room startled McLaren. Not because it was garish or messy but because it wasn't the décor he would have associated with the muscular Aaron Unsworth. And it also seemed better fitted in a bedroom of the 1940s. Sheer, frilly curtains bracketed the front window, ruffles edged the throw pillows on the sofa and chairs, a pair of ceramic pug dogs claimed the center of the fireplace mantel and was surrounded by ornately framed photos. The entire room seemed ephemeral, done in shades of pink, powder blue, and white. McLaren stared at the door leading, most likely, to the bedroom hall, expecting Cary Grant or Joan Fontaine to emerge.

"Please, don't stand on ceremony." The utterance

burst McLaren's dream. Motioning him to a seat, Aaron tossed his packet of cigarettes and his lighter onto the table. The sound of a guitar being tuned came from somewhere within the house. "My son, Fraser." Aaron sat opposite McLaren and arranged himself against the sofa cushions. "Some big event he's practicing for, I think. Or maybe just to impress his girl." He pulled one of the throw cushions from behind his back and set it on a neighboring chair. "I don't smoke in the house because he has asthma."

"Sorry to hear that. I hope he's managing all right."

"As long as he takes his medication and stays away from polluted air…"

"Might not be so easy to do, but I suppose there are places that pose no problem for him."

"Thankfully, yes. And more and more businesses are going smoke free, too. Not that it keeps him out of them. He just has to go easy and take a fresh air break if it gets too bad. But you didn't come here to talk about Fraser's health problem."

"You want an answer to your question." McLaren had one quick mental argument with himself before he replied. "I haven't heard from a family member. I was asked by one of your neighbors to look into it."

"Who shall remain anonymous, for whatever reason. Does this neighbor have an emotional tie to Kent Harrison?"

"Nothing other than wanting to see justice done."

"So, the family's not offered a reward, then."

"If they have, I'm not aware of it. Where do they live? Do you know?"

"His parents live in Australia. They emigrated just after Kent was killed. I think the shock was too much for them, like they wanted to get away from reminders. You know. The village, the pub he frequented, the events at the castle, his song played on the radio... Well, it's understandable, isn't it? Why have all that around you to rub salt into the wound? You can't heal. They're also rather elderly and not in the best of health. Mr. Harrison has a brother in Sydney, so they went to live near him. Family support, I suppose."

"So all these reminders...they lived here, then?"

"Yes, but across town, on the northern side."

"Not on *this* street, then. Not as close as you lived to Kent. Not next door, as you are."

"No. Not next door, as we used to be. But *close* neighbors."

The emphasis on the word told McLaren more about their relationship than just the proximity of their houses.

Aaron reached for the cigarettes, then shook his head and stopped. "That's about it to his family, other than his ex. No kids. Oh, there's Kent's younger brother. He lives on the Isle of Lewis, in the Outer Hebrides. I always thought that rather odd. Such an isolated part of Scotland, those wild islands. But he's a web designer so I suppose he can live most anywhere. You don't have to actually be in contact with your clients for that, do you?"

"Kent's parents and brother aren't concerned about the case? They're not pressing the police for an arrest?"

"Perhaps some memories are too painful to keep alive. Sometimes it's best to let the wounds heal."

He agreed. But if there were ill feelings in the family, like hatred between two brothers...

Aaron pulled in his lower lip, exhaling slowly. His

eyes softened, as though he were staring at something over McLaren's shoulder. The guitar tuning continued.

"Nice painting," McLaren said, hoping to nudge the conversation into high gear. Time crept onward. The sun poised on top of the western ridge of hills; soon it would topple over the rim, leaving the valley in shadow that would thicken into blackness. Several homes had already turned on table lamps near their front windows. The circles of golden light, just distinguishable now, would strengthen as the gloom increased, becoming small oases and lighthouses for those homeward bound. "Did you do that?"

"What?" Aaron half turned in his chair to distinguish which picture was singled out.

"That small one above the mantel. The sunset. Stanton Moor, isn't it?" Of course it was. No other monolith looked like the moor's famous Cork Stone. But he needed to prod Aaron into talking.

"Yes, that's the moor. It was done last year."

"It's very good. Who's the artist?"

Aaron lowered his head, rubbing the side of his face. His reply was barely audible. "My wife."

"Really? She's very good. Does she exhibit anywhere, have anything for sale?"

"I wouldn't know. She left us last year. One year and one day ago."

Silence settled over the room, absolute but for the sound of the guitar chords being clumsily practiced. McLaren glanced at the painting again, then at Aaron. "I'm sorry. I didn't know."

"Why should you? It wasn't on the evening telly." He picked up the pillow and hugged it to his chest. "I thought I'd be over it by now, but..." He exhaled loudly as he rubbed the back of his neck. "Fraser's done a better job than I have at putting this behind him. Not that he'll ever forget his mum. Sorry. This isn't the time to air the family secret. You're here about Kent Harrison."

"I'd like to know if you heard anything, perhaps saw something unusual that night. Your house is the last in the row, nearest the wood where his body was found."

"Do you suspect me of the crime, Mr. McLaren? Or of having a hand in this? I think I'm entitled to know your line of supposition if I'm going to divulge anything and possibly open myself to further questioning from the police. And I assume," he said, relinquishing the pillow, "that you'll be in touch with them should you learn anything explosive."

"I don't owe the police anything." The words came out harsher than McLaren had wanted, but he couldn't stop his feelings, couldn't stop revealing the hurt that subject engendered. He took a breath, then proceeded rather more even-toned. "I look into cold cases on my own, because someone asks me to," he explained, suddenly astonished that he had come to this point, to admitting this might become a new career for him. He had quickly come to think of himself as a repairer of dry stone walls, hardly recalling his years as a police detective in the Staffordshire Constabulary. It had been deliberate, this shoving aside of his former occupation. It coincided with the removal of most of his police knick-knacks and mementoes to the darkest recesses of his attic, and with the near-hermit life he had constructed for himself. Including shutting out Dena, his former fiancée. McLaren stared at the painting, and felt the kinship of hurt with this man. But Aaron hadn't shut himself from the world as McLaren had tried to do. He had his son and his job to keep him anchored. And evidently loved his wife enough to keep the room as she'd decorated it.

He cleared his throat, drawing Aaron's attention back to him, and said more calmly, "I'm just doing a preliminary investigation. Sometimes people recall little things somewhat later that seemed too trivial to mention at the time of the original inquiry." Or life situations change, he thought. Friendships break, family members drift away, threats or other situations fade so that a person feels free or compelled to speak.

"I doubt I can remember anything now that I didn't tell the police then."

"Kent Harrison's body was discovered in the wood, I guess you know."

"Yes." Aaron's gaze shifted to the front window. The road ended just beyond his house, the last in the line of houses before giving the village up to grassland and forest. "That's what the police said when they questioned me."

"And you heard nothing that night? I ask because that seems unusual."

"We were next door neighbors. Yes. Therefore, I was in a position to hear something."

"Yes." He said it without implying Aaron had been withholding information from the original inquiry. Merely a simple statement that set the facts in concrete. Staring at Aaron's impassive expression, McLaren added, "No car coming and going? No one walking? No conversation, no matter how quiet it may have been? You saw no one you didn't know? Some stranger who may have suggested that something odd or suspicious was about to happen?"

"Sorry. I didn't hear a thing. Didn't see anything out of the ordinary, either. It was a Sunday night. I do remember that. Fraser and I were still coming to grips with my wife being gone. We didn't hear anything."

"You were home, it sounds like."

Aaron pressed his lips together, glaring at McLaren. Silence fell between them for a moment before Aaron's indignation shot into the air. "You're implying I need an alibi."

"Do you need one? Have you a motive for killing Kent?"

"I've no motive, but the police have thrown innocent men into prison before now. But no, I didn't wish him dead. I don't wish anyone dead. I haven't that sort of anger or hatred in me. I got along fine with Kent. A lot better than I do with some of my family members, if you need to know. And though that's not a prerequisite for the side job, I'm the president of his fan club."

"President…"

"I don't make a practice of talking about it because it seems silly to many people. More in line with a younger person. But I admired Kent's music from the first I heard it. Then, when the club formed and grew, he needed someone to take charge of it, so he asked me. I suppose it came about because we did know each other, being neighbors, or that he trusted me. But there you are. First and only president." His index finger and thumb pulled at the corners of his mouth.

"I had no idea Kent Harrison was that popular."

"Oh yes," Aaron replied in a rush of enthusiasm.

"We've been in existence about a year and a half. Around the time 'The Swans' Song' came out. A little before it, actually."

"Were you at his last Sunday performance?" McLaren eyed the man, wondering if he were always so energetic or if it was the result of talking about Kent.

"Certainly. Not only because I felt it my duty as club president to support Kent but also because I admired him as a fine musician and singer. A style all his own. Creative and yet true to earlier music and its roots. He did nothing cheaply or demeaning, nothing that poked fun at our forebears or his fans. He was a true gentleman, a fine individual."

"Do you have a shop or building for the club headquarters?"

"The office is situated in my house. In the back room. There is no clubhouse or other official site. We have discussions online, offer Kent Harrison products such as beer glasses and guitar straps through our website, have an annual get-together at a music festival. Things that can be done via computer, mainly, except for the yearly gathering. We continue our existence now, mainly, to assure continuation of Kent Harrison's memory and his recordings, of which there are an appallingly few number. And now, sadly, we'll hold a memorial for him. I have no idea if it will become an annual thing."

"How late did you stay at the Minstrels Court?"

"Until he finished his set."

McLaren smiled. "Yes, I expected that. What I meant was, how late did you stay at the Minstrels Court after Kent had concluded his set? A few minutes, until closing…"

"Not long. No insult intended to the event organizers. It's a grand idea, certainly, but by the time Kent had finished and I had talked to a few club members, it was going on to ten o'clock and I had an early start to my day Monday, so I packed up my tent and crept into the night, as it were."

"Did you see Kent in the car park? Perhaps you saw someone with him, or heard a conversation he had?"

"I only wish I had. I'd be able to help the police solve this dreadful murder. No, I walked straight to my car. I had two other club members with me, and I had to drop them at their homes on my way home."

"When did you got in?"

"Not much before midnight, I shouldn't think, though I didn't exactly consult my watch. One member lives in Buxton, which was an easy enough drive. The other lives in Leek." He looked out of the window, as though envisioning the drive he had taken. "I have never yet figured out which is the swiftest route to or from Tutbury. Take the A520 into Leek and then shoot north to Buxton, or take the A515 to Ashbourne, then the A523 into Leek and proceed to Buxton on the A53." He sighed and then refocused on McLaren. "Well, it probably doesn't make much difference. I'm more than happy to pick up anyone I can. An audience crowded with club members must have been very supportive for Kent."

"May I have the names and contact details for these two members who rode with you?" McLaren held his notebook and pen toward Aaron, who slowly accepted it. "If you don't mind."

"Oh, not at all." He hastily scribbled down the

information and handed the pad and pen back to McLaren.

"Can anyone substantiate when you yourself arrived home?"

"No. Fraser was in bed, asleep. I had a cup of tea and then turned in. It'd been a long day and I was bushed."

"I suppose you have a lot of people walking down your lane. You know." McLaren motioned toward the front window. The flowering shrubs and pavement had faded into dark green shapes in the early dusk. "Walkers, picnickers, maybe people wanting to do some nature photography. They must come often. I've seen the car track that goes westward from your lane. They must drive up the hill a bit before they park."

Aaron got to his feet and moved slowly about the room. He stopped at the window, placed his left hand on the frame, and peered into the dusky light. "The Council's talking about fixing a chain there, so they can't drive on that piece of land. It's private property."

"But they haven't yet."

"No."

"So last year people could still drive close to that section of the wood."

"I suppose so. Yes. But I didn't see anything like that. No one driving, nor any cars that I don't know. I don't stand at my window and keep track of cars that drive out there."

"Of course not." McLaren hoped to appease the man. "You've got a son to take care of, a job that must demand a lot of your time, and probably other pressing things."

"Yes, the job does. But I couldn't work at anything

else. You know how it is."

McLaren nodded. In spite of his resentment over his treatment at his former job, the Detective still lived in him; he loved the chase and the feeling of justice that washed over him when the criminal was convicted and sentenced. "Did Kent have any of his friends over to his house, do you know? Anyone from his school?"

"You ask me because, living next door to him, I might have seen his friends and can identify them." He reached again for the packet of cigarettes, swore, and set a book on top of them.

"Logical, isn't it? I know my neighbors' friends and family. Know their vehicles, too."

"I don't know about any friends or colleagues over at his house that evening. Simply because I wasn't paying attention."

"But nothing odd registered with you."

"No, but he could have had someone over from Tutbury Castle, I suppose. He was rather chummy with some of them. I probably could recall names of his friends if you think it's important, but right now…" He shrugged as though his shoulders ached. "Kent did like to have people over from time to time. That was part of who he was."

"How often was this?"

"I have no idea. I don't keep track of my neighbors' private lives."

"Anyone come over regularly?"

"Like every Saturday for poker, or for lunch after church?"

"Yes."

"Intimating that someone keeping such a regular schedule would not cause undue alarm on the street. Or even register in my mind as being here at The Time in Question."

"Something like that, yes."

"Sorry, but no one comes to mind. It seemed to be a haphazard influx of friends and co-workers. Nothing obvious."

"Those people you said he sometimes had over...did they come because Kent performed during the Minstrels Court event? He made particular friends from there?"

"That, sure, but people also dropped in because he was a popular entertainer. He had a lot of fans. Sometimes he'd invite them over, sometimes they'd just show up on his door step." He paused, his gaze diverted to the small painting. "You know. People chat you up, show an interest in your art or music or woodcarving, and next thing you know you're talking to them over a cuppa about your creativity process and the subjects that inspire you."

McLaren left, wondering if Aaron was still in love with his wife, wondering which of the couple was enamored with the great boulder on Stanton Moor, a boulder that nearly mimicked the large rock where Kent Harrison's body had been found.

Chapter Ten

The boulder where Kent Harrison's body had been found haunted Dena as she drove back to Buxton. She hadn't been one of the curious last year who had visited or photographed the area when the police had released the scene for public use. But she did recall it from her previous walks through the wood. Not that she seemed to get much time to do that now, but she had during her childhood—short meanderings barely into the copse to collect October-tinted leaves; sunrise strolls when the dew-laden grass hugged your jeans; star-studded summer nights around a fire, telling ghost stories and proclaiming plans for the future. That time seemed long ago, hardly more than a gray haze in her memory. Jobs and school and disappointments in love had a way of bullying out the less urgent events in life, even if those events were more important to your emotional well being than landing a job. You could live without looking at a beautiful painting or feeling the crunch of dry leaves underfoot, but was that life really full?

Dena stopped her car in a lay-by and pulled out her small notebook from her shoulder bag. She added the notes—brief as they were—to the others in the book, the people she had talked to in connection with the Kent Harrison case. Her pen moved quickly over the page as she summarized the meeting with Fay Larkin. Kent's girlfriend: slim and hazel-eyed and efficient. Able to keep an office running smoothly, managing doctors, patients, and emergencies, but barely clinging to sanity. A robotic shell, nearly useless in the Information Department. Between crying spells and repetitive statements of his fine character and helpfulness, Fay had said only that her life was over and she didn't know how she and her child would survive. "We were going to be a family." Fay had choked the words out between sobs. "He wanted that as much as I did. Maybe even more because it was getting late in life for him to have a family. Late for me, too, for motherhood. He was forty-five and I'm not far behind him. This baby meant everything to him." She had closed the session after that, too upset to talk further and the crying baby needing her attention. That had been thirty minutes ago, Dena realized, glancing at her watch. Thirty minutes that hadn't produced anything other than frustration for her, and distress for Fay over the dredged up memories.

Her mobile phone rang and she answered it eagerly as she glanced at the caller ID display.

McLaren's voice slipped into her ear in a caress of warmth and love. "Can you talk?"

"When it's you, always."

"I mean, you're not driving, or have someone with you…"

She heard the hesitation in his voice, as if he could see her having tea with her friend, afraid he was interrupting something. "No, Michael, this is fine. Did you want anything special?"

"You."

She fought the temptation to sing "A-Rovin' on a Winter's Night," and instead replied, "Thank you."

"I mean it, Dena." He paused again, but only

slightly, for his heart must have been speaking when he rushed on. "I must have been insane this past year, leaving you, shutting you out of my life. I'm more sorry than I can ever say about that, about wasting those precious days. I just want to tell you how much you mean to me, how glad I am that you're back in my life, that I'll try to make it up to you."

"You don't have to, Michael. I know you were going through hell. It's enough that we're together again."

A faint sound, as if he were taking a deep breath to tell her something else—or sighing in regret of the lost time—slipped into the silence. He coughed and mumbled an apology, following it by a dull scraping as if he had reached for a heavy mug and was dragging it across the tabletop toward him. There was a sharp clink of metal against ceramic—his ring hitting the mug, perhaps, or a spoon stirring the beverage—and then his voice, strong again in his ardor and apology.

"I want us to be together, Dena. As long as I live."

"So do I, Michael."

"I know you're busy tonight, but what's tomorrow look like? I thought we could have dinner together— either at a restaurant or my place. You decide."

Dena's soft laugh floated over the phone to McLaren. "You're willing to cook for me?"

"I love you. Doesn't that prove it?"

"More than a declaration on bended knee. Super. I'll take you up on your handcrafted meal, then. What time?"

"Tomorrow's Tuesday…"

"Good."

"I know the day. I was just thinking out loud,

figuring out my interviews and what time I'd be back home."

"I like a thinking man."

"I think if there are many more interruptions…"

"Okay. I'm silent. What time?"

"Oh, eight. Does that interfere with anything you've got going?"

"Even if it did, I'd rearrange my schedule. Thanks, Michael."

"You haven't had dinner yet."

"No, not that. For wanting me, for loving me again."

"I never did stop loving you, Dena. Even through this nightmare year, I still loved you. I just couldn't do anything about it."

"You have now." She rang off, recalling Fay Larkin's grief at Kent's death, her despair at the family that would never be, at the love ripped from her life. Dena closed the phone and put it back in her bag, shutting her heart and mind to the frightening images of she and Michael in a similar scenario. Life wouldn't be that cruel to Michael, would it? Not after he was fighting his way back from the abyss created by Charlie Harvester.

She flipped over the notebook cover and leaned to her left to grab her bag. The notebook slid onto the floor as she searched for her lipstick. She found it, gave her lips a quick swipe of the red cosmetic, then sagged against the back of the car seat. Traffic zoomed past on the main road, stirring up dust and the scent of rain, but all she was conscious of were the words whirling about in her head. Was she helping Michael by talking to people? Or was she harming his investigation? Dave

Morley hadn't been exactly ecstatic to talk to her. Nor had the others. Was she building walls that Michael couldn't scale when he talked to those people?

Cursing her amateur meddling, overcome by regret and love, she picked up her mobile again. Better tell Michael what she'd done. Maybe he can mend fences if she caused problems. She opened her phone and began punching in his number before unconsciousness claimed her.

Chapter Eleven

The next morning McLaren's footsteps thudded dully on the bare soil, a trail worn through the grass that carpeted the courtyard of Tutbury Castle. A few freestanding towers and a stretch of crumbling, roofless rooms were all that remained of the castle's former glory, a life of nearly nine hundred fifty years that had seen cycles of ruin and restoration, depending on the reigning monarch's bent. The successions seemed to have been stopped, ending with the hulk that stretched before him. He sighed, the waste of national heritage and architectural beauty upsetting him. Yet, some people cared. Like castle curators and tour guides and archaeologists. Maybe other people learned to care through them, or through school classes. Shaking off the feeling, he shooed a fly from his arm. The day would be another hot one. He squinted at the sun that seemed to sit on the broken rim of the South Range. Mimicking or exceeding Monday's temperatures. He hoped that the bottle of water in his car wouldn't be too hot to drink when he left the castle. He had parked in the shade, but the sun traveled.

He eyed the beer vendor, again wishing he had brought the water with him, and walked on. The courtyard was only partially filled at this early hour, and the breeze ran unrestrained over the grass and banked against the castle walls, dragging away part of the heat already building in the objects. It would get even hotter later on, when the tourists filled the castle grounds, bent on enjoying themselves at the Minstrels Court gala. He skirted the vendors setting out their wares and opening their fabric booths. The bold colors shone even brighter in the strength of the sun.

McLaren passed the performance stage, a long wooden rectangle raised four feet from the ground. A proscenium had been created with lengths of sequined and silky fabric and an overhead banner of large pennants, which fluttered in the warm breeze. A wooden stand holding large poster-sized placards that could be changed to announce the presenting performing act, stood to stage left, near the edge of the forestage, a footlight trained on it. The fabric, flags, stand, and flooring were in hues of maroon, wine, lilac, and silver, with black accents of lettering and embroidered fanciful beasts. All very medieval looking. McLaren glanced at the woman taking a lute from its hardshell case. The bright yellow plush case lining caught his attention, seeming out of place in the forest of reds. All very mood-inducing.

The South Range loomed larger than life as he left the stage and booth area. Most of it was little more than a shell, a broken silhouette against a pale blue backdrop. A tower capped the left-hand end of the Range, a piece of history tourists could climb and feel, if only for a few minutes, a link with past lives. A red brick building bookended the opposite end, contrasting in color, texture, and time to the tan stone of the main section of the building. It snuggled against the Hall, its long, sloping roof giving it a sleepy air. But that was deceptive, for it held the tearoom and gift shop.

Ignoring the urge for a glass of water, McLaren entered the main building and found himself in the Great Hall, a two-storey affair with fireplaces, glass-paned windows and wooden floors.

"Mr. McLaren?" The caller stood at the head of the staircase, little more than a dark figure in the dim light. "I'm Clark MacKay, castle curator. We can talk in my office, if you'd like." He stepped back and motioned for McLaren to join him. The creak of the wooden steps as McLaren ascended conjured up images in his mind of Henry IV and James I, the torchlight stretching shadows behind them. "I appreciate you coming at this early hour," Clark added when McLaren stopped in the hall.

The room was larger than McLaren had thought. Loftier, too with superb wood timberwork. Framed documents and pictures dotted the tan plaster walls. Ahead was a person-tall fireplace, presumably large enough to roast a calf or lamb, but which now sat empty and bracketed by wrought iron candle stands. A panel of floral embroidery done in tans, creams, and greens claimed the head of the stone fireplace opening. An area rug in cream, navy, and cranberry hues stretched parallel to the fireplace and continued the colors in the wooden chair in the corner, red-canopied and throned on a carpeted dais. Waiting for Mary, McLaren thought, wondering again how the Scottish queen had lived in captivity. Waiting for the past to reincarnate and free her. She seemed to inhabit the hall—the interior of the canopy sported her coat of arms, items for daily use dotted the walls. But more importantly Mary herself appeared to welcome him. A white dress, complete with dark blue kirtle, pink bows, and white-ruffed collar, stood to the left of the fireplace. The costume could have been real, with the embroidered lion and unicorn on the edges of the long tunic. It could be Mary, except that it had no head, hands, or feet. He glanced once more at the long sleeves, expecting a jeweled finger to show itself, then followed Clark into his office.

"I'm glad you could accommodate me," McLaren said as Clark closed the office door and hurried around him. "I know it's short notice."

"Better short notice than short change in the till, I always say. So." He clapped his hands and rubbed them. "Anything I can do to help. Tuesday mornings are usually fairly quiet."

"The weekend influx has gone."

"Except this week, of course, we're holding the Minstrels Court, so we expect folks all eight days. But that's still an hour away." He gestured toward the table near the window and stroked his mustache. It was as flamboyant as his personality. "Anything? Tea or coffee?"

McLaren declined and took the offered seat facing the desk.

The office seemed to be made of bookcases, for they consumed two entire walls and part of the third. Two large windows let in enough light so that the brass shaded desk lamp need not be used much. Photos of castle events and famous entertainers crowded in between the windows and took up what space the larger posters didn't. A computer, printer, and telephone perched on one section of the desk.

"I find it useful to work here, just off the hall." Clark settled in his chair. He was large, rather than heavy, and he filled the area physically, his hands and arms obliterating the sides of the chair, his torso nearly masking the chair back. McLaren felt the man also filled the area authoritatively, for an underlying hardness colored his sentences, even when he jested. "I'm close to the gift shop, and I can pop out occasionally to answer any questions the visitors in the main hall might have."

"Good idea." McLaren glanced at the bookcases crowded with historical information. "Your events seem very authentic, from what I hear. And now that I see how much research you evidently do for each one—" He broke off as Clark handed him a brochure.

"An events calendar for the castle. We've something going on most weekends. A rather nice mix, I think, of Renaissance fairs, music festivals, ghost walks, historical lectures, and reenactments. And those aren't all military battles," he added. "We demonstrate and lecture on cooking, medical treatment, dress, architecture, and crafts. The craft demos are very popular, as you may imagine. Again, we have a good representation, such as straw work, embroidery, candle making, illuminated manuscript writing, paper making, jewelry making, and wood carving."

"Quite a list."

"These are as accurate as we can make them, too. Each practitioner is well known in his field and is, of course, responsible for authenticity, not only in technique but also in design. But you want to know about last year's Minstrel Court, right?"

"If you recall anything about Kent Harrison on the day he was killed. Perhaps someone became angry with him, either a fellow musician or a fan or a member of the castle staff. Maybe someone was constantly jealous of him, for whatever reason, and his emotions got the better of him that night. Anyone at all whom you can recall who might have held a grudge or disliked him."

Clark frowned and picked up his pen. His fingers rubbed the smooth barrel, evoking an image of Aladdin rubbing his lamp in desperation. "I felt so bad about that. Still do. To die like that…so young, too. I just couldn't believe it when I heard about it." He shook his head, as though still in disbelief, or wishing to rid his memory of the event. When he spoke, his voice was strained. "Such a nice chap. Extremely popular, you know. With his audiences and in his private life, too, I'm told."

"You had no dealing with him, then, outside the castle?"

"No. He was a regular at the Minstrels Court. Do you know about that?"

"Not really. I've never attended."

"You must!" Clark's voice took on the enthusiasm. "It's glorious! We run it annually the same weekend each summer. As you can probably tell from this morning, it's focused on entertainment that would be found in John of Gaunt's court at that time. He began it in the 14th century, if I'm not insulting your intelligence. It was so popular that it continued annually for three hundred years."

"Music, miming, dancing."

"Yes. But also juggling and acrobatics. Envision jesters cavorting through the area, minstrels singing, tumblers and dancers. John of Gaunt's original Court lasted for several weeks, but we've scaled ours down to eight days. I've learned that his festival eventually got so wild that a special court was convened to punish wrongdoers."

"I suppose, with all these entertainers vying for attention, it did get a bit rowdy."

"Our Minstrels Court is nothing like that, of course. Quite tame in comparison, even with the jousting. I don't believe that was part of the original festival, but we added it as a visual learning device."

"So, Kent Harrison performed the night he was murdered." McLaren jotted an entry into his notebook. "What time did he wrap up his act?"

"They had the last slot that night, so they wrapped up at half past nine."

"Remarkable memory you have, Mr. MacKay."

"Not really. I simply recall it because I'd spoken to the police so often about that. I didn't get to hear him that time, though. I was in a meeting with Sheri Harrison, one of our castle tour guides, until eleven o'clock."

"You work long, odd hours, then."

"Same as the police, Mr. McLaren. Kent appeared with his sometime singing partner, Dave Morley, for that session."

"The two of them weren't a regular duet, then."

"No. Kent was the main act, if you want to call him that. Dave would come on for a set comprised of anywhere from six to a dozen songs. Then Kent would continue as a solo."

McLaren considered the similarities between his folk group and the Kent-Morley venue. He said, "Was there any difference in popularity when Dave joined him? You mentioned earlier that Kent was very popular with the crowd."

"Dave didn't really detract or add anything, I don't

believe. Not in the way you mean, not in popularity. Dave added a nice harmony to Kent's melody line, and the second instrument was nice. The sound was completely different when Dave sang with Kent. I can't call it better or worse. It was just different." McKay shifted from one foot to the other, as if anxious to be on his way.

"So their audience didn't prefer the duo, for example, to Kent's solo stint."

"Not that I could tell. Though they were quite good. Extremely popular. He'd taken to singing 'The Swans' Courtship' as his encore, did you know?"

Probably sang it for his last song before he died, McLaren thought. His swan song. "The woman who sang with him on the recording didn't appear for that number, then?"

"No."

"Did they have their sights on doing this as a career?"

Clark inclined his head and looked thoughtful. Footsteps crossed the wooden floor beyond his office door and faded into nothing before he replied. "I doubt it. More like a serious hobby."

"Just fun, then. Something to bring in a bit of extra money."

"I should think so, yes. After all, you've got to begin early in the business, don't you, if you want to turn professional?"

"And Kent was in his middle forties, if I recall. What about Dave? How old—"

MacKay shrugged, as if he'd never thought of it. "I don't know. Forty, I'd say. Maybe younger. If so, just slightly." He pulled a photo from a file on his desk and handed it to McLaren. "One of their publicity shots."

The men were dressed in their Renaissance outfits and gazed at the camera. "You're probably right. Fortyish. Beyond the age of having a shot as a career, if he's just starting now."

"Might be. Then again, people always have that dream in their hearts, don't they?"

"Did Dave ever appear as a solo act?"

"I only saw them here, at the Minstrels Court. I have no idea."

McLaren made a note to question Dave Morley, then asked if the two had been mates or just singing partners.

"Again, I don't know. But it would have to be more than acquaintances if you're in business together."

"Because Dave and Kent weren't a permanent duo, you mean?"

"That, certainly, but also because I never saw them eat together or leave together. But I suppose they could have done. I didn't stand and watch them constantly. You can ask some of the vendors and musicians who have been here for a while. Musicians are a close community, especially ones who sing early music. They know all the backstage goings-on. The vendors, being here the entire day, see a lot. Their booths are in an area adjacent to the stage."

"I'll ask around, thanks."

Clark lay down his pen and sat back in his chair. The sunlight slanted through the window, illuminating the moisture on his forehead and his blond hair. "I do hope you are successful in your investigation, Mr. McLaren. As I said, I liked Kent Harrison. So many others did, too. I'd like to see the person responsible for his death punished."

"I'll try my best." He got to his feet, folding the brochure and sticking it into his trousers pocket. "Well, as I said, if you happen to think of someone who might have been jealous of Kent Harrison, or had a quarrel with him, please let me know. I know a year is a long time to remember something, but if you do, I'd like to know about it."

Clark stood up, banging his knee into the side of the desk. He grimaced and rubbed the muscle. "You'd think I'd learn. I'm constantly doing that."

"One more question..." McLaren watched Clark's expression slip from affable to wariness.

"Yes?"

"Have you installed CCTV cameras throughout the castle? Or in the car park?"

Clark blinked, and replied rather slowly, "Why, no. We have it budgeted for next year, though. Is that a concern?"

"No. It might have been helpful."

"Yes." He grimaced, as though embarrassed by their inability to help.

McLaren held out his right hand. "Well, thank you for your time, Mr. MacKay."

"Certainly, though I didn't do much, did I? Just seemed to rabbit on about the Court."

"Maybe something will occur to you later."

"I doubt it. There isn't anything to tell you about anger or jealousy or quarrels. Kent Harrison was such a likable chap, never made an enemy, always helpful in whatever way he could be."

"His helpfulness extended beyond giving Dave Morley a set on stage, then."

"Certainly! Kent coached pupils at his school. His friends came to him for personal problems. I know because he made a joke of that. But he also had a remarkable memory for people. He'd bring folks together to help each other."

"In what way?"

"Well, I don't know all of them, but I do know he introduced Ron Pennell to Aaron Unsworth. Ron's an herbalist. He has a booth every year at the Minstrels Court. He's also in business for himself. He's a garden designer and consultant."

"Kent introduced Ron and Aaron because Ron wanted to learn to cook?"

"Could have done, but I doubt it. Aaron Unsworth is a chef, a highly skilled one. But he wanted to write a cookbook containing recipes that used all natural ingredients. Being a next-door neighbor to Aaron, Kent knew of Aaron's project, and introduced Aaron to Ron. I don't know the status of Aaron's cookbook, if it's published or even finished, but I don't think Ron would be your killer. What would he have to gain?"

Precisely what I'm going to find out, McLaren thought as he made his way to the vendors' tents. Who wanted Kent Harrison dead?

Jo A. Hiestand

Chapter Twelve

Who wants me dead? What else could it be if not my death? Ransom? Am I kidnapped? Dena turned her head and was instantly assaulted with a wave of nausea. She felt as though she were on some grotesque fair ride—a chairoplane or up-and-down roundabout, or devil's wheel. Something that tilted and spun more violently than a merry-go-round or a big wheel.

Her hand went to her forehead as she pushed herself up to a sitting position. The pain in her head erupted behind her eyes and in her ears, showing brilliant fireworks and setting off sirens. She remained with her left arm stiff and propping her upright at an angle, trying to make sense of the throbbing that multiplied into hundreds of drums and gongs the second she moved. Days seemed to pass as she fought to keep down her stomach contents. As the screaming faded she slowly opened her eyes.

A small room, she thought, her eyes still half shut against the light and the blazing images. A small room, but where? Dena carefully opened her eyes, testing the pain and the noise inside her head. When nothing more intense than a rocking sensation washed over her, she looked about.

It did seem to be a small room, for a tiny window was set into the wall to the right. The door opposite the window was closed—probably locked—and painted the same color as the walls, a pale beige that hinted at a house or institution. A school? A warehouse? Another door, smaller than what she considered to be the main door, was set into a neighboring wall. Nothing but a metal chair and a paper bag occupied the room. And the faint aroma of fish and chips that mingled with musty stonework. She leaned forward, careful not to jiggle her head, and got on her hands and knees. With small movements, she crawled to the chair.

The journey took forever, the throbbing in her head and the ache in her knees giving it the feel of miles. The floor, cold against her palms, turned into an unyielding snowfield. Even in the insipid sunlight, it threw brilliant reflections that hurt her eyes. The ceramic tile ran smooth and hard beneath her, light green and flecked with darker green and white. Again she thought of a school and warehouse. But the floor appeared to be new, unscuffed, and highly polished as befitted an area newly laid. Or barely walked on.

At the chair, she sat, cross-legged on the floor, and grabbed the bag. A green and blue logo consumed most of the paper front, bringing a bit of normalcy to her nightmare. Ordinarily she shunned this takeaway restaurant chain, but she laid the bag on her lap and rolled back the folded top. The fish and chips aroma rushed out, beckoning her as emphatically as if she'd been Samson succumbing to Delilah. She hesitated only momentarily, negating her concern that the food was poisoned. They would have killed her outright. Dena reached into the bag for a piece of plaice. They wouldn't be keeping her alive, feeding her.

She ate more quickly than she had intended, barely chewing before she swallowed each mouthful. The fish was still warm, and she had a sense of it being light and crispy on her tongue. A capped Styrofoam cup emblazoned with the same company logo held water, and Dena drank greedily, finishing most of the contents before she set the cup back on the chair seat. She grabbed several chips—thick cut and slathered with vinegar—and pushed them into her mouth. Her teeth crunched into the crisp exterior as she gulped and reached for more. This time she chewed slower, aware of the skin on the potato slices, the roughness of the salt, the smell and sting of the vinegar as it washed against the raw skin inside her cheek. She finished the fish.

There was no napkin proper in the paper bag—an oversight by her thoughtful abductor. Dena licked her fingers then wiped them against the folded paper circling the exterior of the cup. Feeling better, she moved the cup to the floor next to the crumpled paper sack, and eased onto the chair. The cold metal bit into her back and for the first time she realized she must be in an occupied building. No one would run the air conditioning for one person.

This thought stilled some of the fear inside her. Wherever she was, she wasn't alone. If she were in a public building, would anyone hear her if she called for help? But if she weren't, if she was in her captor's house, would her cries antagonize him? Would he come in and beat her into silence?

Dena needed to know where she was. Probably not the location, as a specific town or building, but general area. Then she could deal with her captivity.

Turning her head toward the light, she stared at the window. It was set high on the wall, as if making room for a tall bedroom chest of drawers or bookcase. Or shelving to hold supplies, she added. A storeroom? A hospital? But wouldn't a public place need an Exit sign above the door? There was none, she realized, but that did little to set her in a specific place. She turned back to the window.

The light eased through the rectangle in pale yellow streams, broken by shifting shadows across the glass pane. If she knew where she was, which way the room was oriented, she could figure out if it was morning or early evening. It can't be Monday. Didn't this happen on Monday?

She tried to think, to remember what she'd been doing, where she'd been before she woke up here. Had she been here a few hours or a few days? Did anyone even miss her? Would anyone find her car?

She stretched out her legs and pulled up the bottoms of her trousers. Rotating her legs slowly she checked her skin. A small deep blue bruise tattooed the outer side of her right calf. Probably hit it on the car door when he dragged her out. She checked her arms and gingerly fingered her neck and face. She felt no cuts or dried blood. The bruise seemed to be the only physical souvenir of the abduction. Other than stiff muscles, she corrected herself as she bent her knees again.

She placed her left hand on the chair seat and pushed to her feet. She stood for several seconds, wary of fainting, but the room remained still. Too still, for she heard nothing. With her knees, she nudged the chair to the window, again traveling slowly, for she didn't want to bend over and risk blacking out. The window seemed even higher now that she stood at it, but she centered the chair below it and placed her foot on the seat. As Dena eased herself up, she grabbed the windowsill and peered outside.

An eye level view of black asphalt striped in white paint greeted her. Several cars were parked within the confines of these strips but the majority of the tarmac was empty. A small building appeared at the farthest end of the car park, for that's what it seemed to be. Trees edged the left-hand side of the area, but what lay to the right Dena couldn't see. A vigorous clump of daylilies leaned against that edge of her window, obliterating further view.

She must be in a basement. But where, and in what type of building? Her fingers gripped the edge of the windowsill; she stood on tiptoe, trying to see farther to each side. Tarmac covered nearly all the expanse before her, coming up to the window just inches below its bottom edge. Daylilies swayed in the breeze, alternately throwing the room into shadow and light.

Now that she could give a description, vague though it would be, she realized she could ring up Michael. Or 999. Even if she couldn't get an address, couldn't the police trace her mobile phone call, figure out the area from where it came? Surely that would lead them to her and she'd be rescued.

She looked around the room. Her handbag wasn't there. She patted her pockets. No mobile. She'd laid it on the car seat when she'd finished talking to Michael. No help would come. Sagging against the windowsill, she gave in to the fear and cried.

Minutes crawled by. Maybe it was hours. Dena wasn't sure. Time became measured in the creep of the sunlight across the floor, the beat of her heart, the breaths she took. No sound reached her ears but her own sobbing. She was aware only of her desperation, fear, and the cold room. And the presumed images of her demise.

She was not going there, she told herself as the first wave of panic waned. She would not die. Michael would find her. Of that she had no doubt. She choked back the last of the tears, took a deep breath, and, standing on tiptoes, looked outside again.

Several cars had arrived and were parked far enough away that she could see them entirely. The area still wasn't filled, and as she wondered if it eventually would be, a car rolled into her view and stopped. It parked quite near Dena, for all she could see were the left rear tire and wing. A slight sway of the car body— perhaps caused as the driver got out—a dull thud and muffled footsteps, and suddenly a pair of Oxfords and brown trousered legs walked into view.

The nearness of the person so startled Dena that she stared with unbelieving eyes. It wasn't until the person had passed the window that she pounded on the glass.

It had no effect. The legs didn't turn to come back. The fear that she had thought conquered broke from within her and she pounded the windowpane again, screaming to the unknown person.

This time the legs reappeared. Or, more correctly, another pair of legs, for these trousers were navy blue.

She slammed her palms against the pane and yelled as loudly as she could. No face peered through the glass, no voice replied. The legs remained in front of her, so close that the trouser fabric touched the glass. She pounded the glass again, screaming with all the air in her lungs. Was he deaf? Did he have an iPod plugged into his ear so that he couldn't hear her? Again her fist slammed the glass and again she got no reaction.

Her hands slid down the glass, aching and red from the abuse she'd forced on them. She relaxed, settling down onto her feet. Her toe and calf muscles hurt. As she bent to massage her leg, the trousered leg outside the window lunged forward. The other leg remained where it was but bent slightly, as though the person was reaching or lifting something. Seconds later she heard scraping, as of a heavy ceramic object being pulled across a rough surface. Her view was cut off by a large terra cotta flowerpot holding an exuberant boxwood evergreen. Another pot, jammed full of hostas and more daylilies snuggled up to the boxwood. Her vision of the outside world had been effectively cut off.

She crumpled onto the chair, hugging herself in the realization that the landscaper was most likely her abductor. Why else would he obliterate her communication with the outside? She leaned forward, heart racing, trying to think, desperate to know where she was, needing to escape. It was while she was thinking that she blacked out.

She came to slowly, pulling herself from her dream back into the reality of the beige room. She was quickly aware of being cold, and when she moved she discovered she was lying on the floor near the chair. Her hand went to her head, feeling for injuries from her fall. There were no bumps but her head throbbed. Not like a concussion. More like a bad headache. She got onto her knees, leaned against the seat of the chair, and stood. Time to explore her surroundings.

The room behaved itself on the whole; only the

floor angled off at odd degrees as she staggered to the main door. But she made the journey in short steps, shuffling rather than striding, and grabbed the doorknob. The gray metal was as cool as the tile floor had been and startled her. She turned the knob and pulled. The door remained closed. She turned the knob the other direction. Still closed.

The other door wasn't locked. She found the light switch inside the black opening after a few seconds of fumbling and switched on the overhead light. The area was closet-sized, painted in the same pale beige as the main room, but held a small wall mirror, toilet and sink. No window or air duct offered an escape route.

Dena glimpsed her reflection in the mirror. The image momentarily startled her, and she jumped, stifling the yelp nearly as soon as she uttered it. She was shocked at what she saw. The disarranged hair didn't bother her as much as the red marks on the right side of her face. From banging against the open car door when he hit her, or from sleeping on the floor? Her fingers gingerly traced the redness. The skin had swollen slightly and was tender. Perhaps it would turn into a bruise. Wouldn't she look lovely when Michael saw her?

The thought of McLaren rescuing her cheered her briefly. She stared into the area in front of her, and a balloon-accented conference room suddenly transposed itself in the space. It was the opening night of the fundraiser for the tiger sanctuary; she worked as a volunteer at the silent auction. McLaren's sister had contributed a painting and he was there to bid on it. The sounds and images washed over her, pulling her back to the moment they'd met.

"You've been returning to the bid sheet every few minutes, sir. Are you interested in the painting?"

"Yes. It's rather nice, isn't it?"

"One of the best ones I've seen of Bolton Abbey. Have you put in a bid?"

"I'm trying not to, but I think I'll have no choice." He had laughed at that moment, as though he shared a secret with someone. "The artist is my sister."

"Gwen Hulme?"

"Yes. This is a first for her."

"Surely not painting. She's awfully good for a beginner, Mr. Hulme."

"It's McLaren."

"Pardon?"

"My name's Michael McLaren. Hulme is my sister's married name."

"Oh! I'm sorry. How stupid of me."

"That's all right, Miss…"

"Ellison. Dena Ellison."

"I'm not married."

"Excuse me?"

"You glanced at my left ring finger. I'm not married."

"If I did, Mr. McLaren, I…it wasn't intentional." She had stuttered, suddenly embarrassed, yet amazed he'd picked up on her eye movements. Had he also noticed the heat flooding her cheeks?

"I shouldn't have said anything. I was having a bit of fun at your expense. I apologize. Unfortunately, it's a nasty habit of mine. My sister can tell you more details, if you're interested, or other stories bordering on mortification. But you'll have to schedule some time for it. There are too many to hear in one sitting." He'd laughed again, a warm ripple that melted her heart.

"Let's call it even, then. I won't say I make a habit of scrutinizing fingers, but I obviously did just now. Normally I'm quite conventional. I'm a volunteer at the tiger sanctuary."

"I wouldn't call that a conventional calling. Do you like it?"

"Oh, yes! I've worked there a little over a year, but this is the first time I've worked the fundraiser."

"It's my first time here, so we're even." He had grinned, and the humor gleamed in his eyes. "How much longer do I have to keep my eye on the clock?"

"The bidding closes at nine."

"Good. Only another ninety-three minutes to stay vigilant."

"You're wanting to leave?" She remembered her disappointment, wanting him to remain until the event's closing at ten. His loyalty, sense of duty and humor appealed to her, and she'd wanted to develop a relationship with him.

"Not especially. I'd like to look at the tigers. Would I have time in ninety-three minutes to see them and still dash back here to place the high bid? I don't know exactly where the place is."

"If you had a guide to show you a short cut to the sanctuary and then through the office and lab to the compound, you could do."

"A round of applause, then, for insider information. Shall I drive, Ms. Ellison…"

The voices faded, the balloons and streamers disappeared, and Dena was back in the beige basement room, feeling terribly alone and desperate for McLaren's strength and humor.

This wasn't doing her any good. She relinquished the last vestige of the images. Michael wouldn't wallow in this sentimentality. He'd be figuring out how to escape... Giving one last look at herself, she flashed a courage-inducing smile. Then she turned off the light and closed the door before climbing back on the chair.

For all of her captor's great plan, Dena could still see outside and she held on emotionally with renewed fervor to the link with the world. The flowerpots were angular and trapezoidal in shape, leaving gaps between their neighbors through which she caught snippets of her previous view.

The sun had moved during the time she'd been asleep, for the light had strengthened and altered its whitish hue to egg yolk yellow. Shadows beneath the trees, flowerpots and cars had deepened to black, hugging the foundations and roots of their hosts. Noon or early afternoon, Dena thought before realizing she'd been unconscious throughout the previous evening. Hadn't she been talking to Michael around teatime yesterday? Hadn't she set a time for dinner at his house tonight? The sense of elapsed time frightened her, angered her, spurred her into greater resolve to escape or summon aid.

She had discarded the idea of smashing the window with the chair legs—she wouldn't be able to lift the chair above her head and reach the window without something to stand on. She was considering tearing a piece of fabric from her clothes and shoving it under the main door hoping some passer-by would see it and investigate when the door opened.

She clutched the sides of the chair, simultaneously frightened and anxious. A sliver of bright florescent light slanted into the room. A gloved hand angled around the edge of the door and laid a bulging paper sack on the floor before retreating into the light and shutting the door with a finality that spoke of continuing imprisonment and despair.

Chapter Thirteen

There's a finality about this place, McLaren thought as he left the South Range and walked into the open courtyard. Not the ruins that speak of despair and uncaring people, but the belief that it will survive. As long as Clark MacKay has anything to do with it, McLaren thought, glancing at the vendors opening their booths for another day's sales.

McLaren crossed the grassy expanse, searching for Ron Pennell's tent. The sun hovered higher in the sky and had burned off the early morning dew. The short grass was dry and stiff beneath his shoes, mutely testifying to the July heat that seemed to draw the moisture and energy from every living thing.

He found Ron's booth at the beginning of a row of crafts and art vendors. Of medium height, graying hair and blue eyes, Ron smiled on seeing McLaren, perhaps expecting an early sale, then looked surprised as McLaren introduced himself.

"Yes, I knew Kent." Ron talked over his shoulder as he arranged pomanders and sacks of herbs and dried flowers on the table. The sunlight shone through the bottles of *enfleurages* and tinctures, casting delicately colored rectangles on the tablecloth. Ron straightened the line of conserves—small, squat glass jars of honey-jellied flowers and herbs—and added, "Nicest man you'd ever hope to meet. I was so sorry to hear he had been killed. He introduced me to Aaron Unsworth. He wanted to write a cookbook featuring recipes that used a majority of natural ingredients. Flowers, spices, herbs, leaves."

"More healthful," McLaren supplied, eyeing the variety of herb-flavored vinegars.

"Definitely."

"Was Kent a customer of yours?"

"A customer?"

"Yes. Did he ever buy some of your ointments or teas? Maybe try something unusual, like galingale or angelica or calendula? I thought since you knew each other, he might have tried flowers or spices in his cooking."

"Kent bought chamomile once. He had a long bout of stage jitters. The chamomile is good for settling the nerves."

"Did it do the trick, do you know?"

"Sorry, I don't. He had bought rather a large amount, so whether he was just imagining stage fright, or if the chamomile helped, or even if he just got over it himself, he didn't buy any more. At least not from me." As though underlining the possible personal insult, he pushed up the sleeves of his shirt.

McLaren made soothing sounds and added, "Sorry you lost future sales."

"I'm glad I could help him, do him a favor for once. Kent was always helping others. As he did for Aaron, helping him in a roundabout way with his cookbook."

"And did you? Confer with Aaron Unsworth, I mean."

"Yes. We've had several meetings. I let him have

some of my recipes, with the stipulation that he note in the book where the ingredients could be obtained, and gave him other resources for recipes. He's finished with the writing, but I don't believe the book is published yet. Next month, I believe. Unless it's been held up at the printer."

"And when did you help Aaron?"

"Late last summer. Into the autumn. Aaron'd been considering the cookbook idea for some time, but he never did anything with it. Maybe he hadn't the time until last July."

When his wife left him…

"Anyway…" Ron straightened up from the table and looked at McLaren, "that's all I know."

"You didn't see him leave the night he was killed, then. Or hear an earlier argument he may have had with someone here."

"No."

"Do you know what time he actually left the castle? Maybe you saw him in the car park?"

"I've no idea when he left either place. It's easier for the musicians to pack up and walk out when they've finished. Most of them just have an instrument. When it's closing time we vendors have to put away our wares, take down our signs, and stow any outdoor tables and chairs and tablecloths inside our tents."

"When did you finally leave?"

"Sometime a little past eleven-thirty. Clark MacKay saw me. He always walks around the area, making certain everything is all right, checking to see if anyone needs help and has left the castle before he locks up. He waved and we exchanged a few words as I was making for the main entrance. The car park attendant saw me, too. He and a few of the security officers Clark hires for these large events were standing near the ticket booth. There weren't that many of us here at that time and the car park was nearly deserted. That came out during the police investigation."

"Do you know when Kent's musical set finished? Not precisely, but some idea? Perhaps seven o'clock, half past eight, ten?" He waited, mentally crossing his fingers that he'd get a lead.

"Sorry. I didn't pay any attention to who was performing. I usually don't. I suppose I shouldn't say this, but after so many years selling here the music's become little more than background noise. There's always a crowd of people in the vendors' area. If I'm not answering questions or making sales, I'm watching the people at my tables. Theft," he added rather reluctantly, rubbing his arm. "It's a shame sellers have to be like that, but that happens."

McLaren agreed that theft seemed to be on the rise.

"So, you can understand why I didn't know when Kent or any of the performers left the area." He watched McLaren examine a small bag of dried mint leaves. "Very useful plant, mint."

"What else can you use it for besides mint sauce?"

"*Many* things. Medicinally to treat stomach ailments such as cramps, nausea, vomiting and colic. For fevers and reduction of arthritis and chronic joint pain. As a facial wash and an additive in toothpastes to ward off bacteria and viruses. You may also get the same protection against bacterial growth by chewing on the leaves after eating starchy or sugary foods. Mint is helpful as an herbal bath and foot soak. In cooking you can make mint vinegar, a delightful mouthwash. Also it's used to flavor teas and baked goods. Many perfumes and oils for massages include mint in their ingredients." He tapped the front of the bag, drawing McLaren's attention to the writing on the label. "Some of those uses I just mentioned are listed here. Many people are surprised to learn that there are more than three thousand types of mint, the best known being lemon balm, horehound, catnip, lavender, rosemary, and sage."

"Sounds like a wonder plant, all right."

"It is, for the most part. But like anything else natural, we always recommend using caution. You may be allergic and not know it. That's why I advise you consult your doctor before you eat or use any type of herb. Pregnant and nursing women, especially, should talk to their doctors before they use any mint. This applies to cosmetic preparations, medicinal use, as well as in foods."

McLaren turned the bag over and read the back sticker. "Is this for making tea? I don't want to buy the wrong kind. You have a recipe here on the label."

"It's very good for tea. That's why the recipe is included."

"I suppose Aaron devoted a large section of his cookbook to mint, if it has all those uses."

"I don't know. I gave him what recipes I had and, as I said, referred him other sources. I don't know what he did or didn't include in the book. There are hundreds of recipes."

McLaren pulled his wallet from his trousers pocket. "I'd like to buy this."

"You're under no obligation to pay for my information." Even if the phrase came off businesslike, his voice held a suggestion of gratitude.

"I realize that. I still want it. I like mint tea."

Ron accepted the money, slipped the purchase into a logo-covered paper bag, and thanked him. "I appreciate the sale. My address is on the back label, if you should wish some more and can't locate me at a certain venue."

"Thanks." McLaren put away his wallet. "I'm just wondering. Did you and Kent initially meet here, or had you known each other before you came to the Minstrels Court?"

"We met here. He came to my booth and we struck up a conversation." He smiled and tugged on his shirt. "I thought Kent intelligent, good humored, and kind. He mentioned he was one of the musicians appearing here and I wandered over to the stage area to listen to him sing. He had a magnificent voice, pure and strong that sent shivers coursing through your body when he hit high notes. A great performer, too. He knew how to work a crowd, had some funny dialogue. He threw out handfuls of his guitar flat picks to the crowd as souvenirs. Sometimes he made a little contest of it."

"How's that?"

"The person who caught a certain pick would get a free autographed CD. Things like that."

"Do you know how he designated the specific pick? Cut part of it off or pasted a decal on it?"

"I'm not sure. I don't think he cut off anything because his picks already had a hole in them. I was in the audience once when he threw them. I asked him about it later. I thought it so odd." He paused, smiling as if he remembered. "He said his hands sweated so much from the lights and his nervousness that he punched a hole in the center of each pick with a paper punch. His thumb and index finger could then touch when he held it, you see, and the pick wouldn't slide around in his fingers."

McLaren nodded. "I do the same thing."

"Just an instance of his popularity, though he didn't have to give away things to be so well liked and sought after. I know for a fact." Ron lowered his voice and moved slightly closer to McLaren. "Ellen Fairfield was after him." He raised his eyebrow and nodded, underlining the implication.

"Who's Ellen Fairfield? An ardent fan?"

"Yes, but not in the way you're imagining it. She's the curator at Rawlton Hall. She's trying to set up historical events and fetes like Clark has done here at Tutbury. She's been after Kent for years, it seems."

"Trying to lure him to her place so the crowds will move over there."

"You got it. How she did rabbit on, too. Telling him of the extra money he'd make, the great promotion she would do. I thought what she was telling us was mostly rubbish."

"So she was trying to lure other performers and vendors to her Hall, then."

"Too right. Kept coming around bothering us. I thought she and Clark were coming to blows one day. She wouldn't leave off. But she calmed down and we didn't see her for a while."

"I suppose she did this all the time, appeared at the other events held here at the castle."

"And other places like Rawlton. She went farther afield than Staffordshire. But I have heard she liked to frequent Tutbury. She had a good eye for talent and for what sold well. I know she was just looking out for her own job, but it got up Kent's nose, her pestering him all the time. And him a nice chap. Always helping people. That's one of the things I liked most about him."

"Do you know anyone in particular he helped?"

"Well," Ron said, "the only person I know specifically is Dave Morley."

"His sometime singing partner?"

"That's the one. I didn't know the particulars about the act, but I know what Dave always said."

"And what was that?"

Ron straightened a row of bagged herbs. "That Dave needed Kent to boost his career."

****

Luckily for McLaren, he found Dave Morley in the stage area. It had just gone half past nine and the festival wouldn't open for another half hour, but Dave was getting ready for his performance. He was still in his street clothes, but his costume—short doublet with dagged sleeves, opaque hose, and pointed-toe shoes—sat on top of his guitar case. A battered brown trilby, frayed around the front edge, perched on the back of his head. Not doing much for sun protection, McLaren thought. Probably vain about a balding spot. Dave sat on the edge of the stage, guitar resting on his right thigh. His head was turned and lowered over the guitar body as he tuned, listening intently to each string as he plucked them separately and slowly. He sat up, startled, as McLaren walked up, calling his name.

Dave rested his right forearm on the bent side of his instrument and gazed inquisitively at McLaren. "Yes?"

McLaren introduced himself, then nodded at the

guitar. "That's a nice instrument. I probably should have stayed with nylon strings, but I changed to silk and steel a few years ago."

"Folk, right?"

"Yes," McLaren said, astonished.

"Popular choice among folkies. I use nylon since I play mainly early music."

In the brief silence a teenaged boy lumbered up to them. He seemed to be still growing, for his height hadn't caught up to his large hands and feet. Thick, curly hair offset his scant beard. He hung back, chewing on his thumbnail, and looked at the two men.

When Dave noticed him, he nodded. "Hi, Fraser. What's going on?"

The boy took a few steps closer before stopping a yard from Dave. He cleared his throat nervously, then asked if Dave had time to help him with a problem.

"Not right now." Dave glanced at the clock backstage. "I go on soon."

The boy pressed his lips together and sighed heavily.

"See me after my session, if you can stick around. Ta." Dave nodded as Fraser thanked him and walked to the nearest row of chairs in the audience section.

"He a pupil of yours?" McLaren watched Fraser select the perfect spot to view the concert.

"No. Not really. He's a wannabe and he grabs anyone he thinks can give him a boost in the field, teachers and event planners included. You've got to be firm, tell him you can't help him, or he'll cling to you forever." He grimaced, as though he'd experienced it.

"Did he cling to Kent?"

Dave snorted as he wiped down the strings. "When

he could, but I don't think it was too often. He accepted Kent's food and guitar picks but didn't give anything in return, if I'm to believe Kent. And I have no reason to think otherwise."

"He could change when he's a bit more secure with his ability."

"Whatever ability he has, he could do. Unfortunately, he's got Big Time aspirations and no talent. But I help him when I can. He wants to play guitar and sing. But between you and me…" He scrunched his mouth and shook his head.

"He's not Aaron Unsworth's son, is he?"

"Yeah. You know him?"

"No. Just that his name sounded familiar. Not many Frasers around."

"I think I'm his last resort."

"Oh yes?"

"He wanted Kent to help him on the road to fame, but when that didn't work…" He shrugged, as though suggesting any port was good in a storm.

"Hope he makes it."

"It's an awful tough career. There aren't many successes."

"Kent seemed to be on the verge. If you've got another minute, I'd like to talk to you about him."

Dave's right arm straightened and laid across the body of the guitar, pulling it nearer to him, as though a wall to ward off unpleasantness. "What about Kent?" His eyes narrowed as he examined McLaren's face. "If it's about his death, I already talked to the coppers last year. I didn't know anything about it."

"I understand you discovered him approximately twenty-four hours after he went missing."

The man straightened, his voice tightening. "What of it?"

"Nothing. I'm just trying to get the facts correct. You'd been ringing his home and mobile phones prior to that, though. Beginning Sunday night when you left the Minstrels Court, correct?"

"All that was in the newspaper account at the time, but yes. I tried getting him on both phones but he never answered. I finally went out looking for him Monday night."

"And you found him in the wood near his village."

"I was lucky."

"I agree. It was half past ten at night, dark. Dark enough in the village and the field, darker still among the trees. How'd you find him?"

"What do you mean how did I find him? I looked for him. I saw him. He was lying next to that big boulder."

"Just like that? You didn't hunt in the village or get someone to let you into his house?"

"What are you hinting at?" Dave scooted to the ground and stood up, his hands around the guitar neck and holding the instrument vertically in front of him. "He—I couldn't get him on his phones so I went to his house. I knocked and rang the doorbell. There was no answer. I thought it odd because his car was parked in his driveway. I asked his neighbors if they'd seen him. They said no. I went back to my car and got the torch from the glove compartment and started looking around. I knew he liked to walk in the wood, so I went there. He could've gone there after our gig Sunday night, to clear his mind and think, or he could've gone Monday some time. I didn't know, of course, but I knew it was a favorite spot of his. So I looked. He—I saw him right away. He was in plain sight, like he had just dropped over dead. Maybe he had, for all I knew. Heart attack. I didn't know but I was scared. I rang up the police and they came and took over."

He related this while still holding the guitar upright, his words coming quickly in his agitation. Now that he was finished, he merely stood where he was, waiting for McLaren leave.

"Why'd you wait so long to look for him? He was a business partner of sorts, you two were friendly enough."

"I already talked to some woman about this." His tone announced his annoyance. "Why are you bringing this up again? Didn't she tell you?"

Great. Dena's little jaunt into Sherlock Holmes-land is already messing up my investigation. He glossed over Dena's sleuthing. "I assure you, Mr. Morley, I'm not working with anyone. My inquiry is entirely on my own."

Dave eyed him as though he didn't quite believe McLaren.

"So, if you don't mind telling *me*...never mind this woman...why did you wait so long to look for Kent? You know how it looked to the police. To most everyone," he added, thinking Dave Morley had earned his premier position beneath the spotlight.

"Yeah, I know. But we weren't brothers. Or Siamese twins. We liked each other well enough, but we weren't best mates. So what if he didn't answer his phone Sunday night? I thought it a bit queer, since he'd told me to ring him up, but stuff happens. Life gets in the way. Maybe something else came up, or there was an emergency. I didn't know. I don't have a copy of his calendar. We didn't do things together, like pub-crawls or taking in a film or walking the Tissington Trail. We led separate lives. It was no big deal. I thought I'd talk to him on Monday."

"Did you eat together when you were performing?"

"You mean, did we picnic together or go to a pub afterwards?"

"Just what I said. Did you eat together? I don't know about you and Kent, but I'm always ravenous after a performance. All that energy goes right to my stomach, I guess. I'm ready for a sandwich or steak, something more substantial than beer. You didn't have a sandwich together, perhaps backstage, or grab something from one of the food vendors here at the castle?"

"I guess we must have done sometime. Sure." Dave ran his index finger along one of the guitar strings, causing faint squeaks as it vibrated. "Why wouldn't we? I can't recall any specific times, but we probably picked up fish and chips or a pastie along the way."

"You're awfully vague about it."

"It's not something I put in my diary, for God's sake! If we were hungry, we got something to eat. I didn't perform all the time with him, you know. He was the main draw. I just appeared infrequently. We were friends but not that close."

McLaren let a group of chattering teenaged girls walk past before he spoke. "I'd think even an acquaintance, and you were more than that, would be concerned about his absence that Sunday night. Forget the partner angle. You weren't exactly enemies, for

God's sake. Didn't you have the least bit of human decency to be worried about him, about anyone who hasn't answered his phone for twenty-four hours?"

"It's not as easy as you make it sound! Nothing's that black and white."

"Really?" McLaren's voice took on an edge. Of all the self-centered, unfeeling berks he'd ever encountered... "You hiding something, Mr. Morley?"

"What?"

"You're hard of hearing as well as forgetful?"

"You've no call—"

"I'm talking about a murder, Mr. Morley. The murder of your friend and occasional singing partner. Though from the impression I'm getting, I'd phrase it as the murder of your occasional friend and singing partner. What really happened? You two have a dust-up? You fight about billing order or repertoire or something?"

"No! We never did."

"Is that why you don't want to admit you followed him Sunday after leaving the castle, continued the argument, and killed him? Were you that bloody cheesed off that the argument escalated into murder?"

"You're wanting me to carry the can for Kent's death. Well, I've news for you, mate. I'm not about to. Because," he added quickly as McLaren began to speak, "I didn't do it. I wasn't watching from the wings, wanting Kent to die so I could grab the spotlight. What do you take me for? I loved Kent as a friend. Why would I want to kill him?"

McLaren eased off, having accomplished his objective. "Surely, if he didn't answer his phones by the next morning—"

"I couldn't do anything. You've got to understand this." David clasped his hands and practically whined. "I was stuck, unable to do anything further. Well, not what I *wanted* to do, not right away. I-I'm a clerk in a music shop." He fumbled for the right words. "We—I didn't have the luxury of taking off work whenever I like. I started my shift first thing in the morning and worked all day Monday, until I left the shop for the Minstrels Court. I figured Kent would be there for our set. He wasn't. It was the first time in the four years we'd sung together that he missed a gig. I was anxious and panicky. I didn't know what to do. I didn't know if I had enough material to fill an entire slot. I could hardly think. It was late by then, Monday night, eight o'clock. We were supposed to go on at any minute. All I could do was get through a solo set, hoping Kent was just late, that maybe he'd had a flat tire or had been sick or something. I finished the set three quarters of an hour later and he still wasn't there. It was so odd, so unusual for him to forget a performance date. By that time I was convinced he was sick. Maybe too ill to get to a phone. He was my pal and I cared about him. When I'd finished talking to some fans, had changed from my costume into my regular clothes and had driven to his house, it was ten o'clock."

"And then you talked to the neighbors, looked around the village, and then went into the wood." He said it with a hint of skepticism in his voice.

"Yes. The wood was dark. There was no bonfire or candles or torches anywhere. But he sometimes sat in the dark like that. You know…stargazing, looking at the moon and waiting for the night birds to sing. He was like that. Loved the natural world. So I didn't really think the police or anyone would imagine it odd that I would go to the wood to look for Kent, even look at night."

McLaren nodded, relaxing in the mental image. It would seem strange to an outsider or someone wrapped up in city life, but he often sat outside on his stone wall or on the grass, looking at the night sky, listening for owls or nightjars to cry into the stillness.

Dave glanced at McLaren, then cleared his throat. "Anyway, that's why I went straight way to the wood when I couldn't rouse him at home. I sure didn't expect to find him dead." His tone had softened and the volume had decreased to hardly more than a whisper as he finished his narrative. The eagerness McLaren had seen in Dave's eye when introducing himself had died, replaced by a dullness that spoke of sadness.

Dave removed his hat and crushed it in his hands. Showing reverence during prayer, McLaren thought. Or hanging onto a floating bit of wreckage.

McLaren let the silence drop between them as he considered Dave's account. It sounded reasonable, something a timid or indecisive person might do. But was that Dave Morley? He didn't seem like it now. Merely a sad individual, perhaps regretting that he hadn't acted more quickly at the outset, perhaps fearful McLaren was stirring up trouble. But McLaren knew many people who sported a Jeckle-and-Hyde personality—soft-spoken, perhaps timid, when at work or in public, self-confident and personable when performing...or doing something he loved. So Dave still was not eliminated as a suspect. He may have needed Kent to boost his own career, but jealousy sometimes doesn't take long range plans into account.

****

Fraser Unsworth lounged on the grass near the stage, humming to himself and playing air guitar. He nodded when McLaren asked if he could talk and, McLaren thought later, looked annoyed and embarrassed.

"So, Fraser, you're a guitarist, I hear." McLaren settled opposite the teen and plucked a blade of grass.

"I'm trying to be, yeah." Fraser laid his hands in his lap and shifted slightly so the sun wasn't in his eyes.

"It's a slow process. I play, and I'm painfully aware of it." He wriggled the fingers of his left hand, hoping the pun was understood.

"You ever hear Dave?"

"No. Nor Kent. I understand he was quite good."

Fraser nodded and leaned back, his arms supporting him. "The best. That recording of his was a smash hit on the radio. I learned his arrangement and played along with it."

"Super way to learn. I used to mimic several folk musicians when I started. I probably spent more on CDs than I did on clothes or food." He wrapped the grass around his finger, then let it flutter to the ground. "What do your parents think of your guitar playing?"

Fraser glanced to his left, focusing on something. "Dad's okay with it. He likes folk. He's prez of Kent's fan club."

"How about your mother?"

Fraser shrugged. "She never said. When she was with us, she spent more time on her painting and lining up exhibitions at galleries. Mainly local stuff, but she went to Munich a few times. I guess she had a good following there."

"Are your mates impressed with your playing?"

Fraser sat upright and grinned at McLaren. "Yeah. I'm the best one in our group. My girl's always asking me to play."

"Did she like Kent's music?"

"Yeah. She turned me onto him, actually. She was a fan before I'd ever heard him, probably for a year or more. She'd stay out till all hours when she attended his gigs."

McLaren said that's how he'd been when he first latched onto a group or musician he liked. He let the conversation drop as he stretched his long legs out in front of him. "I guess your dad keeps late hours at Kent Harrison events, being fan club president." He plucked another grass blade, threw it over his head, and watched it float down. "He mentioned he came home late the night Kent last appeared at the Minstrels Court. It must cut into your time together if he's gone so much."

"It's not so bad. I stayed up so we could talk when he got back. I was upset. I wanted to talk about mom leaving. We went into the back and talked for about an hour."

"Well, I'm glad you got some time with your dad." McLaren got up, stretching, wished Fraser good luck, and walked to his car.

Chapter Fourteen

So, what is his long-range plan? Dena wondered as she finished the last of the meal. *He's got to have one. He can't keep me here forever. Wherever I am.* She put the cling wrap, paper napkin and juice container into the paper bag and crushed it into a heap before depositing it in the waste bin. The meal had been a homemade affair—the cling wrapped sandwich, mismatched plastic utensils and juice carton spoke of items from someone's kitchen cupboard. *Does it mean, then, that her abduction was more impulsive than planned? If so, why? What had she done to instigate this? More to the point,* she thought, getting up, *has her captor negotiated with her dad over her release? He's got to be waiting for a kidnapping payoff.*

The thought did little to cheer her. Did kidnappers always release captives unharmed after they were paid?

An icicle of fear pricked her back. Dena saw herself left in the room, no food, no air, no light. She was tied up and thrown from a car, left to freeze in the wintry wilds of Kinder Scout. She was knocked unconscious to breathe in carbon monoxide fumes in a deserted garage. She was shot in the head as Michael ran up to her...

She trembled, her mouth quivering as she fought to control her imagination and emotions. Of course this was absurd. She watched too many films, read too many novels. He was feeding her, wasn't he, whoever he was? He hadn't thrown her into an abandoned, filthy warehouse or kept her bound. For whatever reason, he was treating her well, with respect, keeping her alive. She pushed back a strand of hair, somewhat comforted by this explanation, and wandered over to the window.

Although the view was virtually obliterated, Dena got on the chair and strained to see outside. Whether the car park was deserted or filled, she couldn't say, and she found herself disappointed in not knowing if others were nearby or if she were alone. The light had lessened, a faint yellow tinted with hints of pink. The flowerpots appeared more three-dimensional than they had earlier, the sunlight lingering on the western-most sides and leaving the opposite sides in shadows that would slowly advance to hide everything. The thought of night suddenly frightened her and she eased off the chair, plagued again by the fear of the unknown. I'm supposed to sleep here? Without a blanket? She wrapped her arms about herself, shivering, unsure if the thought of a cold night on a cold floor bothered her more than spending the time alone in a vacant building.

She sat down, scooting to the edge of the seat, unwilling to let the cold of the metal seep into her back. She would be chilly enough lying on the floor without hurrying her discomfort. Leaning forward, she tried to think—of the reason for her kidnapping; of her father, at his home in Manchester and who was blissfully going about his daily routine; of Michael, who might be unaware of her predicament, yet would be dangerously obsessed to find her.

Despite her previous caution to avoid the chair's cool metal, she slid backward and sagged against the chair back. She was aware of nothing: no temperature, no sound, no shifting of light as McLaren's face floated before her. His hazel eyes held her gaze, caring and concerned, intense in his love and determination to find her. She heard him speak, though his mouth remained smiling. Words that reassured her of her rescue, that whispered of his love, that offered her an anchor of hope in the storm had threatened her sanity and spirit. He moved, and the sunlight caught a flaxen streak in his dark blond hair. His arms went out to her, offering refuge and warmth and healing. She got to her feet, ready to go to him, when the door to the room opened. No sound came from the space beyond the door, no voice or footstep or running machinery. She seemed to be floating in a bizarre landscape where time had ceased to function and the sole inhabitant stared mutely at her. For, framed in the open doorway, silhouetted against the florescent light in the hallway, stood a tall figure dressed in dark coloring. A rubber mask of a smiling Margaret Thatcher covered his face. His hands were gloved, the left holding a coil of rope, the right holding something dark that glistened in the light. He stepped into the room, not speaking, yet making his desires known with the gesture of the gun.

****

This nightmare couldn't last, Dena reasoned, straining to see in the new darkness that surrounded her, clinging to her like a spider's web. That she'd be able to see through; this blackness is absolute. Thick.

And yet, not quite. As her eyes became accustomed to the dark, pinpricks of light wriggled into her space. The gloom lessened slightly and she distinguished less dark shapes around her. She tried to move but found her arms and legs bound. A rectangle of duct tape secured her mouth. Like a lamb. A lamb ready for the slaughter.

Did a lamb know where it was heading when it was led from its pasture? Did seeing make any difference to it, calm it? She had been blindfolded for the trip to the new location. Her captor had done it neatly, thoroughly, taking no chance she would see where she was being led. And swiftly, perhaps fearing he would be discovered in his shameful deed. The blindfold had been augmented, a fabric bag thrust over her head. That darkness had been complete but not as terrifying as the blackness that now engulfed her. Perhaps it had been the ride here, the knowledge that another living person—no matter if it was her captor or not—was within several feet of her, that she wasn't alone. Perhaps it had been the smell of the July night, warm and sweet with the scents of still warm earth, watered foliage, and blooming honeysuckle. That blackness had given her hope that he still wanted her alive, still had a use for her. The gloom that invaded the new prison hinted at danger.

She struggled to a sitting position, struggled for breath as the exertion exhausted her. A muffled groan escaped her taped lips, bounced off hard walls and instantly stilled her attempt. She sat frozen, half-sitting, half-reclining, listening for a movement in the farther recesses of the room, waiting for a gunshot or a curse, expecting the tattoo of hurried footsteps and the banging open of the door and the sharp slap as an unseen hand struck her face. But as her breathing slowed and the cry faded, no one announced his presence. She tightened her stomach muscles and slowly pulled upright.

Though what good it did, she couldn't say. Unless it was that she felt more in control of her destiny. Sitting upright, like a human being, instead of lying trussed on the floor and waiting to die.

Dena looked around, trying to discern her location. The darkness painted everything uniformly, giving no depth or detail to the area. Rocking back and forth and scooting her legs by inches to the right, Dena maneuvered in a tight circle, viewing the entire space. Nothing stood out; nothing suggested the identity of the place. Other than the faint dots of white light when she returned to what she assumed was her original position. She could be anywhere.

And yet, that wasn't true. She was sitting on carpet. She felt it through her shoes as her feet had pushed against it to sit her up; she felt it through the seat of her trousers as she wriggled around in a circle; and with her fingers if she bent slightly backwards. A fitted carpet, not the hard, cold ceramic tile of her previous captivity. A room-sized carpet, otherwise it would have bunched beneath her as she fought to sit up. Therefore, a room frequently peopled. The realization that she hadn't been dumped in a garage or basement, that she was in an office or residence, comforted her. But it did nothing to reveal where she was—or why she had been kidnapped.

And it did nothing to diminish her fear.

She tried to think as McLaren would, putting the pieces together to form a picture of her kidnapping and her dungeon. Ignoring the 'what,' she asked herself the five remaining questions that formed the basis of any inquiry.

How was she taken? Easy, she thought, aware of her aching scalp. Clobbered on the head. But how was she physically brought here? In a car. Well, some vehicle. She had been blindfolded but awake, aware of what was going on. She didn't know the length of the ride before she'd regained consciousness, so she couldn't estimate the distance traveled, but she did recall sounds and road surfaces. Smooth tarmac, a great number of bends to it. Which suggested an A or B road, not a motorway. Which also suggested she was in a village or town. Longer episodes of straight travel would hint at a city, or at least suburbs. And there had been a constant, though sporadic, sound and brief hesitation in the car... What was that? What did that signify? Gear changes.

What else had she heard? No lorries lumbering by, no horns honking, no sheep bleating, no bell towers chiming. Nothing to say 'I'm near a church or the waterfront.' And no car radio announcing the time, call letters or music. No conversation from the driver to her or anyone else.

But surely there had been a second person. Wouldn't it be easier and faster if two people transported her from her car to the kidnapper's car? They'd want to do it as quickly as possible, to avoid being seen.

Her car... That answers the next question.

Where did it happen? Yes, as she sat parked in the lay-by. But there was another 'where' to answer. Where was she now? Besides indoors, in a carpeted room. Was it another room in the same building, or a different building? She'd been in a residential area that harbored a school or office. She knew that much because she'd seen the car park and the group of houses along its farthest end. It was a well-attended school or office because the car park seemed to be filled; plus, those pots of plants and flowers were alive and healthy. They wouldn't be so well tended if the place bordered on dereliction.

Right. She'd figured out the "where" and "how it happened." What else?

When did it happen? Must've been Monday afternoon, just after speaking to Gwen on her mobile.

What of the kidnapper? Who could it be? Dena hadn't seen him…or her…or them…before being knocked unconscious. So she had no description like Michael always joked about: narrow-set eyes, weak chin, scruffy beard. She hadn't see anyone when she was moved from the vehicle—the blindfold took care of that. She had no idea if her captor had an identifying mark or if she'd injured him. There hadn't been a chance to fight him off at the beginning, and when he moved her from his car two people had been involved. Her hands, arms and legs were tied, so no joy there. No sounds of a doorbell ringing, or whispered commands between two people. Though she had sensed being carried down a short flight of stairs, and around a corner. Their footsteps echoed, as though they were walking on a hard surface, like linoleum or terrazzo, which would go with the school or office. But who could it be? Obviously he wanted to remain unidentifiable—the dark clothing could conceal a male or female frame; the gloves disguise size, skin color, work history, and gender; the mask removed any positive identification; the mute gestures eliminated recognition—of someone she might know, of gender.

Could a woman have done this? Would she have the strength to shift me, twice now, from vehicle to vehicle, from vehicle to prison? But that doesn't preclude two people involved in this, as it seems to necessitate since I was carried originally from the car to the office. Nor does it preclude that it's someone I know, whether acquaintance, family, or friend.

An acquaintance I could accept, though why abduct me? A family member or friend tinges the act of kidnapping with the taste of jealousy. Or revenge. But revenge for what?

Dena sat upright, afraid of the answer that already barked at her.

Revenge? WHY? The question consumed more than her mind; it enveloped her with an unstoppable shaking that suddenly gripped her body. If it's revenge, *what did I do?*

She needed to know who'd carried out her abduction, and where she was being held. The answers might allay some of the questions—or destroy her emotionally.

She considered getting to her knees and inching around the area, feeling along a wall—if she came to one—with her shoulder or the top of her head. But she quickly abandoned the idea. The unknown room, wrapped in darkness, could hold anything, things she might not want to bump into or confront. The childhood terror of stretching out her hand during a game of Blindman's Bluff and feeling a dried blowfish rushed back at her from this new darkness, shrieking with a thousand taunts that bounced off the walls. She would stay where she was, content with the progress she had made in identifying her kidnapping, yet hoping that morning would bring light and a greater revelation.

****

147

The man pushed back his dinner plate and stared at the unfinished steak, bits of salad, and chunks of the cheddar scone. He'd been hungry during the meal preparation, ravenous when he sat down. But the remnants stated otherwise. Well, he'd give it to the trash bin. Or to the birds.

But he made no move to get up. Something bothered him other than the peculiarity of his diminished appetite.

The phone rang, disturbing his internal questioning, and his hand slapped down on it. He glanced at the caller display before answering. "Yes?"

"Can you talk?"

"I'm alone. What's the problem?"

"Nothing. I fed her and she's peaceful enough for tonight."

The man sighed, clearly exasperated. The call underlined his growing sense of anxiety. "Then why ring me up? The police aren't breathing down your neck, are they?"

"Not yet."

"What does that mean? Are you expecting to be questioned formally?"

"I guess anything's possible."

"Look. We agreed when we grabbed her that we'd see this through. Now you sound like you're rethinking this. If you do a runner and leave me with her, I'll hunt for you. No matter if it takes my entire bank account or the rest of my life, I'll find you. Got it?" He laid his free hand on his thigh to stop its quivering.

"I'm not having second thoughts. You know I'm in this as deep as you are. I just want to know how long we're going to have her. Feeding her a few meals is one thing, but keeping her hidden, seeing to her...physical needs is another. We didn't consider everything when we decided to snatch her. I didn't, at least. Now it seems like it'll go on eternally."

"Need I remind you why we did this?" the man snapped. He tried not to betray the inklings of fear and regret that grabbed his soul. Without knowing it, his partner echoed the man's feelings. And it bothered him to have his emotions exposed.

"I'm well aware of our reason, thank you."

"Then quit complaining. We won't have her around much longer."

"You're not going to...get rid of her. I didn't bargain for that."

The man leaned back and stared through the dining room window. Moonlight glinted off his car. He felt he was in the showroom, drawn to it, mesmerized by the sleek finish and the gloss black accents, seeing it for the first time. It'd been a prize he'd wanted forever, a psychological boost during his depression. Maybe it could help him again... He sat up and his voice rose slightly in pitch. "Yes, we're going to get rid of her but not in the way you think. Stop mimicking a crime show on the telly and think for once. We'll drop her off somewhere. We'll be shed of her and she'll be scared off her investigation. She'll not be hurt and we'll still escape any suspicion in any of this."

The voice on the other end hesitated, as though the caller gave the proposed solution careful contemplation. "Drop her where? No place where she could get hurt."

"What the hell do you take me for? Of course she won't get hurt. I don't relish the thought of killing anyone. We'll keep her blindfolded and drive her north, maybe a hundred miles or so, and leave her in a park or forest. We'll tie her hands but make sure she can get free. I'll put some money in her pocket and she'll be able to get to a pub or house and phone for help."

"Won't she be scared alone outside in a park or forest? Will she be safe?"

"We'll drop her off just before sunrise. She won't be there long. She'll be fine and she'll be so thrilled at having escaped the enemy camp that a few insect bites won't bother her. Now, quit crying."

"I guess it sounds all right."

The man relaxed now that the immediate future seemed resolved. He got up and took the dinner plate into the kitchen. "Sure, it does. It's best for her and it's good for us, too. Let me figure out a spot to leave her and I'll ring you up in a day or two. I won't be long. Don't worry."

"You better not be long. Every time I go there to feed her I'm afraid the cops are going to nab me. I'm not cut out for this."

"You think I am?"

"No. It's just getting to me. She's a nice lady. I like her." The voice whined in concern, irritating the man.

"I like her, too, but what the hell has that to do with anything?"

"I hate for her to go through this, that's all."

"She won't much longer. I'll bring her breakfast as usual tomorrow and I'll let you know when we can release her. Okay?"

"Sure. Ta."

The man closed his mobile, laid it on the table, and walked outside with the plate.

Chapter Fifteen

McLaren thought the familiar urge he had that morning would bring light and a revelation. He silently acknowledged that he was at a dead end. Perhaps this was the reason the case had gone cold, he thought as he drove to The Split Oak. Perhaps he just needed a pint in his favorite pub and a chat with his mate, Jamie Kydd. Police detective or not, Jamie might point out something in McLaren's haze.

It wasn't particularly late—just coming on to four o'clock—but McLaren felt as though he had no brain left. He stopped at Rawlton Hall, hoping to speak to Ellen Fairfield, the curator, but was told she was in Beresford Dale. "Taking a bit of time for herself. She's been working that hard," was how the assistant conveyed it.

McLaren thanked her and drove the fifteen miles back north.

He took the small road north of Alsop-en-le-Dale and hit the B5054 near Hartington. The Dale, a serene glen of high cliffs and trout-laden pools, carved a place for itself on the River Dove. McLaren turned onto a lane and soon came to the river. He parked in a wide area alongside the road. A black Land Rover Defender sat under a tree.

McLaren got out and glanced at the immediate area before sauntering down to the Dove. A wooden bridge, one-person wide and sporting a waist-high railing, spanned the stream. The opposite bank opened onto a pasture; cliffs curtained the far end.

He crossed the bridge, thinking Ellen would be strolling in the sun, but after several minutes' walk through the high grass and getting no response to his calls, he re-crossed the river and took the path bordering the bank.

Early twilight hovered in the Dale, the steep cliffs holding the sunlight at bay. Shadows wallowed at the cliff bases and in the thickets on the western side, while the eastern face held onto the light dawdling halfway up its heights. The land was cooler along the water; dampness hung in the air, and he wondered what it would feel like in winter. Ferns poked from crevices in the rock wall, their leaves glistening from the mist. Moss coated tree bark and rocks, and threw its musty odor into the air.

He stepped over a fallen log and entered the Dale proper. Clumps of burdock and other river plants crowded the river's edge, some leaning precariously close to the rushing water. On his left, vines and branches dangled from the cliff face. This section wallowed in shade, for sunlight seldom hit it,. He glanced at the cliff tops, alive with birds and trees and bright light before pushing a few of the more emphatic branches out of his way. The earth and sand were wet where boulders threw water onto the path and he stepped over the areas, careful not to lose his footing on the dampness. His back-slid along the rock face, and he called again.

A woodpecker drummed on a tree before taking flight.

McLaren stopped opposite a rectangular boulder stuck upright in the center of the river. He gazed at the cliff top, trying to discern from where the rock had fallen. It must've happened years ago, for the vegetation and trees blanketed the peak in dense green.

The river bent to the left but the path stopped. He walked a few feet into the bushes, thinking the river bailiff was overdue in keeping the pathway clear. But the plants packed the meter-wide slide of land. There'd probably never been a path here, he reasoned, and walked back to the bend.

The river gurgled louder and tumbled faster here as it slid over a reef of rocks. From this point to the opposite shore, a line of stepping stones led across the river to the path. He hesitated, judging the river's depth and swiftness, then rolled up his trousers and waded in. The water was only inches deep.

Reclaiming the path, he walked slowly, looking for evidence that someone had recently come this way. He called Ellen's name again, but his words broke against the rock faces or dissipated into the air. He was on a fool's mission, he told himself when he stopped minutes later. The path had meandered slightly east, out of the river's sight, leaving several dozen meters of flower-carpeted land between him and the water. He looked around, wondering if Ellen was at the fishing temple. But unless she was an invited guest, she couldn't get into Charles Cotton's cottage. It was kept locked to discourage unwanted visitors.

McLaren swore at the waste of time and turned back. His steps were faster, betraying his eagerness to redeem the remainder of the day.

His pace didn't slow when he came to the crossing.

Annoyed with Ellen and with himself, he stepped off the bank. His leg slammed into something, his foot slipped on a rock, and he lost his balance. He crashed into the river, unconscious.

****

The Dale had grown darker by the time he came to. Sunlight hovered on the eastern cliff edge, painting the tops of the trees in a splash of ochre. In the gorge, along the river, dusk had settled, and the wild things that belonged to the night started to stir.

McLaren sat up, unsure where he was or what had happened. He stared at river, bewildered as to why he lay in it. He moved his hand, disbelieving the silt and bits of plants he stirred up. Water ran down his back and from his hands as he pushed to his feet. He bent forward slightly, feeling the water's resistance on his lower legs. He trudged toward the bank from which he'd fallen, the riverbed uneven beneath his shoes.

He curled his fingers around a rock half embedded on the edge of the path, grabbed the trunk of a sapling, and clamored back onto the land. He turned toward the river, partially bent over and breathing heavily, and stared at the area where he'd lain. The river stretch was a confusion of rushing water, large rocks and half-submerged logs. How bloody lucky he'd been. If he'd landed a half meter either way, he'd either have drowned or split open his skull. He shuddered at the narrow escape and took several deep breaths before he looked at his leg. A thin line, angry and red, marked his encounter with some foreign object. But what had it been?

He searched the bank, rooting among the rocks and vegetation, and found a length of wire. One end held firm to a tree trunk, the other to a metal rod. The wire sagged from its encounter with his leg.

McLaren pulled up the rod, slipped off the wire, then yanked the wire from the tree, anger overriding his judgment. The wire obviously hadn't been there when he crossed over. Someone had hidden here and deliberately rigged the trap.

He stood on the bank and surveyed the area. The dusk was too heavy to see properly; the air held numerous midges and mosquitoes, their wings a blur in the heavy light. He swung his arm, breaking up their cloud, tucked the rod into his belt, and waded to the original bank. Once again gaining ground, he picked up a stick and held it in front of him, sweeping it like a sightless person with a cane. His shoes plopped against the soft soil and squished with each step. As he stopped to dislodge a pebble from his shoe, he cursed Ellen, his unknown assailant, and the pain in his head.

He was tempted to get into his car and collapse against the padded seat, but he spent a quarter of an hour walking around the meadow, letting the heat from the grass partially dry his clothes. When he finally drove off, the black Defender still sat under the tree.

****

The dampness that remained in his clothes bore into his skin as he turned the car onto the B road. He had no idea how he looked but he smelled of river water. Not the best aroma for having a pint with Jamie. Maybe he could wash off at Dena's. After all, he was about a ten-minute drive from her house.

He put a CD in the player, a recording of Beethoven German dances, remastered from the LP featuring conductor Edouard Van Remortel, needing the solace of great music to soothe his mind. There'd been music at his retirement party when he left the job last year. A hastily arranged affair with "Auld Lang Syne" playing as a background to the jokes and well wishes. But one officer's eyes held his real feelings, and McLaren had read the disingenuous we'll-miss-you loud and clear. He hummed along to Beethoven, but the Scottish song echoed in his mind.

He made a sharp right opposite the village of Parwich, and drove down the smaller road sandwiched between the A515 and the River Dove. Kirkfield, Dena's village, presented itself as he crested the hill.

The main road wasn't yet crowded with the cars of workers returning home from their jobs in the surrounding towns. If crowded was the correct word, McLaren reconsidered. But the road did hold a few late returning shoppers and the occasional tourist. McLaren parked in front of her house and jogged up the front walk.

The house was in keeping with the others in the row—stone façade, flower boxes underscoring the front windows, and small front gardens in a riot of summer color. And as old, for the length of dwellings had not altered in external appearance since built in the 1700s. A grandfather oak near the house's front corner spread its massive boughs over the roof and upward to heaven, as though simultaneously offering protection and blessing. McLaren lifted the heavy, brass doorknocker—surprisingly warm to his touch—and rapped at the door.

While he waited for Dena, he glanced at the garden, a well-kept harmony of warm colors—orange day lilies, red roses, pink geraniums, yellow daisies, and marigolds, with an accent of white Queen Anne's lace by the birdbath. A sense of envy claimed him as he took in the weeded perennial beds and mowed grass. But the emotion left as swiftly as it had come. He was content with his strip of daylilies and wild flowers that grew uncorraled along the stone wall. He hadn't the gardener's heart even if he did revel in nature. Weeding was a chore, not a loving gesture. He sighed, knowing he'd have to be content to gaze on other's gardens, and turned back to the door. The house remained silent.

Maybe she was still at the animal rescue center. McLaren glanced at his watch. Or stopping at a girlfriend's before coming to his house. He knocked once again, louder and longer, but the door remained closed.

He got back into his car and closed the door. But the key remained in his hand, his gaze still on her house. The disappointment at not talking with her welled up in his soul until he thought his heart would split. He wanted her wise counsel, the uninvolved view, the impartiality of an onlooker. Plus, if he were honest with himself, he wanted to be with her. Now that he had put the year's estrangement behind him, he wanted her love and companionship. He wanted to step back to the intimacy and belief they had had before they had separated, before he had pushed her away. He wanted to pour his heart out to her and hold her.

But the unopened door delayed the moment. Telling himself he would do that over dinner, he started the car and drove to Somerley, thinking three hours had never seemed so long.

The Split Oak in McLaren's home village hadn't yet filled with the home-going crowd when he walked into the main room at five o'clock. Those who were there sat at small tables that formed a U-shape at the end of the room, and stood in clusters, examining packets and books and jewelry and talking "price" with the costumed people at the tables. All very medieval, McLaren found himself thinking, mimicking the phrase from earlier in the day. Appropriate to the pub's interior of polished oak paneled walls, old porcelain pitchers and age-yellowed maps. Waving to the publican, he nodded toward the group. "What's all this?"

They seemed to blend with the pub's interior, for the costumes were of the Middle Ages. Of the type that Ron Pennell had sported that morning at Tutbury Castle.

"Escaped all this before, have you?" The publican, a brawny man in his late forties, held the glass he was drying up to the light and squinted at it. Dissatisfied with his job, he applied the towel again to a stubborn spot.

"Must have done. I feel underdressed."

The publican glanced at McLaren's trousers, shirt, and tie, then went back to his glass drying. "I wouldn't worry. No one will arrest you for indecent exposure."

The man was dying to know about the eau-de-river and his damp clothes, McLaren thought, but mentally applauded the man's good manners. "Fine. Now I can get a good night's sleep."

The publican's laugh bounced off the oak-paneled walls. "It'll get busier toward seven, eight tonight. But only the main players come costumed."

"Fine, but what's it for?"

"Oh, didn't I say? It's the Minstrels Round."

"*Round*?"

"Aye. An annual event for students going on to sixth form or university. The Minstrels Round helps sustain the scholarship for those kids who need financial help. Folks come, donate to the scholarship fund, indulge in a bit of medieval fun by learning some history, partake of food, buy a trinket or two from the various craftsman, listen to the musicians…" He paused in his explanation to place the glass in the overhead rack, then picked up another and began drying it. "I'm told it's all authentic—the food, music and such. I wouldn't know, being as I'm not much of a scholar. But it's a nice time for everyone and the music's good. Guitars, lutes, harps. That sort of thing. Old stuff."

"Authentic." McLaren looked at the mandolin lying on a chair seat.

"So they tell me. I'm surprised you haven't come before, you being such a fan of this sort of music."

"Is it held the same time every year?"

"Same weekend, yes. It's been going on for several years. A teacher at a school in Ashbourne organizes it. That's him in the Robin Hoodish outfit. Teaches history."

"This is a bit far afield to be holding an event for Ashbourne, isn't it?"

"Oh, they have this Minstrels Round all over Derbyshire. They've set up a regular schedule. August in Hathersage and Bakewell; sometime in May in Matlock, Bath, and Tideswell; a spring event in Buxton… If you're interested, they've no doubt got a schedule printed up."

"So the scholarship is for any student?"

"There are particulars. Most likely has to live in Derbyshire, but you can find that out. I guess they have to want a certain career." He set down the glass and rested his hand on the bar top. "I mean, with all these performers dressed up like folks from Round Table days, the scholarship ought to go to a medieval history buff or budding musician, don't you suppose?"

"Can't see why they'd drag all their items here if not." McLaren bought a glass of wine, thanked the bartender, and joined Jamie at his table. "You ever see this before?" he asked as he settled into a chair. They sat a corner opposite the medieval group, where the light was dimmer and they could talk without being overheard. Most every patron's attention was focused on the Round, anyway.

Jamie set down his beer glass and shook his head. "Must have been lucky. Never even heard of it. Whatever happened to you? You smell like—"

"I cooled off in the River Dove."

"You should've done it without your clothes, Mike. Maybe you can borrow something from one of those blokes. They seem to have on a few layers. You run into them before?"

"Get a schedule before you leave. Then you'll know where to catch them up."

"It's rather nice. Should be good music later on." He took a sip of beer. "You want to eat something and stay for a bit?"

"Can't. Dena's coming for dinner. I have to get home soon and cook."

"Special occasion?"

McLaren shrugged, trying to make it appear a casual event, but his heart was racing. He downed half the wine, needing time to still the tremor he felt in his throat, then told Jamie about his investigation.

"You've spoken with most of the major players." Jamie leaned back in his chair. "Unless there's a colleague or two at Kent Harrison's school, or a mystery man you don't yet know about, I'd say you've done rather well."

"I'm going back to the school," McLaren explained. "The headmaster is away, but I set up times to talk to some of the faculty who knew Kent rather well."

"Then I don't see what your problem is, Mike."

McLaren set the glass down but kept his hand on the stem, as though needing an emotional anchor. "I feel like I'm missing something, like there's a big secret, and I'm the last person to know about it."

"There usually are secrets in a murder case."

"But something more than the killer's identity. Like everyone is lying to me, only I'm too stupid to know."

"Well, if it will give you an edge on your suspects, you might want to know that the only things that came to light in the original search of the scene where Kent's body was found were a guitar pick and a grommet."

"Grommet?"

"Besides the usual rubbish of our uncaring public, I mean."

McLaren nodded, picturing the scene and the others he'd processed as a young constable. All the refuse of indifferent people—cigarette ends, water bottles, food wrappers, beer cans, used facial tissue… "A grommet—like from a ruck sack?"

"Shouldn't think so. It was small. Like on a belt buckle, shoulder bag strap or shoe."

"And the pick doesn't particularly mean anything.

Lots of kids probably use the spot for get-togethers and singing." He thought a minute, looking at the mandolin. "What kind of guitar pick? Anything unusual?"

"You're the expert on that, Mike. It just looked like a guitar pick. Flat, plastic, tortoise shell color and pattern. No hole, if that's what you're asking."

"Does nothing for me, no." He pushed the glass away from him. "Not much closer to a solution than we were before."

"I guess the medical report is old news to you."

"Why? Anything more than what Cheryl's already told me?"

"You've talked with her, then. No, nothing new. Not if she didn't say anything."

McLaren nodded. "Cyanogenetic glycoside in his stomach, death by asphyxiation some time between ten o'clock and midnight on Sunday night."

"He was strangled."

"No signs of manual strangulation. Garroted," he added, somewhat reluctantly. "Not exactly in line with fair play."

"Kent had to have been jumped, I suppose, because there's an indication on his skull that he'd been hit with a rock. At least that's the official consensus."

"There are certainly enough rocks at that spot, yes." McLaren paused, tapping the glass with his index finger. "You know what this reminds me of?"

"I know I shouldn't ask, but I will. What?"

"That time I was talking about those two murder cases and Harvester butts in with his attempt at a solution."

Jamie lowered his head slightly, nodding. "I remember you telling me. What an inept attempt

Harvester gave. Are you sure he graduated?"

"My partner and I were discussing the possibility of the same killer for both murders, since they happened two hours and one mile apart."

"Right. Two shop employees at the first scene, and three at the second. Seemed a logical assumption in the beginning."

"Which is what Harvester clung to, quite vocally, I recall. He was all for calling it a serial killing right off the bat, whereas my partner and I opted for two different killers. The two employees were shot execution style, the desk, cash register, and safe filed. The three at the second scene were tied up and stabbed, and a length of rope was left there."

"Same type as used on the victims, yes."

"I was telling my partner that this first murder looked like an experienced killer who was after money, perhaps to finance an escape. He knew not to leave any living witnesses. The second scene appeared to be of an intimate nature. Knifings tend to be that, up close and personal, unlike the distance of a gun to the victim. Also, the unused length of rope told us the killer had come expecting someone else. When he didn't find the fourth person, he left. The knifings also suggested rage, each victim sustaining nearly a dozen wounds."

"But Harvester didn't like that, right?"

McLaren skewed his lips at the corners and snorted. "What do you think? Papa's boy who got through police school by whispered favors and implied threats? I don't think Harvester cared that the victims' deaths were different. He just saw the time and distance connection and went with that."

"How'd it turn out? I don't recall you telling me."

"When we had arrested the killer who shot the two people, Harvester rabbits on about charging the bloke with the second murder. It was all I could do to make him listen to my explanation as to why we looked for someone else. He wanted to wrap it up fast and neat."

"Probably to impress his dad." Jamie rubbed his nose, as though he could smell the stink that would've followed that catastrophe.

"Luckily, my chief inspector hammered home the logic of the two killers."

"Saving Staffordshire Constabulary the embarrassment. How'd Harvester react?"

"Typically. A week later I find a coil of rope on my desk chair."

Jamie let out a swear word. "Subtle, ain't he? What a berk. You didn't take it for a hint that he'd like to do that to you, did you?"

"He hasn't the nerve. I just smiled when I next saw him. I think my silence drove him bonkers."

"Serves him right, the berk. Someone ought to knock some sense into him."

"I know a few dozens blokes who'd pay to do the job. They'd bring their own hammers or rocks to do it, too."

"Well, you're got your own rock. Kent," Jamie said, bringing McLaren back to the subject of the singer's death. "Using the rock to knock him unconscious was a nice touch. Knocked Kent out so he couldn't fight back. So the person got bloody well close enough to him to do that, at least, even if he was jumped. Not a fight, because there were no defense wounds on his body."

McLaren snorted. "There's always that pesky

problem of how his body ended up in the wood. His car was at his home, remember?"

"What's to prevent some chap from following Kent home from the Minstrels Court, or arranging to meet him somewhere?"

"At his house, most likely."

"Anyway, they meet up, walk nonchalantly to the wood and, Kent being off his guard because he's set up the rendezvous—"

"—is taken unaware when the bloke jumps and kills him," McLaren finished. "Fine. A lovely scenario, but again…who?"

"Dave Morley, Kent's sporadic singing partner, said they were to have talked that night," Jamie reminded McLaren.

"I heard. I don't suppose they actually met and Dave's just a tad sketchy with his memory."

The musician sat on a stool, tuning her mandolin. The notes were drowned out by the conversation coming from the Minstrels Round area.

"Lies, faulty memories—doesn't make much difference. You still don't get any truth, no matter what year you look into the case."

"Speaking of time…" McLaren stood up as he glanced at his watch.

"The frying pan calls, I know. Give Dena my best, Mike." He reached for his glass as McLaren left the table.

McLaren strolled up to the man in the Robin Hood costume. In his late fifties, McLaren thought, glancing at the crow's-feet angling out from the dark eyes. Yet muscular and trim.

The man looked up from the beer he was sipping,

put it on the table behind the stack of pamphlets, and wiped his hand on his doublet before extending it in a handshake. "Sorry. I try not to eat or drink while there are people about. But I was thirsty."

"Perfectly all right."

"Trevor Pennell. Glad you stopped by."

"Pennell? Any relation to Ron Pennell?"

"You know him? We're brothers."

"Is he here?" McLaren turned slightly to glance around the room.

"No. He's meeting with a client. Something about redesigning a garden. Is that how you're acquainted? Has he done work for you?"

"I could probably use his expertise, but no. I met him at the Minstrels Court. He seems extremely knowledgeable about herbs."

"He is. I'm amazed at all he knows."

"You're not of that bent, I take it."

"I'm into history, but we both like the good olde days, as Ron puts it."

"Just different aspects of that age."

"Right. Are you new to the Minstrels Round? I don't recall seeing you here before. It's a fairly tight-knit community, so I know most interested parties."

"No, I've not participated." He introduced himself and stated he was investigating Kent's death.

"Ah, yes. Kent Harrison. Did you know him? No? Too bad. He actually came up with the idea for the Minstrels Round. He taught music at the school where I teach. Grange Hall Performing Arts College. He saw how attracted some kids were to the pageantry and the Middle Ages in general."

"Kind of an outgrowth of the Narnia books and

Dungeon and Dragons and so forth?"

"Precisely. He started demonstrating some of this in his classes. They were immensely popular, so this scholarship thing grew out of that."

"It seems like a good way to help students attain the funds for university."

"It is. But it's just another feather in Kent's cap. He was always helping people. He had such a passion for music, and for teaching in general. He infected his students with the joy of the era and with learning. He'd take them to the Minstrels Court for a day, proclaiming that they absorbed more by seeing and being in the correct atmosphere than a week's worth of book study could produce. He'd bring back things from the event and use them in his classroom. He was a superb teacher. I could have easily been jealous of him, of his popularity, but he was so unassuming, that I couldn't. So Ron and I try to keep his charity going and echo his enthusiasm in my own students."

"So your brother knew Kent, then."

"Yes. Liked him, too. There isn't much that Ron and I don't share, which goes for friends and hobbies. We've not let our age differences come between us. I guess we're as close as a lot of siblings."

Which doesn't preclude bickering, animosity, jealousy and anger. How many cases had he worked where one sibling killed another due to such an emotion? Or a child attacking a parent, or one spouse against another? He let the comparison fade as he asked, "Has anyone else at your school taken up Kent's method of teaching, either going to the Minstrels Court or doing something hands-on like that?"

"I'm about the only person. As I said, history is my

specialty. Sixth form students. I lecture at the Minstrels Court, too, but my passion—as was Kent's—is for the hands-on stuff, though his projects did backfire a few times." McLaren must've looked interested so Trevor went on. "One of Kent's neighbors, Aaron Unsworth, phoned in complaints to the police several times. The kids were at Kent's house to work on projects or learn guitar. And acoustic guitar, at that!" Trevor screwed up his mouth and exhaled loudly. "In this day of electrics and rockers and special effects...and they were interested in acoustic guitars and lutes. Anyway, Kent was only trying to teach his students, for God's sake. It wasn't like they were boozing it up in the garden and yelling. I mean, how loud can a few acoustics be?"

"Perhaps something else was bothering Mr. Unsworth."

"I'd give him the benefit of one bad evening, but he complained several times. Kent chalked it up to jealousy."

"Was he jealous of Kent's musical ability?"

"I shouldn't think so, but I don't know. Probably just a mean old buzzard without many friends."

McLaren thanked him for his time, then drove home to start dinner.

****

The trout, covered in a crisp oatmeal batter, was ready for frying as soon as Dena got there. The broccoli, water chestnuts, and carrots sautéed in the skillet—the slivered almonds and Worcestershire sauce would be added in the last minutes of cooking. Lettuce and baby spinach were mixed for the salad and kept cool in the fridge. All he had to do was warm the rolls in the oven before they sat down to dinner.

He paused, a dishtowel over his shoulder, and looked around the dining room. A blue tablecloth and matching napkins perfectly complemented his mother's white china; a white pillar candle waited in the hurricane candleholder; a bunch of red roses beamed from their glass vase. Everything was under control and running along smoothly. It just lacked the guest.

He picked up the water glass on the table—a cut glass goblet handed down through his family—and downed the cold liquid. His palms sweated and his heart raced. It was just Dena, for God's sake; it was just dinner. She'd been over many times previously. He put the glass back, unaware of the drops of water running off the glass' base and onto the tablecloth. Should he refill his now or should he just wait? Maybe he should have just got a single long-stemmed rose and laid that across her dinner plate—would she think that more romantic than the vase of roses? And the silver serving bowl for the dessert…he hadn't had time to polish it. Would she notice? Would she think he didn't care enough of her to shine it up?

Although very well off, Dena took people as she found them, equally content with bread and butter or fancy fare for tea. That was one reason he loved her. His fingers traced the edge of her napkin. He knew that now, knew it as deeply as he knew the sun rose in the east. He loved her with a fire that burned within him, with an ache he could not placate if they were apart. At dinner tonight he would tell her, ask her again to marry him.

McLaren walked back into the kitchen and gave the vegetables a stir. He glanced at the wall clock and lowered the heat. If they burned he had only frozen peas to fall back on. And while there was nothing wrong with peas, the broccoli and carrot dish was a family recipe and would impress Dena.

He opened the fridge and checked on the chocolate mousse. He tapped the cling wrap draped over the top of the dessert. Firm. He smiled and closed the door.

At eight o'clock he turned on the CD of Claudio Arrau playing Liszt etudes. The haunting strains filled the house. Arrau's mastery of scales and arpeggios sounded like liquid gold on the piano.

At two minutes past eight he lit the candle and dimmed the overhead light. The table jumped from Ordinary to Romantic.

At five past eight he turned the heat under the vegetables to the lowest setting.

At ten past eight he filled his water glass, removed the dish towel from his shoulder, and hung it on the handle of the over door.

At twelve minutes past eight he took the salad cream from the refrigerator and put it on the table.

At a quarter past eight he rotated the wine in the wine cooler's ice bath.

At seventeen minutes past eight he lifted the phone receiver. The dial tone assured him the line worked. He replaced the receiver and sat on the edge of the sofa cushion in the front room and looked out the window.

At twenty-five past eight he rang Dena's home phone number. After ten rings the answering machine clicked on and he left a message, hoping she was on her way and that she hadn't forgotten their date.

At twenty-six minutes past eight he called her mobile. It rang until he hung up.

At half past eight he phoned her father. No, he

hadn't heard from Dena in several days. No, he didn't know where she was but he'd have her ring McLaren if she phoned or showed up. McLaren next talked to the few friends he knew. Ditto Dena's father.

At a quarter to nine he contacted the nearby hospitals. No one resembling Dena or having her name had been admitted. He phoned her house again fearful she was hurt and couldn't answer. He left another message, this time voicing his growing fright. He rang her mobile again, got no answer, and left his third message. He hung up, his body frozen poker stiff, his mind racing. Three minutes later he slumped against the sofa, concern for her safety no longer paramount in his feelings. He stared at the candle flame dancing in the dimly lit room. Had she changed her mind? Was she sitting in her home, looking at the phone's caller ID, not picking up his calls on purpose?

McLaren stared at the road skirting his front garden. No car headlights approached his drive. The tarmac lay undisturbed and quiet in the dusky light. Suspicions whispered in his mind, fueling the pain exploding in his forehead. He rubbed his neck, trying to ease the growing tension and, in so doing, his fingers touched his necklace. He rolled the strip of leather beneath his fingers, then felt the ceramic and wooden beads. Like worry beads, rolling them between his fingers and his palm. Each caress produced Dena's face or voice or laughter. His hand slid from the necklace and fell heavily onto his lap. He sagged against the sofa and closed his eyes.

At half past nine he blew out the candle, scraped the vegetables and fish into plastic cartons and put them into the refrigerator. He turned off the kitchen light, turned off the dining room light, turned off the front room light, turned off the music. The house plunged into darkness as complete and heavy as his soul. He wandered into his bedroom, sat on the edge of his bed, and took off his shoes. Without bothering to wash or undress, he fell back onto the quilt and stared out his window. The willow at the front garden was barely visible against the black sky. A bank of clouds streaked before the wind, racing for the sprinkle of stars in the eastern sky. The world beyond was silent except for the occasional rasp of a tree branch against the side of the house. He turned onto his side, his eyes staring into the darkness, hearing Dena's warm voice as she accepted his dinner invitation, wondering if it had all been a trick to get back at him for their months of separation.

A verse of a song crept into his mind. He usually sang it with fervency, looking at Dena if she were in the audience, imagining her if she was absent. Either way, he considered it her song, his declaration of love. His hand slid beneath his head, cradling his body as well as his thoughts. The lyric and tune spun around him, drowning him in feelings. "I'll love you till the seas run dry and the rocks all melt in the sun. I'll love you till the fires freeze and the streams no longer run."

He pulled his knees to his chest, feeling hurt, betrayed, and alone.

Chapter Sixteen

McLaren woke early the next morning after a fitful night. His sleep, when he finally dozed around half past four, had been punctuated with dreams of Dena— taunting him, playing hide and seek with him, mocking him. He sat in bed now, aware that he was in his clothes, aware of his mussed hair and the staleness of his mouth. Swinging his legs over the side of the bed, he saw it was quarter past five. He showered, shaved and dressed as fast as his headache would allow him, then stumbled into the kitchen.

The remnants from last night's supper littered the room, tacitly ridiculing his romantic effort. He ignored the used mixing bowls and skillets, and heated up the leftover coffee.

The liquid was hot, nearly scalding his throat when he drank it minutes later. But he needed the heat to jolt him awake and think through last night. The replay of their earlier conversation convinced him that Dena had neither forgotten their date nor had deliberately not shown up. She didn't hold grudges or get even. And, he reminded himself, she had instigated their reunion, phoning him last month. Dena didn't play around with people's emotions. He stared at the bubbles on top of the coffee in his mug, watching them cluster together. He took another sip. No, car trouble was not an option, as she would have phoned to say she'd be late.

Therefore, the alternative was that she was ill.

But she would have phoned. Something was decidedly wrong. Something had happened to her.

That suggestion both frightened him and prodded him into action. Any dregs of self pity, of thinking she hated him and had deliberately stayed away, were erased in his unshakable conviction that her absence was beyond her control. She needed him.

The recorded messages on both her home and mobile phone numbers chilled him now that he realized she wasn't cruelly playing with him. Her voice smiled to him over the phone receiver, asserted that she loved him. Getting no answer, he hung up, his mind racing. Where was she? What could have happened so that she was unable to contact him? The hint shook his very core; he rang up Jamie. It was time for professional help.

****

Jamie answered in a sleep-drenched voice but jerked fully awake on hearing McLaren's voice. "What time is it?"

"Three minutes to six," McLaren said. "Sorry for the ungodly hour, but I need your help."

"You must, calling at this hour. Hold on." He turned to his wife, who stirred beside him. "It's just Mike."

"Just so long as it's not police work," Paula mumbled before pulling the sheet over her head. "You need your day off."

Jamie stood up, the handset of the cordless phone in his hand, and walked into the kitchen. He turned on the coffeemaker, grabbed a mug from the cupboard, and leaned against the corner of the worktop. "Okay, I can talk. What's wrong?"

"Dena's missing."

The coffeemaker belched into the quiet. "Dena. How do you know? What happened?"

McLaren related the night's event and his conclusion. "You know her. She wouldn't set up an elaborate charade like this."

"There's still no answer at her house or on her mobile, you said. Did you ring up her dad this morning?"

"No. We left it last night that he'd tell her to get in touch with me if he heard from her."

"Did you check the hospitals again? Maybe she was brought in last night."

McLaren admitted he hadn't. "But she'd have her ID with her. Surely her dad would've been notified, and he would've called me."

"Could do, I suppose. You call the hospitals— that'll at least erase one possibility. I'll look around, see if I can find out anything. Do you know what she was doing yesterday? Was she meeting a friend, or going shopping? It would narrow my search."

"She was talking with some people connected with the Kent Harrison cold case—she thought she'd have to do a bit of carrot-dangling with me. I don't know whom precisely she contacted, but it would have to be those named in the newspaper articles of the time. She wouldn't have any way of knowing the minor players."

"So," Jamie grabbed a pencil and pad of paper from the message center, "people like the ex-wife, his girl friend, Dave Morley and Ron Pennell."

"I spoke to some of those, but only Morley said a thing to me about Dena preceding me."

"Don't know if they would, particularly. Dena's just asking questions as a curious citizen. You represent The Law, no matter if you're once removed. Anyway, you don't know what results she got, do you? Maybe no one aside from Morley spoke to her."

"That's true. She told me she was meeting a girlfriend in Buxton. She didn't have anything particular to say."

"So, she didn't tell you that Clark MacKay ordered her out of his office, for instance."

"I've got nothing to go on except when I last talked to her, she sounded like she was in her car."

Jamie's tone sharpened. He looked up from his note taking, the pencil point still on the paper. She could've been anywhere. He already felt tired with the myriad possibilities of the hunt. "Did she say where she was headed?"

"She said she could talk, so she wasn't driving. But the acoustics didn't sound right. You know, the full resonance of an enclosed space versus the thinness that the outdoors produces."

"Were there any sounds you could identify?"

"Like a chiming clock tower bell, or ducks quaking or a train horn? Nothing. Ducks would have steered you to Howden Reservoir, I guess."

Some distinguishable sound would've been nice, but quacking ducks could also mean Carsington Water, not to mention other lakes. He sighed. A nice train whizzing by would've helped immensely. All he'd have to do was look at the map of rail routes, ring up Network Rail and tell them the time. He shook his head, imagining the needle they were about to hunt for and all the haystacks in the country... "Well, don't worry,

Mike. I'll find her. I'll start with the key personnel in the case and work out from there. Luckily they aren't scattered all over Derbyshire, so I'll try the areas around her house and the castle first. I'll find her," he repeated, hoping McLaren would believe it.

"Sure. I know you. That's why I rang you up instead of going through the regular steps. You'll find her."

He rang off, giving Jamie his promise that he'd call the minute he heard from Dena—and getting Jamie's promise should he find her. He also promised he'd try to work on the case.

"Keep your mind occupied," Jamie said. I know you, Mike, he thought after hanging up. I know you'll rush around the country like a mad man, trying to find her. Or go insane. Or slit your wrists in your depression.

Which was what he and Dena had feared McLaren did last August.

Jamie leaned against the wall, the image and conversation of that event welling up in his mind. Dena had rung up, frantic because she couldn't raise McLaren by phone or at his house. Jamie had searched the residence and the outbuildings, eventually finding his friend unconscious and bleeding in a field and carrying him back.

Jamie roused himself from the recollection, looking again at his kitchen, briefly unsure of where he was. The memory of that day clung to him, the event as sharp now as it had been ten months ago. He'd never talked with his friend about what had happened, never asked if the wound was the result of an accident or a deliberate suicide attempt. McLaren had never referred to it, either, merely thanking Jamie days later for finding him.

The voices and mental images evaporated, and Jamie stared out of the window at the just-risen sun. Had the emotional pain been so great at that moment that death was preferable to dealing with the disillusions of prevailing justice? Was that hurt with him now? Was he still considering his two choices?

****

Clark MacKay grabbed his briefcase, locked his car door, and shuffled across Tutbury Castle's car park. The sun slanted with a vengeance over the eastern edge of the nearest tower, shoving morning shadows toward the west, as if they sought cooler climes. He ran the tip of his tongue over his cracked lips. He could nearly taste the heated air. The ground, packed hard by millions of visitors and the summer drought, threw back dull, nearly imperceptible thuds beneath his shoes. A clump of grass crowding the railing post nodded in a breath of wind, and he glanced at the sky, hoping to see a rain cloud. But the blue expanse stretched unblemished from horizon to horizon. He sighed. Another unbearable day under a baking sun.

He approached the gatehouse, tired of July and the struggle to retain a modicum of comfort, but turned as he heard his name called. Ellen Fairfield hurried after him, her cheeks bright pink and her forehead shiny with sweat.

"Ellen?" Clark paused, astonished to see her, and see her on his turf, as he equated it. She wore a pink blouse and tan suit, but carried her jacket, already shed in acknowledgement to the enthusiastic temperature. A thin gold necklace winked at him in the sunlight, half-hidden by the collar. He eyed a bead of sweat sliding along the chain before disappearing beneath the blouse, and wondered how hot the afternoon would be. And if it would affect castle attendance.

She nodded at his greeting and pushed back a strand of limp hair. Perspiration dotted her hairline, looking vaguely like tiny diamonds.

Already feeling the heat rising from the dry grass, he loosened his tie. Is my face as red as this, he wondered, and squinted against the sunlight. A voice bounced off the castle wall to the right and was answered by another.

He measured her approach by her labored breathing, and was tempted to extend his hand as she angled up the last meter or so of the approach, but shoved his fist deeper into his pocket. The help might be misconstrued as a warm greeting. So he merely looked at her and drew himself up a bit taller. "Whatever is the matter, dear? Are you all right?"

"No." She took several deep breaths and looked back at the car park, as though she hadn't noticed the number of cars when she arrived, or was looking for something specific. "Is there someplace we can talk? Without being overheard?" she added as a groundskeeper passed them on a riding mower.

Clark gave her a half smile. "Whatever it is, it must be monumental to root you out of Rawlton Hall and into the enemy camp, as it were."

"Now's not the time to be cute, Clark. Or for us to remain divided. I don't care about our past competition. We need to join forces."

"The proposition is tempting, of course, but without knowing what you're wanting, I can't commit."

"Then, let's talk, as I suggested." She half-turned toward the car park. "In my car?"

"Dear, as much as I like your Mini, I think I'd be more comfortable in my quiet sanctuary." He patted his ample girth and inclined his head toward the entrance. "After you."

Their footsteps thudded on the drawbridge—now permanently horizontal over the grassy moat—and across the courtyard. The scents of warm soil and sun-scorched grass, more pronounced in the chunks of sunlight coating the land, rose in tiny waves of heat. Clark tried to swallow, desperate for something to alleviate the dryness in his mouth, and fixed his attention on his office window. He hadn't remembered it being such a far walk. Was this how it felt to die of thirst?

He felt marginally better on entering the South Range, the main building housing the great hall and smaller rooms. That feeling bordered on energetic as he climbed the stairs and settled in his office—him at his desk, and Ellen in the chair reserved for guests. The coolness of the room refreshed him, and he chatted about noncommittal things until the teakettle went off the boil. But his attempt at conversation failed, for Ellen remained mute. He set a mug of tea in front of her, claimed his chair, and swallowed a mouthful of tea before settling back. "Now, what's so mysterious, darling? I've got a staff meeting in forty-five minutes."

"If you're more concerned with ruling your little kingdom than in staying out of prison, fine."

"What the bloody hell does that mean?"

"Just that someone's poking around in the Kent Harrison case. Dena Ellison, I think she said her name is. She's asking questions that could be dangerous."

Clark took a sip of tea and visibly relaxed. "Is that all? Why does that threaten you? Haven't you been a good girl?" He winked, and Ellen stiffened at the innuendo.

"You never were good at humor, Clark, and this isn't the time to start. This woman talked about Kent's murder and implied I knew something of it."

"What of it? If your hands are lily-white, you've nothing to fear, as far as I can see."

"But she's in law enforcement, or something like that. Don't you realize what that means?" She waited for the implication to hit Clark.

He nodded and spoke slowly as he thought through the perceived outcome. "He sends rain on the just and on the unjust, dear. I, too, have been questioned about Kent, if that gives you comfort. Though I doubt we can request adjoining prison cells, but we can wait to see."

Ellen stiffened, her tea ignored. "You mean she also came here?" She glanced around, perhaps believing Dena lurked in one of the corners.

"Not her, no. Michael McLaren. Do you know him?"

Ellen shook her head, her eyes shining with fright and panic.

"He's a former police detective."

"If he's former, he can't do anything, can he?"

"I haven't a clue. Don't cops, whether ex or current, stick together and talk?"

"You think he's going to relay his information to someone?" Her fingers wrapped around the edge of the desk and she leaned forward. "If he's not a cop anymore, will anyone believe him? Isn't whatever he learns, or thinks he learns, labeled as hearsay?"

Clark shrugged and downed another swallow of tea. "This is out of my league, Ellen. I don't know what they do when they get together at their watering hole. But I don't think it bodes well for anyone with whom McLaren or that woman talk."

Ellen stood up, her right arm stiff as she braced herself against his desk. "This is all your fault, Clark. You've brought this misery on both of us, and you better have a way to get us shed of it."

"Me? What did I do? I merely answered his questions when he was here. I didn't send him or that woman to you. I don't know what you expect me to do about any of this, either. Seems to me this investigation, if you care to call it that, is already underway and unrelenting. You might as well try something easy, like stopping the sun from rising tomorrow or swimming the Pacific Ocean, because McLaren has the decided characteristics of a bloodhound."

"Don't get flippant, Clark. We're both being questioned by cops, and whatever status they have, they'll be believable. They could be hired by Kent's family or they could be sent out by the constabulary."

"Hardly makes much difference, either way." Clark set down his mug and rubbed the back of his neck.

"I know cops. Once they've got an idea, they run with it. And whoever's under their magnifying glass hasn't a chance." She sat down abruptly and looked startled as she hit the hardness of the chair seat. "There has to be something we can do to shift the spotlight from us. But short of leaving the country or assuming another identity, compliments of a bit of plastic surgery, I can't think."

Clark scratched his chin, his gaze on the castle courtyard. The groundskeeper had begun on the area near a curtain wall. "That's not a bad idea, Ellen."

She frowned, her mouth partially open. "What? Which one? I didn't really mean we could do it. I'm just…trying to think of a way out of this."

"You could become this Dena Ellison dame."

The words were uttered so quietly that Ellen blinked, unsure if she'd heard him correctly. "Me become Ellison?"

He shifted in his chair, leaning his forearms on the edge of his desk, and nodded. "Sure. Oh, the plastic surgery doesn't have to be spot on. Just good enough to pass for Ellison momentarily so you can get close to McLaren."

Ellen sniffed and screwed up her lips. "You've got to be joking. Anyway, as I said, your sense of humor needs some work."

"It's one way out, if you're willing to take a chance. And I think we need to take a chance if we're to rid ourselves of this…leech."

"So I get made up as Ellison. Right. And then what? I'm no killer, Clark. I may want to make a killing with my own festival at the Hall, but I don't go in for murder." She reached for the tea, then evidently thought better of it and laid her hand in her lap.

"Your fete triumphs aren't quite the same thing, dear, but I'll let that pass." He broke off, his gaze again on the courtyard. "You know, I just realized why you're worried about this."

"I told you why. You should be, too."

He went on as if she hadn't spoken. "You're worried because you killed Kent."

Ellen bolted to her feet, glaring at him. "You're daft!"

"You killed Kent and you're afraid Ellison or McLaren are getting too close with their investigation and will soon arrest you. Am I right?" He flashed a grin and stirred his tea.

Her face drained of color and she slowly sank to her chair. The sound of the mower filtered through the closed window. "I wasn't near the castle the night Kent died. You know that."

"That may be, dear, but you could've killed Kent elsewhere. There's nothing in the rule book that says you had to have dispatched him back stage or by the crumpet sellers or in the car park. In fact, I don't believe he was knocked off here, if I recall the case correctly. You could've just as easily met him somewhere and killed him there. Hmm?"

"That's the stupidest thing I've ever heard! What's the saying, Clark? What's sauce for the goose..." She seemed to take comfort in the idea, for she sank against the chair back, her fingertips stroking the smoothness of the arms. "I think you're trying your damnedest to pin this on me. And I wouldn't doubt for one second that *you* killed Kent." She looked steadily at him, as though judging his guilt.

"Now you *are* clutching at straws, dear. But drowning people do that, I'm told."

Ellen shrugged but kept her gaze on him. "Can you prove you didn't kill him? Or perhaps you hired someone to do it. That works just as well."

Clark rubbed his forehead. The conversation was out of the realm of reality, and he felt ill from the topic. But he also felt nervous, though he wouldn't let her know. She'd made some good points, as sick as they were. The investigation was progressing too quickly for him to stop, and he had the impression that McLaren would keep on until he found the killer. Or dropped dead… Clark took a deep breath, swallowed, and hoped he could keep his voice steady. "You've overlooked one important thing, darling, in your rush to name me as Kent's murderer."

"I don't think so."

"Besides having an alibi for the time in question, I had no motive." He grinned as Ellen frowned. "It usually comes down to that, doesn't it? There's normally something to be gained from getting rid of someone. But I'd eliminate my own bread and butter, as it were, if I killed Kent. He was a huge draw at the castle. He brought in a great deal of money. I'd have to be insane to overlook that. But what about you, dear? You're so eager to name me as murderer, we've overlooked *your* motive."

"And what has your overworked brain come up with? Something stupendous, I hope. I'd like a good laugh."

"The old cliché, darling. If you couldn't have him…" His right eyebrow shot up as he waited for her reaction.

The phone rang on his desk, loud in its intrusion and alarming in the suggestion. Clark blinked rapidly, feeling the tension increase, and grabbed the receiver. Still looking at Ellen, he said, "Clark MacKay speaking."

"Mr. MacKay, this is Don. From the bakery."

"Oh! You're up and about early."

"I want to let you know that we've had a spot of

trouble with our van, so the delivery will be an hour or so late. It's unfortunate, but I hope it won't cause a problem in the tearoom."

"Why, certainly, I understand. No trouble at all."

"We're reloading the items onto another van, so it shouldn't be too long."

"Whenever you get here is fine."

"Thank you for consideration. I'd like to give you two dozen lemon scones in appreciation of your kindness."

"I look forward to your arrival. Thank you." He hung up and made a note on his day planner. "To quote you, dear…what's the saying? Speak of the devil." He grinned as Ellen blanched.

"McLaren?"

"I'm sorry I have no prize for you. Yes. He wants to drop by. We'll make a chummy threesome, though he doesn't know you're here. Still, I've no doubt it'll be a pleasant enough surprise for him."

Ellen grabbed her handbag. "He's coming now?"

"Soon. We've time to finish our chat before you make your escape. I don't think he's on your trail…yet."

"I-I think I was hasty in my accusation, Clark."

"Oh yes?"

"I thought about what you said while you were talking just now."

"And you've realized the error of your assumption, I take it."

She nodded and gave him a tentative smile. "Motive *is* important, and I don't think you have one any more than I do."

"Unless there's a secret I've kept from you. I

could've topped Kent for some other reason."

Ellen started to speak, but drew in a breath and seemed to change her mind about something. "I don't believe you're that deep, Clark. You lead a rather transparent life. No, we have to figure out who could've killed Kent. It's to our advantage to solve this so the questionings stop."

"You're saying we can't stand too much scrutiny."

"Well, we're in the same predicament, aren't we?"

"I'll refrain from answering that, since I don't know what dark enigmas you may be hiding, dear. But I wouldn't mind if McLaren or that woman focused on someone other than us two." He removed his tie and undid his collar button. "Do you have any particular person you'd like to see arrested?"

"I know so few people who are involved in this."

Clark frowned, thinking she sounded regretful by her lack of potential victims. "How about Dave Morley?"

"That sometimes singing partner of Kent's? Do you really suspect him?"

"He's as good a killer as anyone. He's got motive enough. That's what you wanted, wasn't it…motive?"

Ellen smiled and stood up. "I hate to leave this unfinished, but if McLaren's coming, I don't want him to see me. We can wrap this up later today. But in the meantime, be thinking how we can trip up Dave Morley." She went to the door but kept her hand on the knob as she turned back to Clark. "And if that doesn't work, maybe we can make it look like a certain ex-cop is the killer."

Fine, Clark thought as Ellen quit the room. But what's to stop me from nudging McLaren in your direction? You'd look beautiful in his crosshairs, darling. Or I may keep this personal and take care of you myself. So satisfying. After all, a little less competition would be nice.

Chapter Seventeen

Which choice was better? Jamie repeated an hour later, getting into his car. He had showered, shaved and dressed faster than he thought possible at this early hour. But McLaren's fright had crept over the phone. And for Michael McLaren to be shaken to the depths of his being meant that he loved that person very much. More than his own life.

They had discussed at length about involving Official Channels, a polite phrase McLaren mumbled between his clenched teeth. Jamie knew his friend's real opinion, knew how he actually referred to them. But he also knew this was the proper way to proceed. Jamie leaned in that direction, reminding McLaren that with more manpower, police dogs, early press coverage, and local radio appeals Dena would be found faster than with their own makeshift two-man search. And since the circumstances of her disappearance implied a high level of concern, a team under the command of a DI or DCI would be put on the case immediately. That gentle reminder alone might have squeaked past McLaren. But hearing the words 'uniform branch,' 'CID involvement,' and 'search teams' opened the floodgates, and all McLaren's pent-up frustration and fear broke from him in a torrent of four-letter words. His maverick streak flared up, and he quickly killed any and all contemplation of constabulary involvement. Did he realize he could be gambling with Dena's safety, Jamie asked. Yes, McLaren had whispered, but he couldn't bring himself to crawl back to the people, however innocent these specific ones were, whom he still associated with the injustice heaped on him last year. Asking for police help, whether it came from Derbyshire, Greater Manchester, Staffordshire or any other constabulary, was akin to asking Charlie Harvester personally for help. Besides, if the Derbyshire lads became involved, word would leak out to Harvester, which was one thing McLaren never wanted. He would look for Dena for the rest of his life, if need be, but he would never let Harvester become a part of the search. It would be like letting the devil into Paradise.

Jamie had reluctantly agreed to McLaren's plea to keep this between themselves. A decision that an hour later already ate at Jamie's heart and gut. He briefly considered ignoring McLaren's entreaty and call in the Force, but that would destroy their friendship. And Jamie would rather die than do that.

So how to begin, Jamie wondered as he turned his car key in the ignition. Search the places or zero in on people she might have talked to? He backed out of the garage, then paused as he stared up the road. Was he about to bring joy or devastation to McLaren? His throat closed up for one brief moment as he imagined McLaren's grief over Dena's disappearance. No matter what his search would reveal, he had to learn where she was. McLaren would do the same for him if Paula were missing.

Traffic was light at seven o'clock when he left his home in Castleton and turned off the B6061 onto the

A6. He had decided to start at Dena's house, maybe ask any neighbors up and about if they had seen her Tuesday afternoon. It was only Wednesday morning, so memories should still be fresh. He settled back, his mind already forming the questions he'd ask, the people he'd talk to. Having a plan lulled him into the belief he was in control.

He made good time to Buxton, for most of the office and store crowd hadn't yet hit the roads for work. He sailed around Buxton's eastern side, passed Morrisons Supermarket, then zoomed between the low, dark stone wall fringing the copse and the River Wye. He was barely immersed in the tunnel of leafy trees and giant ferns when he was once more in the open, headed down the A515 for Kirkfield.

Dena's house looked deserted. Still, he parked, got out of his car, and rang the front doorbell. He listened, barely breathing as he prayed she'd appear. But no sound came from inside the house—no radio, television, conversation, or ringing phone. It was as if all the interior contents had been scooped up, leaving a four-sided stone shell.

The milk delivery—a pint of cream and a quart of milk—sat next to a container of geraniums on the porch. He touched the glass bottle. The milk was warm. So was the cream container. He rang again, then knocked, and after a few minutes, walked around to the back garden. Every window and door was closed and locked, although the curtains and blinds had not been drawn. Because she hadn't returned home Tuesday afternoon, or because she'd left the house this morning before he got here? But he dismissed that idea as quickly as he thought of it. McLaren believed Dena wouldn't play such an outrageous trick; she was in trouble.

No footprints marred the surface of the soil; no torn-off button or spot of blood littered the drive or pavement. No broken or bent plants or tree branches spoke of a lurking kidnapper.

The few neighbors who were out had no idea where Dena was, let alone knew she'd gone missing. Dena's father, on being called, hadn't heard from her. Nor had the relatives he'd talked to. Jamie sat in his car and rang up McLaren to report the lack of progress.

"Hardly a lack. You've established there's no sign of a forced entry into the house, that there was no struggle outside to abduct her, and that no one was lurking near the house."

"But I haven't found her, or even a trace of where she could be." He paused, debating if he should mention the police again. If ever there was a time to ignore past differences and call in the professionals... Jamie's annoyance at McLaren's stubbornness slipped out in an angry rush. "Something's bloody well wrong, Mike, and you need to get the coppers on to this."

"Not yet. This is the first place you've looked. Wait a bit before we do something stupid."

Jamie knew what McLaren meant but purposely misread it. "The only stupid thing, Mike, is not getting the CID involved."

"I don't want anything to do with them, Jamie. We talked about this already."

"Yeah, we did, and I still think you're making the biggest mistake you've ever made. Her house looks all wrong. Something's happened to her. The cops need to be told."

"Because she doesn't answer the doorbell, you're ready to call in the Mounties."

"It's more than that, Mike. It's the whole set-up. Your unreturned phone calls, her missed dinner date with you, her eagerness to get back together. These things don't add up to a simple instance of forgetfulness. You know that, if you'd be honest with yourself. You were ready enough last night to admit it." He sighed deeply before adding, "I don't like the look of it, Mike. Where is she?"

"You're right, Jamie. It smells. I'm not thinking straight." He broke off for a moment, as if trying to made a decision. "Do something for me, will you, Jamie?"

"I'm outside her house right now. Of course I'll do something for you. What?"

"Kick in the door."

"Kick in?"

"Get inside. Smash down the door, break a window. Anything. I don't care. But get inside that house."

"I'll force an entry in the least obvious spot, maybe around the back."

"Fine. Whatever. Do a thorough search, Jamie. For Dena, for any lead as to where she might have gone. A *thorough* search."

"Don't worry."

"I'm trying not to."

"What luck did you have with the hospitals? I assume nothing, or you would've phoned me."

"I *did* have luck. She's not in any of them."

"Smashing! How are *you* doing?"

A brief silence wedged in between their words.

Jamie could imagine McLaren lying on the sofa, a bottle of beer on the nearby table, the curtains drawn against the sun. McLaren had a tenacious hold on his sanity anyway, just crawling from beneath a yearlong bout of depression. Dena's disappearance didn't aid his escape from his emotional quagmire.

Jamie tried again, consciously keeping his voice upbeat. "How are you, Mike?" He raised his gaze heavenward, praying that McLaren would sound focused and determined.

"I'm in hell. How do you think I am? Especially after your little pleasantry. I-I'll go mad without her, Jamie. I want her with me—always. I-I love her more than my life."

"I know, Mike."

A sudden wall of silence fell between them and Jamie had a quick mental flash of McLaren downing a beer. He said quickly, "You still there?"

"Yeah, Jamie. Unfortunately."

"What's that mean?"

A drawn-out sigh answered him.

Jamie shook his head. The day was going downhill fast. He repeated his question.

"I'm not gonna top myself, so don't worry."

"*One* blessing for the day, at least." He glanced at the house, at the front door and windows. McLaren must be near panic, letting me sift through Dena's personal things. He cleared his throat, an idea forming in his mind. It might work, and it might also save McLaren's sanity. "Uh, Mike?"

McLaren's "Yeah?" was barely more than a grunt.

"Why don't you search Dena's house?"

"What?"

"*You* search her house. You need the physical activity. I'll talk to her friends and people she may have interviewed to see if they know anything. Then I'll drive around a bit, look for her car. Your sitting behind a steering wheel won't do anything to relieve your stress. Besides, I don't think it's safe for anyone, you included, if you cruise the roads right now. *You* do the search and let me find her car."

"That'd be fine. I-I'll be right there. I'm dressed. I've got a key."

"If you have a key, I won't wait for you, then. I'll get started looking for her car." He refrained from stating that every minute was important to their search. "Concentrate on your job, Mike, and I'll do what I can from my side. You'll see. We'll find her. With both of us on her trail we'll have some answers very soon."

"Sure. I know. I'll have my mobile with me. Call me the minute you find out anything."

"I will, Mike. Uhh…I know her car—a red MG—but do you know the registration plate number? I'd like to be certain the car's hers if I find one fitting the description." He scribbled down the number, thinking he would call in heavier guns for this job. "Got it." He rang off in the middle of McLaren's thanks.

Jamie started his car, and glanced at the number on his notebook page before screeching away from the curb.

****

McLaren peeled out of his driveway like a British Grand Prix driver charging past an opponent. The gravel splayed in a narrow arc, directed by the urgency of the tires biting into the loose surface. He was on the road and zoomed through the village nearly before the gravel had settled.

On the drive to Kirkfield he talked aloud to himself, as though he were hearing a friend's statement. He repeated the sentence until it became a chant and a prayer, and the road blurred into a gray ribbon snaking between the hills. He was only half-conscious of the traffic, oblivious to the weather, concentrating on the voice drilling into his ear and brain. He found himself breathing in time to the chant, as if that helped with his meditation. Mile after mile the chant buzzed in his ears. "Jamie will find Dena. Jamie will find Dena. Jamie will find Dena…" On and on the cantor sang to him as the villages and farms scurried past him in hazy clumps. "She'll be fine. She'll be fine. She'll be fine…"

But it was more than a chant, more than a childish crossing of his fingers to bring luck. The song was also part emotional anchor and medication, something he could mentally clutch in the midst of this maelstrom. And he needed this buoy for, although he hadn't admitted it to Jamie, he had nearly given in to suicide last night. It would have been so easy to end the soul-destroying ache. So wonderful to sink into oblivion and not feel anything again. Beer and whiskey could do that, certainly, but he needed a permanent fix. Something to guarantee the intense hurt would never again consume him. So he had seriously considered killing himself. Debated, too, about the consequences of living lonely years without Dena.

He'd taken a few sleeping tablets around two that morning, downed them in one quick head-back toss when he couldn't endure the sleeplessness or the dark any longer. The rest of the pills he planned to take in half hour intervals, for he'd heard that the stomach would regurgitate too many taken at once. So he had placed the pill bottle, bottle of beer and Dena's photo on his bedside cabinet, angling the clock to track the half hour intervals, moving the photo to see her face-on when he had lain down in his bed. But Dena's eyes had mesmerized him as he had stared at her; her voice had sung to him, telling him she loved him and would live with him if he would only wait for her return.

It had been a dream, he knew now, driving to Kirkfield. A desperate handhold on that lifebuoy because he loved her more than his life. What would have happened, once Jamie rescued her, when she found out McLaren had ended his life?

So, with more inner strength than he knew he had, he had shoved his fear deep within himself, returned the pill bottle to the mirrored bathroom cabinet—hiding it behind the mouthwash and electric shaver—washed the remaining beer down the kitchen sink, and had downed cup after cup of freshly brewed coffee while walking off the effects of the pills. He'd wandered outside around half past three and sat on the top of the stone wall, the coffee in his hand, his gaze fixed on the sickle moon resting in a puff of dark gray clouds. The air even at this early hour hadn't been chilled enough to shock the encroaching sleepiness from his system, but he kept downing coffee and walking. And uttering ardent prayers to God. He had even succeeded in slowing his racing pulse by the time he reached Dena's house.

The house interior held the quiet air of a deserted place. McLaren called out Dena's name as he closed the front door, praying to hear her answer. But the quietness remained, nearly overpowering. Fear he had never known icicled down his back and he called again,

Jo A. Hiestand

more loudly. Still no answer.

Fighting the impulse to run through the house, he conducted a methodical search room by room. He overlooked nothing—drawer contents, notes scribbled on paper, appointments marked on calendars, condition of her bedroom and bathroom, contents of her fridge, clothes in her wardrobe. He played her recorded phone messages, searched for blood spatter and discarded buttons and muddy shoe prints and cryptic messages scrawled on mirrors or walls or nap of the carpet. He opened every wardrobe, pantry, and closet door. He looked beneath the bed and sofa and behind the draperies. He walked through the basement, moving and peering behind stacks of luggage, disused furniture, and storage cartons. He glanced inside the washer and dryer. He walked through the garage, opened the old freezer, looked behind sacks of fertilizer and potting soil and boxes of terra cotta planters. He poked beneath the bushes circling her house. He walked around her house, noting window and door conditions, shrubbery and flowers, and mulched beds.

Nothing.

He locked the front door and painfully returned to his car.

****

Jamie turned south onto the A50. Tutbury Castle may be off the normal search track, but it and McLaren's case were tied together. The castle and its Minstrels Court event had inspired Dena to involve McLaren in Kent Harrison's murder. The idea wasn't so much of a stretch; maybe Dena had run into trouble there.

But two hours later Jamie mentally posted the

castle and environs in the "no starter" column. He had questioned the car park attendant, castle staff, and booth sellers, driven along every road in the village, and watched for Dena's red MG along the A515 as he headed north again toward Kirkfield. The tarmac thread he followed was slim, for the vast countryside surrounding the thoroughfare could hold its secret quite well if Dena were kept in a barn, machinery shed, or house. Lonely farms, disused coal mines, caverns, cities. Where should he look? She might not even be in Derbyshire any more. He swore at the hopeless task confronting him. A police helicopter search would be nice, but he hadn't the authority to request it. As he stopped in Ashbourne to buy something for breakfast, he realized he was on a fool's errand. Willingness, time and physical availability were fine as far as they went, but the coldness of Reality threw up roadblocks to his eagerness to help. Dena could have gone anywhere: just driving the roads to Derby or Belper or Wirksworth was a challenge, for she could have taken any route, detoured to any village or town farther afield. If she'd made for some place north or east of her house, if she'd gone to Manchester or Sheffield or Birmingham, or even London, he'd never find her in such large cities.

Jamie next spent some time talking to Dena's closest friends. No one had heard from her or seen her recently. Hotels were equally unproductive. He rubbed his head. Just thinking about the hundreds of B&B's in the area gave him a headache. He might find her after a few years' search.

He tossed his half-eaten scone at the sparrows congregating at the base of the old market cross, returned to his car, and rang up McLaren.

"Find her?" McLaren asked, answering on the first ring.

"Not yet." He took a deep breath, then plunged ahead. "Look, Mike, this is a waste of time."

A tinge of anger tinted his words. "What do you mean?"

"I'm one bloke. One man to comb a thousand square miles. There is no way on God's green earth that I can search every house, building, lorry, coal mine, and cave in the county. Even if you joined me, we'd never do it. Not even taking into account that she might be in Nottingham or Bolton or—"

"Okay, I get your meaning." Sounds of his ragged breathing came over the phone.

"I'm not begging off, Mike. You know I want to help. I've already been to the castle, looked around there, scanned the A515 from Ashbourne coming and going. But I can't cover the whole ruddy county. It's impossible." He waited for McLaren to say something, but the silence that returned his statement maddened him. Why the hell was McLaren so pigheaded? Couldn't he see they were playing around with Dena's safety? Jamie tried again, speaking slowly to keep a check on his growing annoyance. "I've phoned her friends. No one's heard from her. You haven't heard from her. It's time to go through official channels, Mike. I shouldn't have to tell you. A missing person, especially when it involves these circumstances and the degree of suspicion we already have, should be taken seriously. You need to include the police." He waited for an explosion of anger, for a scathing opinion of police skills, but heard instead McLaren's reluctant agreement.

"You're right." McLaren's voice sounded reluctant and relieved. "But would you mind calling it in? I-I can't manage that. Talking to…calling it in."

"Sure. I'll let you know if I hear anything." He knew the real reason McLaren wanted to dodge reporting Dena's disappearance. Even if he avoided speaking with someone he knew, he'd have to give his name. And that might be remembered, and the gossip of his former job could start again.

On hanging up, Jamie phoned the Ashbourne police station, one of Derbyshire Constabulary's sectional stations, and relayed the car description and registration plate number. While explaining that the car owner appeared to be a missing person—and one under mysterious circumstances—the dispatcher interrupted him.

"An officer located the vehicle minutes ago. There's no sign of the driver. Nor have there been any reports phoned in to the RAC or nearby garages from a motorist requesting help."

Jamie's breathing nearly stopped. He grabbed a pen and his notebook. "Where? Still in Derbyshire?"

"On a lay-by on the A515, west of Tissington."

West of Tissington on the A515. Jamie had missed it, the village being farther north from his route down to Tutbury. He silently cursed himself for joining the A515 south of Fenny Bentley when he left Kirkfield and, thus, south of Tissington. Was this good or bad news that the car was just minutes from Dena's house? "I know the spot. Please tell the officer not to touch anything. I'll be right there." He rang off, his mind racing. So, where was Dena?

Chapter Eighteen

Where was her release money? Dena wondered. Was her dad still talking amount, or actually getting it? The thought of her paid ransom and subsequent release cheered her until she realized kidnappers didn't always play fair. Once they got the money she might be dumped along a road or tossed into a lake. She was an unnecessary upkeep easily disposed of.

Although still bound, she had struggled into a sitting position. Her entire body ached with the cold of inactivity and a hard sleeping surface. She bent her head forward, stretching her neck muscles and feeling her neck vertebrae strain and pop into place. She got to her knees and arched her back before sinking onto her calves. Feeling better, she glanced around. Morning light crept into the room through a gap between the window and curtain, giving the space shape and color denied her the previous night. Instead of a terror-filled black hole, it had become a pale lilac rectangle. A stack of cardboard boxes filled the far corner. Left over from moving? Was she in a house? The wall color implies a residence rather than an office or warehouse. And if it's a house, she thought, rocking forward onto her knees again, maybe there are houses nearby, with people I can signal.

Hours and minutes had ceased to have any meaning. Her stomach ruled, dividing her waking time into segments of Hunger and Fullness. She judged the march of time by her meals and the light within the room. And though she assumed she had been held captive for two days, she needed to know her location, needed to know if she could signal to anyone.

As if a baby again, she inched across the room, forcing each knee in turn forward. After many minutes she came to one of the room's corners. Angling herself so that her back leaned against one wall and her shoulder pressed the other, she pushed at the walls, using her leg muscles as leverage. She fell several times, once on her knees, and winced at the pain. But she righted herself again and maneuvered into position, pressing her body into the wall. By the time she stood up, she was out of breath and aware of every pain in her body. She hobbled to the window and grabbed the edge of the curtain with her teeth. As she moved her head the curtain parted just enough for her to release the fabric and poke her head between the two panels, letting it lay against her as she looked outside.

Houses similar to those she had seen at her first place of captivity stared back at her, their back gardens well kept and stretching in a line as far as she could see. They snuggled up to each other, giving the impression of older row houses, separated from their neighbors by low stone walls or thick, dense hedges. In front of her, looming large and tantalizingly near, sprawled the garden of the house where she was kept. A path of paving stones led around to the left; a birdbath stood near the back hedge. A wooden bench faced it on the right hand side. Although she didn't know which direction she faced, the sunlight gave the impression of morning, white light illuminating the dew on grass, leaves, and flowers.

Morning. But where was she?

Dena let the curtain fall closed, no better for her knowledge. She could have been anywhere overnight, even out of Derbyshire. How would Michael ever find her?

She pressed her back against the wall and slowly slid down to her buttocks, the pain in her body forgotten as a new realization hit her: she had grabbed the curtain with her teeth—her mouth wasn't gagged. Her captor didn't fear she would call for help. She was alone.

Though tired, she again crawled on her knees to the corner, struggled to her feet, and shuffled back to the window. The room was at ground level. Surely some neighbor would appear eventually in his own back garden—not everyone would be at work. Surely he would hear if she yelled loudly enough.

She measured time in the thuds of unseen doors slamming, the starts of car engines on the street along the house front, the barks of dogs, the distant groan of lorry motors, the twittering of birds.

A figure—hardly more than a shoulder, upper arm and back—appeared in the adjacent back garden barely within Dena's view. She strained on tiptoes to see more but the figure disappeared. She pressed her forehead against the window, desperate to find the person. A score of heartbeats passed before the figure straightened from its bent over position and revealed itself. It started to turn toward her, then stopped and began walking away. Dena banged on the window with her forehead, oblivious to the dull pain, and yelled.

She'd been shouting for nearly a minute when the

door to her room opened, revealing the masked figure. And the inference of trouble.

****

It looks like trouble, Jamie thought, standing at the edge of the lay-by. He'd walked around Dena's car, noting its condition and the ground in the immediate vicinity. The parched earth yielded nothing obvious— no muddy shoe print, no trail of blood, no lost earring. Still, a team of constables would search the area and the car, since he had reported Dena as a missing person, and bag anything and everything. A clue could come from the most mundane object.

A constable wearing a white paper work suit began a preliminary examination of the car. He held up a small notebook and mobile phone in his gloved hands and called to Jamie.

"You might want to see this."

"Something important on the page?"

"Could be."

"Read it to me."

"If it's easier, WPC Fischer can hold it so you can read it."

Jamie nodded as the constable handed the notebook to a young woman who had just finished suiting up. She angled the notebook so Jamie could see the page, holding it and turning pages while he made his own notes. When he had finished, he asked the constable if the notebook had been open when he found it.

"Yes, sir. I picked it up exactly as it lay. Even to the opened page."

"Was it on the front seat?"

"No, sir. Between the two front seats. Her handbag is on the floor on the passenger side. Her mobile is still turned on."

"Could it have slipped out of her bag, do you think?"

"May have done, though it would've had to have been earlier."

"Oh, yes?"

"The bag is zipped closed."

Jamie drew in his breath and stared at the notes he'd made. A list of five names, with summaries of the talks she had evidently had with each person, hinted at her amateur detective game. Had one of these people followed her, perhaps fearing that too much had been said? Did that person kidnap Dena? He grimaced, not willing to consider another alternative.

"You say the mobile is on," Jamie said as the WPC put the notebook into a plastic evidence bag. "Any indication who she may have been calling?"

The constable punched a few buttons on the phone and said slowly, "No. It's just on. Her last incoming call—which wasn't answered—was from McLaren, Michael. Name mean anything to you?"

"What time was that?"

"This morning. Five minutes to six."

Just before Mike rang me up, Jamie thought.

"Something else, sir." The constable held up another evidence bag. It contained a set of car keys.

"Hers?" Jamie glanced at the car's ignition switch. It had no key. A new sense of urgency gripped him.

"Yes. I tried it in the ignition. Anything else, sir?"

"No. That's fine for now. Thank you."

The constable nodded and slipped the mobile into an evidence bag.

Jamie walked back to his car, trying to understand

what he'd seen. Nothing made sense. No woman would leave her key, bag, and mobile if she voluntarily left the car. He said as much to McLaren when he answered Jamie's call.

"I'm still at the scene," Jamie said, staring at the entries in his notebook.

"Do you think she was interrupted before she could complete a call?" McLaren's voice sounded far away and strained, as though he were afraid to voice his thoughts.

"Could be. Or she could have just left it on. You know—most of us have it on. It's normal, Mike. We don't want to miss a call. Especially if we're expecting the plumber to ring or something like that."

"But those names she wrote down."

"Ellen Fairfield…"

"The curator at Rawlton Hall. Right."

"Ron Pennell…"

"The herbalist at the Minstrels Court."

"Fay Larkin…"

"Kent Harrison's fiancée."

"Dave Morley…"

"Kent's sporadic singing partner."

"And Trevor Pennell. Where are you?"

"Still at Dena's house. Why did she talk to Trevor?"

"Why did she talk to Ellen, Ron, Fay, and Dave?" He paused, expecting McLaren's response. When none came, he added, "She wanted to help you, Mike."

The silence, absolute and frightening, filled Jamie's ear and soul. A tractor growled its way out of the dirt lane and onto the road before Jamie said, "Mike?"

"Yeah." His reply was barely audible, yet his voice held steady.

"What are you thinking? You're not going to do anything rash, I hope."

"Define the word 'rash'."

"I'm thinking you need to keep on with what you're doing, Mike, and leave this to me. You're in no emotional state to do you, me, or Dena any good."

McLaren's retort boomed over the phone. "You wouldn't say that if it were your wife who went missing."

"I know I wouldn't! But *you* would if our roles were reversed. You would tell me the exact thing. Because you know that's the proper thing to do."

"Bloody hell. I'm not a copper any more, Jamie. I don't care what's proper procedure and what isn't. I need to find Dena."

"We will, Mike. The police will bring in specialist squads now that it's looking as though Dena was abducted. Your phone, and her dad's phone, will be tapped and monitored for evidence if the abductor calls. They'll set up an incident room, search the obvious locations based on the leads from her notebook, they'll have dogs on standby."

"I know. I've done all that myself when I worked such cases."

"Great. Then you know to give us some time, for God's sake! They just started on this. They've not done too shabbily, have they?"

A begrudgingly given "no" slipped from McLaren.

"And your being or not being a copper hasn't a damned thing to do with this, and you know it. You wanted to by-pass the police—and I know what you told me, you needn't repeat it. But the *real* reason is because you want to find her yourself. You want to repair your fractured relationship in one quick, easy act of heroics and a flash of awe-inducing genius. Commendable but not realistic. Or smart. Dena's life may be on the line and you want to fly around as a lone Mountie and rescue her. Nice, but you can't."

"I'm only saying that I need to do something, for Christ's sake! I can't sit around."

"So you're going to rush around, break down those people's doors, grab them by their throats, and shake answers from them. Just who would that be? The people listed in her notebook? You won't be satisfied to stop there if that doesn't produce Dena. You'll branch out and threaten everyone else you suspect even slightly. You'll look up all the criminals you've ever dealt with. You'll enlarge your interrogation to include their family members because, God help them, someone may be harboring resentment for when you sent his old man down twenty years ago. Only, it took him two decades to figure out how to get to you and kidnap Dena." Jamie took a breath, aware he may have angered his friend, but knowing he had to voice his opinion.

"So I'm supposed to go home, have a cuppa, do some gardening, and wait."

"Yes."

"What's wrong with looking on my own? The cops will never know I'm nosing about. I just might find her faster."

"The most likely thing you'll find is that you'll bring on lies or a lawsuit if you muscle anyone. And that could hinder Dena's welfare, if she's held by one of them." He took a deep breath, letting his words sink into McLaren's mind. "Am I right?"

"Yeah. As usual."

"I'm not keeping score, Mike."

"Go on with your job of work, then. I'm sorry. I didn't mean to come over so…"

"I'll ring you up the minute I hear anything, though you'll probably get a phone call or visit from someone in the job. You'll no doubt be formally interviewed, too."

McLaren made no comment. "Do her notes suggest who may have kidnapped her, or point you in any direction?" He seemed to be pleading for information, to have something on which to focus mentally and emotionally, to use as an anchor in this whirlwind.

"Nothing jumps out at me, no. But this could be circumstantial, you know."

"Like someone *she* talked to then talked to someone else." He stopped.

"I've got the names. The constable showed them to me." He lowered his voice and turned from the police team searching the area. "They don't have to know I'm on the case unofficially. I'll keep going and start with these five. I'm close to Rawlton Hall, so I'll see Ellen Fairfield first. And don't worry. We may be amazed at what I find out."

"Just so you find her. I'll owe you favors for the rest of my life."

Jamie smiled, rang off, and went to see Ellen Fairfield.

****

McLaren decided to talk to Trevor Parnell. Ashbourne, the town where Trevor taught school, was minutes down the road from Kirkfield. McLaren could question the man and be off to talk to Fay Larkin before Jamie knew what he'd done. He'd be helping Jamie and the police, he convinced himself. Besides, in the nightmare he was living, he needed that activity.

A helpful teacher directed McLaren to Trevor's classroom, a room in the academic wing of the building. McLaren knocked on the door, then entered. Colored posters of monarchs from the Plantagenet and Tudor reigns gave faces to the names in the history books; maps of the British Isles illustrated the changing territories of wars' winners; a banner depicting the timeline of one thousand years of major events hung between the two large windows. All in all, McLaren thought, a visual way to learn in this entertainment-demanding culture.

Trevor looked up, plainly startled to see McLaren, but agreed to give him five minutes.

"I won't deny I was jealous of the scholarship funds that Kent received," Trevor said, opening a textbook to a marked page, "but I didn't kill him. If anyone was jealous, it was Fay."

"Fay Larkin?" McLaren asked, surprised to hear her name linked in this manner to Kent's case. "Why? She was engaged to Kent. She had her future all sewn up."

Trevor walked around the room, putting a handout on each student's desk. "That's just the reason. She was in love with Kent. And, being in love and attending his singing gigs, she saw firsthand how he attracted women."

"Women in the audience?"

"And female students. He was good looking. And

211

popular. A deadly combination."

"Like bees to honey."

"More like moths to the flame."

"Scorched."

"Or burnt to death."

"Not literally, I hope."

"No. Just that Fay or Kent made it clear to the attracted female that he was already claimed."

"Was there any trouble?"

"If you mean, did the women riot and burn his CDs, no. But there are always fans who hang on, aren't there? Lurk in the shadows, watch from the wings and follow you from performance to performance. They hope for a little more than an autograph, if you get my drift."

"And Kent?"

"Faithful to Fay, from what I understand. But whether Fay believed that or not…well, you'll have to ask her. How many fiancées in that position would fully trust her man? Or trust that a fan wouldn't become a stalker? Even if the stalking doesn't end in murder, can you trust that it won't end in kidnapping? Jealousy does strange things."

"One more point, Mr. Pennell. I believe Dena Ellison talked to you recently."

Trevor paused at his desk and put down the remaining handouts. His eyebrow lifted and his eyes narrowed slightly. "Sorry, I don't recall."

"You don't recall? You spoke to her on Monday. Not so very long ago."

"That may be, but I don't recall the lady."

A buzz of conversation filtered through the door from the hallway. McLaren stepped toward Trevor, his left hand grabbing the edge of the desk. "I doubt your memory is that poor, Mr. Pennell. Not only do you have to remember the facts of the subject you teach, but you also have to retain students' names and learning progress, school dates, information about the Minstrels Round, your private social life, and other things as well, I'm sure."

"Exactly. Case in point, McLaren. Why should I remember one woman, whom I obviously don't know, amongst everything I have to remember? Why does it concern you?"

McLaren briefly considered telling Trevor that Dena had been abducted, then decided not to. He let the matter slide and thanked Trevor for his time as he made for the door.

****

While he was at the school he decided to speak to Fay Larkin. The drama classroom was in the performing arts wing of the building, a newly renovated section of large rooms and larger fiscal budgets. Several students sat reading, talking, or working on their tablets in the alcoves dotting the hallway. McLaren glanced at each one as he entered the drama classroom.

Fay Larkin, a woman of forty—clothed in sandals, a flowered skirt, and cotton blouse—sat behind at a desk piled with books, various files, a phone, and a computer. A photograph of a newborn wrapped in a Christmassy-print blanket angled out from a corner of the clutter. A whiteboard claimed the wall behind her, and held names and scene descriptions.

"Cute child," McLaren said after introducing himself and stating the reason for his visit. He was already tired of using Kent Harrison as an excuse; he wanted to scream that he was looking for his love.

"Thank you."

"I assume you're Fay Larkin."

"Yes."

"Is this an inconvenient time to talk? I'll be here only a few minutes."

"No, this is fine. The students are working on individual projects, being so close to the end of the term. What can I help you with?" She flipped her long braid over her shoulder and put down her pen.

"I understand you and Kent were engaged."

"Yes, though it seems unreal now."

"I'm sorry for your loss. It must have been a terrible thing."

"Thank you. I thought I'd never get over it. You're so deeply in love that you think you will actually die of a broken heart. But somehow you figure out how to deal with your hurt. Believing yours is special doesn't mean a thing. And being hurt prior to Kent doesn't necessarily help you deal with the current grief. Each ache is different. A divorce doesn't make your current fiancé's death easier to handle."

"You've been married before, then."

"Yes. I think that's what made it so difficult, why the pain of Kent's death was so acute. After one failed marriage you dream that the second one will be perfect, that you've found your soul mate. I thought Kent and I would make the happy-ever-after family. It didn't work out that way. So now I cling to my other elation, the remnant of another joyful time, brief though it was." Her fingers traced the top of the photo frame.

"It's nice that you have a part of Kent to love."

She straightened the photo, turning it slightly away

from McLaren. "It's not—We adopted."

"I applaud your decision. So many unwanted children in the world."

"Yes. It's a shame."

He brought the subject back to Kent. "Were you jealous of Kent's female fans?"

Fay laughed, a quick, light chuckle that spoke of the absurdity of the question. "Heavens, no. I'd been with Kent long enough to see the gaggle of geese around him. That's how I viewed them—geese. Clucking over him, crowding around him, clamoring for a look from him or for an autograph. I'd seen the fans grow as his popularity and fame increased, so a few dozen more simpering females didn't threaten me. Besides, I had nothing to be jealous about. I knew Kent loved me." Her fingers pulled on her earlobe, then toyed with her dangle earring. "You need to find an angry person, Mr. McLaren, if you're looking for his killer. Someone who hated him. All these fans loved him—or thought they did. They wanted a piece of him if they couldn't be with him."

"By a piece of him, you mean…"

"You know." She smiled as she got up and added more names to the list on the whiteboard. "Souvenirs. Something to have and to hold."

"I thought Kent handled that potential problem rather well, throwing guitar picks to the crowd."

"Yes, a nice touch. But everyone got those. To the ardent fan the piece of him had to be something your average person wouldn't receive."

"Which set you apart, made you the envy of your friends who also liked him."

"Yes. Nothing like one-upmanship."

"And that is…"

"Guitar strings."

"What? Like picking up the broken ones after the performance?" McLaren knew that was a treasured object. Go up on stage and pick up the wire strings that had broken and been tossed away, and had been replaced during the set. Some fans even scooped up used Styrofoam cups or water bottles or song lists. Any personal item that brought you closer to your idol.

"I've seen them do that, certainly, but someone went the extra mile."

"You don't mean someone robbed Kent."

"No!" Fay's hand went to her mouth, as though she had said the wrong thing. "Somebody wanted the ultimate souvenir, I guess."

"Kent's clothes?"

"Not quite. The person cut some of his guitar strings—new strings from his guitar, I mean—and ran off with them."

McLaren's head jerked backwards. He hadn't been expecting that. "When was that?"

"I'll never forget it. It was the night before he died. That Saturday, a half hour or so before he went on. He was at the Minstrels Court. He had changed into his period clothes and left his guitar backstage to get a drink at one of the booths. He usually doesn't leave his guitar like that, but he thought it would be safe. He'd be gone just a few minutes. Besides, there were other performers in the area, and a large crowd constantly wandering about. You know, Saturday night."

"Seems like a strange thing to take, strings from the guitar."

"Kent thought so too. Luckily he had time to

replace them. Luckily, too, he didn't have to replace all of them."

"Only a few were taken, then."

"Twelve, ten, eight, and seven. He plays both a 12-string and standard six string." She frowned slightly, tilting her head, and capped the dry erase marker. "Do you know about that style?"

"I play one."

"Then you understand the strings. Kent thinks the fan might have been surprised by someone's arrival."

"Which explains why all the strings weren't cut and taken."

"Either that, or someone was angry or jealous. But we always thought that if that had been the case, the person would've broken Kent's guitar, not simply taken the cut strings. No," she said as she set the marker on the desk. "The strings were cut and missing, like a fan wanted some souvenir."

"But you didn't rule out the jealousy or hatred angle."

"We couldn't since we didn't know who did it. It was an annoyance at the time, and then I forgot about it when Kent was killed the following day. I didn't remember the incident until months later."

"So you don't recall now, thinking through all the people Kent knew, if anyone might have been jealous or angry."

"The only angry person could be Trevor Pennell, I suppose. He and Kent were colleagues."

"Why would you think Trevor could be angry?"

"Kent got the scholarship funds three years straight, leaving Trevor and his project unrewarded. Trevor wanted the prestige that Kent's music events received, wanted the media interviews and the newspaper articles and the letters from colleagues around the Kingdom. Trevor was desperate for that recognition, and wanted it before he retired. Kent always seemed to pick up the jackpot while Trevor stood around uttering empty-hearted kudos."

"Trevor Pennell's close to retirement, then."

"He's another year or so before he retires, he told me. He wanted just one scholarship award before he left the school."

"You mentioned Trevor's project. What was it, do you know?"

"No, but it shouldn't be too difficult to figure out. He dotes on the Middle Ages, which is why he's immersed in the Minstrels Round scholarship and attends that Minstrels Court event at Tutbury Castle. I think he's wanting to stage some big historical event from that time, but I'm not certain. You'd get much better information from him."

"Is there a stipulation about how the prize money should be spent?"

Fay squared up the corners of the stack of books on her desk. "The money should probably be applied toward the project, though I'm not sure, since I'm not part of that. But I do know Trevor needed money for his wife, though. Perhaps he thought that by winning the prize money and making his project a reality it would bring him fame and the fortune he wanted."

"Why was he so desperate?"

Fay's eyes widened slightly. "He needed money, and Kent had just won the school scholarship again. Trevor wasn't in the best of moods."

"Why'd Trevor need money?"

"His wife was—still is—gravely ill."

McLaren bit his bottom lip, mulling over the information.

"*He's* the jealous one, if anyone was, Mr. McLaren."

And would've had a lovely motive for getting rid of Kent.

"Of course, you might learn more if you speak with Trevor's wife."

McLaren said he'd do that. "I'm wondering if you know another woman. She may have spoken to you recently. Probably Monday or Tuesday."

"Her name?"

"Dena Ellison." He watched Fay's expression for recognition. She remained staring at him.

"No, I'm sorry. The name doesn't sound familiar. Are you certain this woman talked to me?"

McLaren took a deep breath, trying to cap his urge to yell. "Yes. A brunette of medium height, brown eyes. Nicely dressed." She always was. He reached back into his memory, picturing her in his home Monday. A description of her clothing would do no good now since he didn't know on which day she'd been abducted. He tried another approach, loath to give up on Fay Larkin. "A soft spoken individual, always smiling, very pleasant personality."

"I still don't remember such a person. I'm sorry. Perhaps she talked to someone else in the school." It sounded like a suggestion, as though she hoped he'd give up and leave.

He glanced again at the whiteboard. The names seemed to be from a play: Everyman, God, Cousin, Good Deeds, Angel, Doctor, Death. "Were you teaching Monday and Tuesday?"

Fay stiffened. She said, rather reluctantly, "Yes."

"Do other teachers use this room?"

"Certainly. But not on Mondays and Tuesdays." She tilted her head slightly, assessing McLaren's reaction. "On Thursdays and Fridays I'm in a classroom in the academic wing." She reached for the open promptbook on the desk. "I can offer no further explanation. I didn't speak to her." She turned to the board, silently dismissing McLaren.

Maybe you're not the only adversary he needed to talk to, he thought as he walked back to his car. Dena could have spoken to someone else but not had time to add that name to her list. The other opponent tied to this case, the complaining neighbor who reported Kent's musical sessions to the coppers. Aaron Unsworth.

Chapter Nineteen

Ellen Fairfield eyed Jamie's warrant card and seemed overwhelmed by apprehension. She leaned against the newel post of the great hall's Jacobean staircase and nodded in acknowledgment to her name.

"I'm conducting an inquiry into the disappearance of Dena Ellison," Jamie said, his voice sounding very business-like. "I understand she spoke to you recently."

Ellen stared at him, as though uncertain if she should admit or deny meeting up with the woman.

"You *did* speak to Dena Ellison."

She nodded at the inference, her hands still grasping the newel post.

"And?"

"She was fine when she left. I didn't watch to see her get into her car, but I assume she was fine. I mean," she said, her throat suddenly sounding dry, "none of the staff found her car abandoned in the car park or anything. So she must have left here without any problem."

"When was this? Do you remember?"

"Afternoon, I think. Mid-afternoon or later. She hadn't made an appointment. She just showed up." Her fingers traced the head of one of the grotesques in the wooden post. "I talked to her for a minute or two, but honestly, it wasn't the most convenient time. If she had phoned ahead for an appointment—"

"What did you speak about?"

"Pardon?"

"Your conversation with Dena Ellison. Surely she came here to talk about a specific topic. What was it?"

"Oh. She wanted to find out if I had any inkling as to why Kent Harrison was killed. He was a musician who was murdered last year. She wanted to know if I'd heard anything that night at Tutbury Castle, assuming I'd been there, which she never bothered to ask. She didn't even have a warrant card, so she had no police authority for any of this. But before I could point that out, she said she was investigating with a friend of hers."

"What did you tell her?"

Ellen inhaled sharply. "I told her I didn't know a thing about Kent's murder, that I hadn't been to the castle, that I didn't know who would want him dead. It was a ridiculous waste of time and frankly I was put out by it all."

"Because she hadn't rung up for an appointment."

"That, yes, but also because she took her role as Sherlock Holmes so seriously. I mean, she isn't a police detective or a private investigator. What right did she have going about asking people questions? I thought her impudent and asking for trouble, and I quickly had enough of Dena Ellison."

Her breathing returned to its normal rate when Jamie left the Hall.

****

McLaren phoned Jamie on his drive to Ron Pennell's house, but got his voice mail. Probably still talking to Ellen Fairfield, McLaren thought, and rang off after leaving a short, frustrated message. He wouldn't allow himself to become hopeful.

Ron, dressed in trousers, long-sleeved shirt, and tie, and clearly about to leave the house, opened the door on McLaren's first knock. He smiled tentatively as he stepped onto the porch and locked the door. "It's Mr. McLaren, right?"

"Nice to see you again." McLaren hesitated ever so slightly, wanting to rush ahead with the question of Dena's whereabouts, but knew he had to tread gently if he didn't want Ron to join the lengthening line of those with selective memories. "I'd like to ask you a few questions about your former colleague, Kent Harrison. If you have the time."

"Kent?" His voice took on a wary tone. "What about him?"

McLaren explained the reason for his visit, then asked if anyone at the castle or Minstrels Court could have been jealous of Kent.

"You're thinking someone was jealous of his popularity with the event-goers? That's ridiculous! No one would kill someone over that. You're wasting your time pursuing that line, McLaren. *And* wasting mine. I'm busy at the moment, anyway, so if you would leave, I'd appreciate it."

"But if Kent's death eliminated him as the recipient of an honor or reward—"

"Look." Ron crossed his arms on his chest and took a deep breath. "I don't know who sent you or set you up for this, but you're round the twist. *Everyone* liked Kent Harrison—students at his school and his music followers alike. Go back and tell his mother to spend her money elsewhere, like donating to the Minstrels Round scholarship. She'll get better results.

Now, I have an appointment with a client."

"You couldn't have been jealous yourself, then."

Ron's face turned crimson. He pointed at McLaren. "You've got a bloody nerve saying that. Anyway, why would I be jealous? The only time I was anywhere near Kent was at the medieval fairs we both happened to attend. And I doubt you could compare Kent's CDs sales and my herbal sales. You'd do better focusing on someone else."

"Like your brother?"

"Trevor had nothing to do with Kent's death. You've been listening to too many students and teachers."

"They might know things you don't, since they work with him."

Ron inhaled deeply, drawing himself up to his full height. "Trevor keeps nothing back from me. We know every detail of each other's lives. He's got no secrets and he sure as hell didn't kill Kent. Now, naff off, McLaren. You're becoming a bore."

"Do you know if your brother ever socialized with Kent outside of work?"

"I've no idea. And I've no idea why that means a damned thing. Ask him or his wife."

"I'd rather ask you about—"

"And I'd rather you shut it. I already told you."

"Sure…about something else," McLaren interrupted, quickly losing what little patience he had left.

"If it'll get you out of here faster, go on. What?"

"Does the name Dena Ellison mean anything to you? Have you heard it lately, or have you spoken to her?"

"And who's she when she's home?"

"I'm enquiring on her whereabouts."

"What happen? She get so drunk she fall in a ditch?" He glanced at his watch and sighed heavily. "How should I know where she is? I never heard of her. I don't want to, either. Now, as I told you before, I must go."

"I'm asking a simple question," McLaren said, his throat tightening. "I'd just like to know if you've heard of her or know her."

"If you weren't as thick as two planks, you'd figure it out by yourself. I haven't seen this woman. Now, leave me alone or I call the coppers."

"Listen, you sod. I asked you a civil question about this lady."

"I told you that I don't know her. And if she knows *you*, then I'm glad I don't know her, considering the company she keeps."

McLaren grabbed a handful of Ron's shirt and pulled Ron toward him. The man yelled and threw a punch at McLaren. McLaren released the shirt, muttered, "Have a nice day," and jabbed Ron's stomach. Ron fell backwards, landing against the door, as McLaren headed toward his car.

Chapter Twenty

Tired and nearly blinded by a headache, McLaren drove home. He squelched the urge to phone Jamie to find out what he had learned from talking to Ellen Fairfield, and if the police were making any progress with their investigation.

He had just turned into his drive and parked when he spotted a car close behind him. A police car. Make that two, he corrected himself as a second one followed the first. The police cars parked, and what seemed like an invasion of animated police uniforms exited the vehicles. Car doors banged, shoes crunched on gravel, and a half-dozen men walked up to the boot of his Peugeot. As they stood there, McLaren swore, glanced at the tools being laid on the ground, and slowly extracted his key from the ignition. He remained seated, considering how best to handle the situation, when a uniformed officer and a plain-clothes detective came up to him.

"Michael McLaren?" The uniformed officer bent slightly to see McLaren's face through the open side window.

I'm dead in the water, he thought, but nodded and wondered if they had come to tell him Dena had been found or if he was going to be arrested for assaulting Ron Pennell.

"We'd like to talk to you about Dena Ellison," the

officer continued. "We understand you know her."

Good. Pennell hadn't the neck to file a complaint. All mouth and no trousers. McLaren glanced from the CID detective to the uniformed officer, and nodded again. "Yes, I know Ms. Ellison. Do you have news of her? Have you located her?"

"Would you mind stepping out of the car, sir? There are one or two things we'd like to talk about. Perhaps inside your house would be more pleasant." He stepped back slightly, allowing McLaren to get out. As he led them up the path and into his house the occupants of the second car began getting into their white crime scene work suits.

Trying to recall it later, McLaren wasn't sure if he had been invited to help the police or subtly manipulated. The hour sped by in a blur of questions, anger, and impatience. McLaren begrudgingly related the abduction facts as he knew them: the uniform officer took notes, and the CID officer asked relentless questions. McLaren handed over Dena's photo, an accurate physical description, and "last seen" information, resenting every disclosure of his and Dena's personal lives and every second of the police presence, yet knowing he contributed to finding her. The detective told him a tap would be placed on his home phone in order to monitor calls. "In case you get a ransom request or other information from Miss Ellison's abductor."

Local radio appeals would be broadcast and an incident room set up to handle the police inquiry. Other than that, what else did McLaren know that would aid them? Perhaps they should make this more formal and continue the interview at the station.

McLaren locked the house door and followed the uniformed officer back down the front path. The detective spoke to one of the white-suited men jamming a metal rod through the soil around the rose bush, then joined McLaren in the police car's back seat. Why did the closing of the door sound like the clank of a cell door?

Jamie could barely contain his anger driving back from talking to Fay Larkin. What the bloody hell did Mike think he was doing? Speaking to Fay in the emotional state he's in? Lucky he didn't get the rocket from her and wind up explaining it all to the police. Though, he'd have some explaining to do when Jamie got hold of him.

He stopped in a lay-by and punched McLaren's number into his mobile. The phone rang several times before McLaren's recorded message asked him to leave his name, number, time he called… Jamie swore and hung up.

****

Dave Morley showed as much enthusiasm as Ellen Fairfeld when confronted with the implication of being a suspect or accessory in Dena's disappearance. He became belligerent and suddenly knowledgeable about law and police powers. Jamie was spared Trevor Pennell's protestations and emotion for the time being, Trevor being in class and unable to be disturbed until classes had recessed for the day.

Which left Ron Pennell in Jamie's immediate future.

Jamie's talk late afternoon with Ron didn't go well, from either person's viewpoint. He had closed the front door of his house and started down the front path when

Jamie came up to him. His shoulders and neck stiffened as Jamie produced his warrant card. At the first question he eyed Jamie through partially lowered eyelids.

"I have no idea what you're talking about." Ron fidgeted with his car key.

"But you don't deny Dena Ellison spoke to you."

"Who the hell is this woman? First some half-crazed berk wants to know and assaults me on my doorstep, now you ask. I wish to heaven I'd never heard the name."

Great. Mike's stirring up more trouble. When Jamie found him he was really going to get a lecture. Jamie mentally counted to ten, desperate to keep his composure. "I'm not partnered with anyone else asking about Ms. Ellison. I'm conducting a police inquiry about her. Has she spoken to you or not?"

"I don't deny it, we talked. It was this past Sunday, I believe. She came up to me at the Minstrels Court. A man and a woman were with her. They'll corroborate that if you think I'm lying."

"What did you talk about?"

"What did we talk about? Are you serious?" He stopped beside his car and pointed his right index finger at Jamie. "Since when is it illegal to have a conversation with a potential customer?"

"That's the topic of your conversation?"

"I don't see what business it is of yours, even if you are a copper." He sniffed, as though smelling something suspicious. "Why are you asking? This is all very odd. I don't know anything about this woman other than she talked to me at the castle. I don't know where she went afterwards, I don't know why she's gone missing, and I haven't seen her since. You'll have to be satisfied with that because I have to leave now." He got into his car and slammed the door, keeping the window rolled up until he turned onto a major road.

Jamie watched him drive away amazed he'd reacted in that manner. He'd experienced witnesses and suspects who evaded questions, but never with a person who was neither. And the old adage that some people didn't like to get mixed up in a police inquiry didn't quite explain Ron's refusal to talk. He hadn't accused Ron of anything; no one knew of Dena's disappearance—except her captor. Jamie's car tires left black marks on the concrete as he sped after the man.

Jamie easily kept Ron in view for not only was the traffic light, but also they had driven only a few minutes. And still within the town.

He parked several cars behind Ron's, on a residential street not far from his house. There were enough vehicles so his own car wouldn't be noticeable. Ron got out, grabbed a picnic hamper from the backseat, and walked up to the house. He let himself in and quickly shut the door.

Jamie waited thirty seconds to be certain he hadn't just delivered the hamper and would come out immediately. But the door remained closed. Jamie jogged to the front door and peered through the large window next to the door; nothing looked unusual. The room held no one. He listened at the door. Silence greeted him.

Jamie rang the bell. No one came. He pounded on the door, determined now that he would stay there all day if he had to—whatever he had to do to unravel this mystery. He was about to knock again when Ron opened the door.

His eyes widened, his mouth opened as though he were about to hit a high C note. A sound like the beginning of a gargle escaped his lips. His fingers tightened around the edge of the door. He stepped back swiftly and tried to close the door, but Jamie was quicker. He was inside the house before Ron could move.

"Anything the problem?" Jamie asked, his gaze darting around the room. Everything seemed in order but there was no sign of the picnic hamper.

Ron took another step backward and forced a smile. His eyes darted to his left, then back at Jamie. "Why no, constable. Why would there be? Something wrong?" He pulled in the corners of his mouth and swallowed, staring at Jamie for some explanation. His head slanted slightly to his left, as though he were listening for something. When Jamie didn't answer, he asked the question again.

"I just thought you might be in trouble. You seemed rather agitated back at your house, and I was concerned about your welfare."

"You followed me here."

"Yes. I wanted to make certain you were all right."

"Well, I am. Thank you for your concern. Now, I really must be leaving." He took a step toward the door.

"You have a key to this house. You and your wife own two houses?"

"No."

"No you don't have a key, or no you don't own two houses?"

"The, uh, houses. We've only the one."

"The previous one? Where I met you several

minutes ago?"

Ron bit his lower lip. Jamie waited patiently, his arms across his chest, his gaze steady. Glancing again to his left, Ron said, "Yes. That's ours. I'm just house sitting this one for a friend. She's out of town for a bit. She asked me to check things periodically, feed the dog…you know."

"Nice that you could do that for her. What kind of dog does your friend have? May I see him? I like dogs."

"Uh, no. He's in the basement. He's not very good around strangers. Sorry."

"Surely it wouldn't hurt just to look at him. From the top step, perhaps? Where is the basement door—by the garage?" He headed for the back of the house, looking for the kitchen. Ron ran after him, calling.

"No! Really! He's a terribly excitable dog. You'll just work him into a tizzy if you look in."

"Surely just standing on the step and looking won't bother him." Jamie stood in the hallway, unsure of where to go, when a scream exploded behind one of the bedroom doors.

He glanced at Ron, angry and surprised, then turned the lock in the doorknob and pushed the door open. Dena stood against the wall, her body turned toward the door. Her hands and legs were tied, but her eyes and mouth were free, the folded bandanas on the floor next to the picnic hamper.

"Bloody hell. My God, Dena…" Jamie gave the swiftest glance at Dena before he grabbed Ron's wrist, handcuffed him and marched him into the room. "Get on the ground," he yelled, though Ron and Dena had no trouble hearing him in the quiet. "*Now!*" he barked. "ON THE GROUND." He twisted Ron's upper arm, forcing him first to his knees, then fully down on his stomach. When he lay facedown on the floor Jamie stood over him for a moment, breathing rapidly in his intense anger. His right hand tightened into a fist and he contemplated—for the merest second—slamming it into Ron's face. Mike wouldn't condemn him for doing it, Jamie thought, his body flooding with hatred for the man at his feet. Mike would do what he was thinking, wouldn't hesitate if he had found Ron with Dena. But he wouldn't condone it either, Jamie realized, and was surprised to discover that he was panting. His fingers slowly relaxed and uncurled as he stared at Ron. He took a deep breath, and, to protect himself and Dena, and to control Ron, he knelt over the man, his right knee on his right ear, his left knee on his back. Still in this position, he grabbed his mobile phone, punched in a number, and asked the police dispatcher to send an officer, police car, and police surgeon to the house. After ringing off, he grabbed Ron's forearm, forced him to his feet, and looked at Dena. "Wait here for a minute," he told her, pausing in the open doorway. His voice, hard and flat, retained the dregs of his emotions. "Can you do that? You won't be afraid?" He studied her as she said she'd be all right. Nodding, he turned back to Ron and led him from the house.

During the wait for the officer, Jamie refrained from talking to Ron. He didn't trust himself to remain professional; his anger threatened to destroy what composure he had left. Instead, he logged onto a police site and obtained information about the house: who owned it, who resided there, history of the owners and residents—if they had previous trouble with law enforcement or with neighbors, occupations of all involved. In short, learning everything he could about the occupants and why Dena would've been taken there.

****

After he turned Ron over to the constable, Jamie jogged back into the house. He heard a voice singing 'Cold, Haily, Rainy Night.' An odd choice, since the song dealt with love betrayed. But maybe not, Jamie reconsidered. The song served as the theme song for McLaren's folk singing group. Perhaps it brought McLaren closer to Dena. Jamie hurried to the bedroom. The words came in spurts, the phrases separated, perhaps from pauses for breath. A note or two cracked or faded into silence, but the lyric came back more forceful seconds later. Jamie came into the room as Dena sang 'Soldier, will you marry me?'

"Don't give up your day job." Jamie forced a lightheartedness into his voice to ease the tension. He hurried to her, assessing her physical condition.

Tears cascaded down her cheeks and her voice quivered when she tried to speak. Jamie shook his head, indicating she shouldn't exert herself, and reached for her, then hesitated, torn between wanting to hug her or untie her first.

"I won't sing anymore, *ever*, if you'll—" Her voice broke and she abandoned her joke as Jamie hugged her.

"God, Dena. I can't believe this." His voice choked; he tried again. "Mike'll be ecstatic. I'm kind of glad, too, by the way." He grinned and cut the rope. As he flung it against the wall, he asked if she was hurt.

A tear slipped off her chin and she tried to smile, but her lips trembled. She pressed them together, stopping the quaking, and shook her head.

Jamie rubbed her wrists and ankles, bringing the circulation back into her flesh, gathered the pieces of rope, and escorted her outside. He then phoned McLaren.

Chapter Twenty-One

Jamie's phone call caught McLaren as he unlocked his front door. He had given his formal statement at the police station, was informed that he may be asked to return for further questioning, then subsequently released and driven home.

The crime scene investigators evidently had finished searching his house, for McLaren counted all half-dozen of them at various places in his gardens, beside the stone wall and in the nearby field. The detective warned McLaren about the searches and added that his car would be seized and examined in the lab. McLaren knew they wouldn't find any evidence of Dena's abduction, but of course the police didn't. Just doing their job, as McLaren had repeated to many people in his time. The fact that this investigating officer and Jamie were colleagues made McLaren's interview less lengthy and less of an ordeal. The two hours had been quite enough, thank you.

He answered his phone only half hearing Jamie's voice, his concentration on the white-suited men abandoning their outside work. The lead CS investigator talked on his mobile and motioned to the others. Why were they disrobing and driving away? Why hadn't they sealed and confiscated his car, or left a chap here until the flatdeck tow truck arrived? Why change their minds? Jamie's first words yanked

McLaren back to the present.

"I've found Dena." He paused dramatically, letting the realization sink in, probably enjoying his role as good news bearer and rescuer.

McLaren managed to cough out a few words before his throat tightened. "Where? When? How is she?"

"In a house. A few minutes ago. Exhausted, on the verge of crying, thanking me profusely, and wanting to talk to you."

McLaren sank down on the front step, oblivious to the July heat baking the earth and the fly buzzing around his head. He switched the mobile to his other ear and leaned forward, staring at nothing, yet seeing Dena's face before him. He swallowed, forcing himself to relax, and asked to talk to her.

When her voice cascaded over the phone, he closed his eyes, mentally thanking God for her rescue and for Jamie's help. When he opened his eyes he realized he hadn't heard what she had said. "Sorry, Sweets? What did you say?"

Her words came out in a rush of emotion, statements, and tears. "I-I'm fine, Michael. Really. Just tired and hungry, mainly."

McLaren got to his feet but could hardly speak, the questions about her wellbeing and her kidnapping swamping his mind. "Jamie said you were in a house. Whose? Where? Are you sure you're all right? You need to go to hospital to get checked over?"

"No."

"Dena."

"No need. The police surgeon just finished with me and said I'm fine."

"I doubt that, but go on."

"I gave a statement to an officer, also. He said something about typing it up."

"Is all this happening at the house where Jamie found you? You're still there?"

"Yes."

"Whose house? Where is it?"

"I don't know. Jamie can tell you."

"Just so you're safe. That's what matters now, dear. Thank God for Jamie."

"He did the whole thing: found me, arrested the…man." She couldn't bring herself to say her captor's name.

McLaren made a mental note to thank Jamie. "You're sure you're okay? Just because the police surgeon has seen you, doesn't preclude you going to hospital."

"Honest, Michael, I'm fine. I'll tell you about it later. All I want to do right now is get a hot shower, a cup of tea, and sleep for a week. I'm still a bit scared, though. I mean, Jamie got the one person, but…" Her tears cut off her words.

"But someone else might be involved in this," McLaren finished.

"Yes." Her answer sounded strange, as though she spoke through quivering lips.

He tried to think like a copper, sift through the unfolding story and his concern for Dena. He was about to insist that she go to hospital, that it would be the safest place for her right now if someone was still looking for her, when Jamie's voice tore into McLaren's ear. "I'll take her to my house, Mike. We've got that guest room. She can bed down there and sleep the clock round. All week, if she wants. She'll be warm, safe, fed, and looked after. Paula or I will be there all the time. Dena won't be alone."

Gratitude welled up with McLaren. "Jamie, I can't tell you how much this means to me. To Dena. You're sure she's all right?"

"You can talk to her later. She really needs some sleep and some food right now. You can see her later. Come over tonight. After tea."

"But she's okay, right?"

"Yes."

"You'd tell me the truth."

"Of course! Look, Mike, I've got to get Dena home."

"Where are you now, Jamie?"

"Ashbourne." He glanced at the house façade and gave McLaren the street address.

"Why there?"

"It's where Dena was held."

"Whose house is it?"

"Steve Howard's. Well, *Stephen* Howard. A friend of our friend Ron Pennell, it seems."

"Ron?" The world tilted crazily as he tried to fit all the names together. "What the hell's going on?"

A pause on the other end of the line greeted McLaren's question.

His anger roared back at Jamie. "What's this Howard bloke and Ron Pennell got to do with Dena's abduction? Does he know Dena? Is he there now? *Well?*" he yelled at Jamie's slow reply.

"Are you driving?"

"What the bloody hell difference does that make?"

"I don't trust you, Mike. You're in a dangerous

mood. You might get into a collision and smash up."

"The hell I'll get into a collision. And I'm more liable to smash the face of the next person I see if you don't tell me what the hell went on." He ran toward his car, his heart rate as high as his anger. "On second thought, no. I'm saving all my energy for Steve Howard. I'll feel much better smashing in *his* face. Before I castrate him."

"Mike…"

"Which is before I tie him up and drag him behind my car on the A515."

"I know you're speaking in anger and intense hatred. I know it's aimed at a name that may or may not be involved with Dena's abduction. And you know I'd react the same way if Paula were ever threatened like this. But you've got to let the law take its course, Mike. You'll only hinder proceedings if you interfere." Jamie exhaled slowly, as though he imagined McLaren laying his hands on Steve Howard. "I arrested Ron Pennell and officers are picking up Stephen Howard, but I don't know how involved Ron is in all this. If he actually kidnapped Dena, if he acted alone, or if he just delivered the meals."

"What the hell are you talking about?" McLaren started the car engine before he asked, "Why did Ron have Dena at that Howard house? Is he involved in the abduction? Are you holding him there? 'Cause, if you are and you wouldn't mind holding him until I get there…"

"Mike—"

"What?"

"This Steve Howard…"

"You said the bastard's associated with Ron." He

exhaled heavily and steered onto the major road. "I talked to Ron a bit ago. He didn't say a damned thing about this Steve Howard chap."

"I don't know if Howard was ever with Ron during Dena's abduction. That's not the issue right now. Not his whereabouts during the last few days, I mean. But he's somehow involved, if Ron kept Dena at Howard's place."

McLaren drove his car around a lumbering lorry and turned onto the A516. He made a hasty mental calculation. "You're still at that house in Ashbourne, right?"

"Yeah. You on your way, then?"

"Another ten miles, I guess." He'd passed the sign indicating the turn off for the A6 south. "I'll be there in quarter of an hour or so."

"Where are you? You must be close."

"Just passing Rushup Edge."

"Rushup Edge…" Jamie broke off.

"Near the Winnats."

"You're not even on the A6 yet, let alone the A515!" Jamie yelled as though envisioning McLaren tearing down the road at 70 mph and wrapping his car around a convenient tree. "What the bloody hell are you playing at? If you're not killed, you'll get stopped for speeding or reckless driving. Look, Mike, I've got to get Dena to my place. She's been through hell and she needs to rest. Meet us at my house."

"That'll take you a twenty minutes' drive up from Ashbourne. Can't you wait fifteen damned minutes for me?" Another few seconds of silence answered him before he said, "Ask Dena. If she's too tired and wants to go to your house, I'll abide by her decision. But ask her, will you?"

Seconds later Jamie said, "She wants to wait here for you. Frankly, Mike, I don't think you deserve her, but that's for you two to settle. We'll wait. We'll be here—whenever you get here. But for God's sake, *slow down*!" He said it with a plea in his voice, as though he knew McLaren wouldn't, that the words wouldn't even register in McLaren's brain.

"So who's Stephen Howard?" McLaren said, marginally calmer. "Do you know anything yet?"

Jamie sighed, sounding as if he was tired of trying to hold McLaren in check. "Never been in trouble with the law, if that's what you mean, and I believe you do. Not so much as a speeding ticket. I checked while I was waiting for the PC and police surgeon to arrive. He owns a van removal company. Howard Fleet. Heard of them?"

"No."

"They're based in Derby. Quite the company. Not only local business, but the continent, Australia, Canada, and the odd one or two moves to America each year."

"With a fleet of large vans, Howard could've shifted Dena anywhere, and we'd never have found her."

Jamie agreed. "Moved out of the country, even. But why? Any idea?"

"If they were holding her for ransom, her father would've been notified before this. I can't quite figure it. Anything unusual about the company?"

"Nothing's been reported. And I don't think they're involved with smuggling illegal immigrants into the Kingdom. Or with any dope runs. Howard seems all

242

above board and a regular businessman. His wife is Sarah Howard. She's employed at Honor Insurance Agents, in the Derby office."

"Nice and convenient. They can ride to work together."

Jamie let the sarcasm pass without commenting. "The firm's headquartered in Manchester but has branches all over the Midlands and Lake District."

"What's the connection between the removers and the insurance agency?"

"Pardon?"

"What's going on between the two businesses that involves Dena?"

"You're trying too hard, Mike. Don't look for villainy under every rock. There's no problem with either company or with the Howards. Steve worked his way up through the industry and formed his own company."

"Who's he to Ron Pennell, then?"

"Ron says he was house sitting for a friend."

Even over the phone, McLaren could hear the quotes around the words. He didn't need to see Jamie's wink or the hand gestures. "The friend being Steve Howard, I assume." He muttered something as he came up to a slower moving driver.

"We'll find out quick enough, Mike. Despite Ron not talking."

"Not yet."

Jamie ignored his friend's veiled threat. "Ron's enjoying the hospitality of the Derbyshire Constabulary. There's no use you puzzling out how to include him in Howard's beating."

"I can always dream, Jamie. Did Dena say how she

was kidnapped? We know where, but how it was done? Did she see who did it? Was it this Howard chap? I can't see Ron Pennell doing it, even if he doesn't have strict hours of employment. He hasn't the conviction of a just cause, never mind if he's trying to protect his own hide." He exhaled sharply, the image of the sixty-five year old man refusing to meld with the strength needed to haul Dena out of her car.

"She hasn't said a thing about it. Now's not the time to ask her, either. She needs—"

"Yeah. You told me. A shower, a cuppa, and some major sleep."

"Those aren't just words, Mike. She's all in. She's been through a hell of an ordeal."

"I know she has!" He barked his frustration as he zoomed around a tractor. "And so have I! I've been worried sick about her. I nearly lost my mind! She's all I could think about, Jamie. What she was going through, where she might be. I didn't want to live without her." This last sentence had been more subdued than the previous anger-filled speech. "Just coming up to Heathcote."

"Not much longer."

"How's Dena holding up?"

"She's fine. She's in my car. Her head's against the headrest, her legs are curled up on the seat, and she's looking at the street. Despite being tired, she looks very peaceful." The silence welled up between them. "I know what you're thinking, Mike."

"Yeah? You taking mind reading lessons?"

"You're thinking if there's one bruise or cut or bump on Dena, you'll kill him. You'll drag him behind your car until he's half dead, then finish him off by beating him. And when he looks at you in the last seconds of his life, you'll smash in his face with a rock. Right?"

"It'd be tempting, but no. If I were caught and sentenced that would leave Dena alone again. She'd be no better off then than if I'd had gone ahead with suicide. And even if I set the scene to look like an accident, I'd still be prime suspect. I'd be no use to her dead or in prison. I won't leave her."

"See that you follow your own advice, then. Where are you?"

"Just coming to the sign indicating Mapleton. Why?"

"I don't think Ron Pennell is the killer, Mike."

"Kent Harrison's killer, you mean? Why? If Ron kidnapped Dena, doesn't that imply his involvement with Kent's murder?"

"Not necessarily. Dena's kidnapping could be a completely unrelated incident."

"Holy hell! How many cases do you want?"

"Less than you think."

"Then why do you think Ron isn't involved in Kent's murder?"

"Nothing concrete. Just a hunch. You know about hunches."

"Just about there, Jamie. Where—Oh. Got you." He braked opposite the house. As he turned off the engine, Dena saw him and jumped out of the car. He ran up to her and grabbed her.

Jamie gave them a minute alone, letting McLaren assure himself that Dena was suffering only from aching muscles and the last vestiges of fright. He flipped his mobile closed, shoved it into his pocket, and walked up to them.

McLaren asked Dena again if she wanted medical attention at the hospital.

"No, Michael," she said, faintly amused at his concern. "A bruise or two, a little knot on my head is the extent of it."

McLaren had her bend her head down while he felt the swelling. His face darkened as he ran his fingers over her facial bruise. "Who did this to you, Dena? Who abducted you? Was it Ron? Steve Howard?" He stopped abruptly, staring at her. "He didn't..." He paused, taking a breath. He tried again, his voice calmer and quieter. "He didn't attack you...in any other manner?"

Laying a hand on his chest, Dena assured him she was all right. "No one came near me. I don't know who grabbed me. It might've been Ron, since Jamie followed him here, but I can't say." Her gaze turned to the front of the house and she seemed to see it for the first time. She returned her attention to McLaren. "Someone fed me, left food for me, I mean, but no one ever did anything else. *Nothing* else."

He nodded and hugged her again.

"I hate to intrude," Jamie cleared his throat noisily, "but I really think it best if Dena get some rest now. You can see her later, Mike."

"After tea time?" he asked hesitantly, his gaze shifting from Dena to Jamie, as though asking permission.

Jamie clamped his hand on Dena's upper arm and led her to his car. He called over his shoulder. "And don't keep ringing me. She needs some serious sleep more than anything else."

246

McLaren nodded and leaned against his car, watching until they turned onto the main road. Sighing heavily, he thought it best to release his tension by talking to Clark MacKay.

Chapter Twenty-Two

Free to focus more fully on Kent Harrison's case, McLaren made a quick stop at Tutbury Castle, thinking Clark's broader view of castle entertainers, event-goers, vendors, and enthusiastic fans might provide the name of a person Kent had slighted. Or, if not a name, some hint of anger that might have been bubbling beneath a calm exterior. Clark's assurance that Dave Morley had shown no resentment over the solo CD hadn't convinced McLaren, and he said so.

Frankly astonished that McLaren asked, Clark said, "Kent made it a point to help *everyone*." He handed McLaren an event flyer. "Everyone wished Kent success and he, in turn, wished that same success for everyone else, no matter their walks in life. It's contagious, you know. You do a good deed for someone and that person in turn helps another."

"What goes around comes around," McLaren said, smiling.

"Something like that. Even Dave wished him the best."

"A strange thing for Dave to say, considering they were a duo. Were they splitting up?"

"Not that I know of. Kent was about to release a solo CD. He had a half-dozen songs on it. I heard the demo. Frankly, I think it would've plunged him onto the charts again and made his name."

"It was that good?"

"Yes. At least, I thought so. And I've heard every musician at every castle event. He dug up some obscure song—from the Renaissance or Middle Ages or somewhere—and gave it a bit of a modern rhythm and some unusual chords."

"How did Dave feel about that? The solo recording, I mean."

"Don't know, do I? But even if he was disappointed, there might have been another CD in the offing—one featuring them as a duo."

McLaren thought he better find out straight from the horse's mouth.

****

Dave Morley's shift at the Joyful Sound Music Shop didn't start for another quarter hour. That's what a clerk announced rather hurriedly to McLaren as the store's phone rang. McLaren mouthed "thank you". A fine Martin D-35 caught his eye and he stood in front of it, wondering if he could take it from the rack on the wall and try it out, when a feminine voice said, "Kent played a Martin, you know."

McLaren turned to find Sheri Harrison standing at the end of the aisle.

"A beautiful instrument. Do you play, Mr. McLaren?"

"Mrs. Harrison." McLaren briefly abandoned the idea of trying out the guitar. "I could ask you the same thing, finding you in this shop."

"Me, play?" Her laugh rippled into the air. "Heavens, no. I'm just an admirer of those who do. Play *well*, I should stipulate. But you must play, and play rather well yourself, or you wouldn't be admiring such a fine instrument. That's not a beginner's guitar."

McLaren raised his eyebrow, unsure of her meaning.

"I don't mean to imply beginners aren't deserving of fine instruments. I meant that a parent wouldn't want to gamble spending so much on a professional quality guitar at the offset of the child's musical adventure. What if it's a passing fancy? What if the child is bent on becoming a ballerina or engine driver the following week?"

"Burning desires often are just flashes in the pan. Do you play something? Piano, perhaps?"

Sheri waved away McLaren's suggestions. "No, but I'll satisfy your curiosity why I'm here. I need to talk to Dave Morley."

"We're both here to talk to him, then."

"You may go first. I know your time is precious. I'll browse among the tin whistles, kazoos and comb-and-papers. Or content myself with looking at the guitar strings and things. Always so fascinating how something as simple as a piece of wire, when stretched so taut, can produce such delectable sounds."

"A piece of magical science."

"I never talked to Kent about the science behind it, but Dave would probably explain it if I asked. I'm just solidifying the memorial for Kent. Making certain Dave knows what he is to do. That sort of thing."

"You're doing this at the Minstrels Court?"

"What better place? That's where we associate him as being."

"Clark isn't in charge of this?"

Sheri pursed her lips and shook her head. "I'm either being punished or doing penance."

"What did you do?"

"I'm exaggerating, obviously, but Clark says I need to get over the bitterness of the divorce, so he's put me in charge of the memorial. You'd think he'd take it on, being castle curator and me just a tour guide, but he insisted I do this. I wish I didn't have to."

He sensed the change of tone in her voice, and wondered if it was attributable to fatigue or evulsion for the subject of the event. Whatever the reason, her professionalism pushed her on with the assignment. "Maybe he hasn't the time, or he believes you'd do a better job of it, since you were married to Kent."

"Do a better job at blackening his name, you mean." She laughed lightly, as though attempting to glide over her feelings. "I'll do a good job of it, don't worry. I'll bite my tongue, slap a smile on my lips, and amuse anyone who asks with family anecdotes and tales of life at home. Don't fret that I'll tarnish the gold. They'll never hear that he had time for students but none for me. Kent will remain the plaster saint of his fans. I can lace my office coffee with DeWar's and my evening cuppa becomes Tanqueray. For the duration only, not to worry." She ran the tips of her fingers over the top of a box of picks. "It'll be character building to see if I can fool everyone. They'll think I was his biggest fan."

"People go through a lot without letting on they're hurting."

"My hurt is that I'm a party to this. Oh, sure, he had talent. I don't take that from him. But it's ridiculous, all this hype. How long's this going to go on…forever? People will forget. Other singers will come along and eclipse Kent. We should drop this now, but Clark wants it. Thank God it's just to be a short thing. Ten or fifteen minutes before the last set on the last evening. Dave and Fay will play two songs that he and Kent were working on for their next recording, and the memorial will end with the recording of Kent singing 'The Swans' Song.' Ludicrous."

"I wish you luck of it, Mrs. Harrison."

She thanked him and wandered off, leaving him alone with the guitars. He had just about decided to take down the D35 when he heard a woman asking if she could help him. He paused, dropped his arms, and turned toward the speaker. A girl smiled at him. Her short-cut red hair set off her blue eyes in an unsettling way, and he found himself staring at her. When she repeated her question, McLaren said he was waiting for Dave Morley.

"Certainly. Though, if you have questions about that guitar I could get another clerk. String instruments aren't my forte. If you'd like piano music, we've got a nice selection."

She looked the type who would hover, trying to be useful to impress her boss. He needed to be alone when he talked to Dave. "Thank you, but I came to speak to Dave. It concerns his late singing partner."

"Kent Harrison?"

"You knew him?"

"Yes. He was my favorite teacher at school. My name's Lorene, by the way. Lorene Guard." She extended her hand, almost shyly, he thought, but appeared eager and hopeful, clinging to the remembrance of Kent's personality and wanting to help. "I still can't get over his death. It was such a shock."

He judged her to be about seventeen years old, the right age for enrollment in the Grange Hall College.

"It was horrible when we found out. None of us could believe it. The whole school went into shock. Mr. Harrison was so well loved and such a super teacher. Nothing's the same without him. Whoever killed him's never been caught. Is that why you want to talk to Dave? Because he knew Mr. Harrison?"

"I'm reinvestigating Kent Harrison's death, Lorene. Old cases occasionally are looked at in the hope that new information has surfaced, or people recall something after the turmoil's died down. I'm talking to those who knew him. Since you knew Mr. Harrison and you know Dave—"

She replied before he could ask. "Dave had nothing to do with Mr. Harrison's death. I know that."

"How?"

"He's not the type."

"Doesn't get angry? Doesn't get jealous…what?"

"Doesn't get emotional. He just sort of glides through life without being bothered by anything—excitement or failure."

McLaren nodded, thinking of several people he knew who took life as it came to them, seeming to accept good news and bad news with equal reaction.

"Dave's younger than Mr. Harrison was. He's also less talented, so he needed Mr. Harrison if he was going to get anywhere with his music."

"Which is why you believe Dave didn't have anything to do with Kent's death."

"Isn't your shift over yet?" A teenaged boy who appeared to be comprised of tattoos and blue denim stood behind McLaren. The question, barked in a surge of impatience, startled McLaren. He jerked around, his cop's instincts in high gear, and stared into dark eyes.

"Another few minutes, Booth." Lorene gestured toward the boy. "This is Booth, Mr. McLaren. Booth Wragg. Mr. McLaren's asking me—"

"Nothing about guitars," Booth said, eyeing them. He glanced at his watch, then at the store clock. "So, when, then? You through on the hour?"

"You know I am." Her face blanched. "I'm sorry, Mr. McLaren. Usually Booth is—"

"What?" He crossed his arms on his chest, waiting for an answer.

Dave Morley entered the sales area from the back room, his eyes taking in who was there.

Booth snapped, "Okay. Your replacement is here. You're off work. You're free to go." He grabbed Lorene's arm, telling her to hurry up.

"Let me get my bag. Sorry, Mr. McLaren." She apologized as Booth pulled her toward the checkout counter. "Good luck to you." She disappeared into the back room, emerged seconds later with her handbag, then followed Booth out of the store.

"I must apologize for that." Dave came up to McLaren. He stared at the door, perhaps expecting Lorene and Booth to reenter, then focused on McLaren. "What a rude berk. There's no other name for him. We've tried to keep him out of the shop, but there's really nothing we can legally do. He's usually here only a minute or so, when he comes to get Lorene. Some times are worse than others. Unfortunately this was one of the worst."

"What sets him off?"

Dave straightened one of the guitars so it lined up

with the rest of the display. "He's insanely jealous of Lorene. Constantly threatens to kill anyone who talks to her." He brushed his fingertips together, knocking off any dust that might have collected on them.

"It appears I got off easy," McLaren said, his gaze on the door.

"Your lucky day."

"Is he dangerous? Have you had altercations with him before?"

"You mean me personally? No."

"So he's never attacked anyone that you know of."

"No. But he could have done, I suppose. I don't really know anything about him, other than he's Lorene's boyfriend. But I *do* think he's whacko. And dangerous. As long as you give Booth no reason to be jealous, you're okay."

"Does that extend to you and Kent Harrison? I heard about the solo CD Kent planned on releasing. That wouldn't have done much for your group, would it? You weren't jealous of his approaching fame, knowing the CD would promote him as a solo artist and leave you in the dust?" Or behind the counter, McLaren thought, taking in the rows of instruments and sheet music. Although not a bad place to work for a music lover, the shop would not shoot Dave into stardom the way a hit single would.

Dave's face turned white and his left hand gripped the edge of the sheet music rack. His dark eyes faded to a duller hue and he stared at McLaren with the look of a haunted man. "How dare you say that! Kent and I were friends, singing partners. I'd be insane to hurt him. We had gigs lined up well into next year. We were going to make a recording. We were on our way as a duo. Why would I kill him?"

"Why indeed. Do you know anyone who may have wanted to harm him? Not wish him dead, necessarily, but maybe angry and got into a fight? Only the fight got out of hand." He left the outcome unsaid, watching the color return slowly to Dave's face.

"Look no further than the piece of dirt who just left." Dave gestured toward the door.

"Booth Wragg?"

Dave sniffed and thrust his hands into his trousers pockets. "Doesn't take a mastermind or detective, I wouldn't think, to see that the boy's round the twist."

"Does that extend to adults, too?"

"Sure. Especially older men."

"Like Kent."

"Yeah. Kent had a reputation at school, as well as elsewhere, of helping people. He'd spend a lot of time talking to kids at the college, helping them with their schoolwork and with their personal problems. They loved him."

"And you think Booth saw Kent and Lorene talking together."

"Why not? It was no secret. Kent talked to most of the students." He walked over to the counter and straightened the jars of wrapped mint candies and thumb picks. Seeing Sheri at the far end of the counter, he waved to her.

"Dave!" Sheri walked up to him. "I was just dawdling over the capos and bottles of polish. I wonder if you could spare me a precious thirty or forty seconds to run over the memorial program." She stopped, seeing McLaren approach Dave. "Sorry. I knew Mr. McLaren was going to speak to you, but I thought you'd finished.

I'll just look around. Don't hurry on my account." She sauntered back to the end of the counter and drew a handful of cork-backed flat picks from the glass jar.

McLaren waited until Sheri busied herself with the sheet music before speaking. "You said a moment ago that Booth was jealous of the time Kent and Lorene spent together. Did you actually see Booth get mad at Kent?"

"Sure. At last year's Minstrels Court. We'd just finished performing, and I was packing up my instruments. Kent had already put his guitar away and stood outside the stage area, but close enough to backstage that I could see and hear. He was talking to Lorene. It was early evening, Saturday. I got my guitar and mandolin packed up and had changed my clothes by the time they'd finished, so they were only ahead of me a few paces—didn't even know I was behind them, most likely. Our cars were parked close together so I could easily see Kent and Lorene get into his car and drive away. I didn't say anything to Kent that next day—Sunday—when we went on again for our set, but I sure wanted to. I mean, the man's personal life is his own. But he was forty-five and she was in her teens. Sixteen, I think." He drew in the corners of his mouth and attacked the leaning stack of flyers for a local concert. "Propriety, for God's sake! He could've been her father and here they go off..." He shook his head, then turned back to McLaren. "Normally I'm all for letting love flow where it will. If a couple finds each other in this mad world, good luck to them."

"But Kent and Lorene's age discrepancy was a bit much."

"It wasn't that so much," Dave said, glaring at

McLaren. His voice took on a sharpness. "Kent was a rat. He had a fiancée. And he was betraying her."

Chapter Twenty-Three

McLaren thought about the betrayal aspect as he stepped onto the street. He hadn't expected to learn that about Kent. Not that any person is a saint, but it was another derogatory remark about the man.

Booth Wragg lounged against a building front several buildings down from the music shop. Waiting for Lorene, McLaren thought, glancing first at the scowl on Booth's face and then at the shop sign. Babes In Arms, one of the newest shops in Buxton, featured clothing for newborns and toddlers, baby furniture and accessories, and a few upscale maternity dresses.

McLaren rang Jamie's mobile, thinking he'd either be at his home, or dealing with Ron at the police station. A few minutes' conversation gave McLaren more information about Booth, and he rang off, wondering again about the judicial system.

Hearing McLaren's approach, Booth looked up, staring at McLaren with unconcealed hostility. He flipped his shoulder-length hair over his shoulder and rearranged the hem of his T-shirt. When McLaren was several feet away, Booth snapped, "You following Lorene?"

The accusation—for that's what the tone of the question implied—stopped McLaren as effectively as if he'd walked into one of his stone walls. He looked at the boy. "Not at all. I'm headed to my car."

Booth stood up, looking like he expected a fight. "Yeah, well, keep on walking, then. Lorene don't want no part of you. Or him," he added, his voice hardening as he nodded in the direction of the music shop.

"What makes you think either I or David Morley is pestering Lorene? Has she said anything to you?"

"No, but she wouldn't, would she?"

"Why not?"

"She just wouldn't." He folded his arms across his chest and stood with his feet slightly apart. "Just telling you nice and friendly, so you don't try nothing, right? Now, push off, old man."

McLaren grabbed Booth's hair and shoulder and pushed him into a nearby alleyway. Slamming him against the brick wall, McLaren released his hold on the hair. He grabbed and squeezed the man's testicles until Booth screamed for mercy. Relinquishing his hold, McLaren angled Booth's face toward him, pressing the back of his head against the wall.

"You want to reconsider your attitude, Mr. Wragg?"

Booth closed his eyes. A tear slipped down his cheek.

McLaren repeated the question, his hand now on Booth's jaw.

Booth opened his eyes and McLaren said, "This is the last time I ask you nicely, Mr. Wragg."

Still silent, Booth tried to turn his head.

McLaren kneed Booth in the groin, eliciting another cry of pain from the man. "Life's full of warnings, isn't it? And what happens when you ignore those warnings?" He tightened his grip on Booth's jaw.

"I-I'm sorry." The words squeaked out from

between his clenched teeth.

"That's better. Life's more pleasant when everyone uses their best manners." He tightened his grip around a handful of Booth's hair.

"I apologize for my rudeness. Sorry. *Really!*" he added, sensing McLaren's anger.

"Apology accepted. Now." McLaren's voice lightened slightly. "Since we're on our way to becoming such smashing mates, we ought to know each other better. I'm an ex-copper. I've beaten up suspects, but no one could ever prove it. I also killed a colleague of mine, but again, I got away with it. Being a detective has those fringe benefits. You know how to muddy a crime scene and eliminate clues." He winked and patted Booth's cheek. "On a more personal note, my hobbies are gardening, singing, cooking...and boxing." He flashed a smile as Booth's face went white. "I mention these things because, as I said, I think there should be no secrets between friends. We ought to know what to expect from each other. Right?"

Booth nodded, trying to swallow.

"And you, Booth? I can call you by your first name, can't I? If we're going to be friends..."

"S-sure. Fine."

"What about you, Booth? Special hobbies?" He cocked an eyebrow, waiting for a reply.

"Uh, Yeah."

"What, in particular? I don't take you for a stamp collector."

Booth tried to shake his head but the pull on his hair was too tight. "Well, I like football and watchin' the telly, and there's a few groups I'm keen on—music groups, I mean."

"Life goals? You and Lorene have any goals?"

"Yeah. I mean, yes."

"Super to hear. You two going to get married, then?"

"Yes."

"Soon?"

"Not so very soon. Well, we don't have a date yet." The tip of his tongue slowly ran across his bottom lip, moistening it.

Like a snake, McLaren thought. But without the reptile's rodent-catching benefit. "You going to live around this area?"

Booth tried to shake his head again. He grimaced. "Uh, no. We're moving."

"I congratulate you both for your rosy future. I hope you'll be happy. I suppose her family's excited about the wedding…her mother especially."

Booth seemed about to say something derogatory, but one look at McLaren's expression changed his expression. "They don't want no part of us. We don't see 'em."

"Sorry to hear that. They out of the country?"

"Blackpool."

"Not too far away that you can't see each other if they wished to."

"Doesn't bother Lorene too much. She's independent."

"Still, she'd want her mother there for her wedding, wouldn't she? No matter their past."

"I-I'm not sure."

"They have a row or something?"

"I don't know. I guess so."

"Not a row over you, I hope."

Booth shifted his eyes to the alleyway arch.

McLaren repeated his concern.

"I don't know. I try to stay out of their fights. People are forever telling us what to do, what not to do. Especially that Fay Larkin b—uh, Fay Larkin."

McLaren hadn't expected to hear the drama teacher's name, least of all uttered by Booth Wragg. "Oh yes? I've talked with Ms. Larkin several times and found her very pleasant and quiet. I wouldn't have thought she'd be telling you what to do."

His gaze still on the alleyway opening, Booth mumbled his reply.

"Sorry?" McLaren's fingers dug into Booth's shoulder.

Booth winched. "Fay and Lorene went off together. To God knows where. All giggly and matey. They leave me sitting at home watching the telly. For months, yet!"

"Frustrating for you."

"At least that's done."

"You don't like her seeing too much of other people, then."

"No."

"Ah, well, love's like that. Each minute away from your woman feels like an eternity."

"Yeah."

"But you're together now."

"It's better now, yeah."

"Oh? In what way?"

"That Kent Harrison...that teacher at her old school."

"The man who was killed last year?"

"That's him. Not to speak ill of the dead, and all

that…" He took a breath, glancing at McLaren's eyes. "But he and Lorene spent a bunch of time together for a while."

"Hard cheese."

"Yeah."

"You didn't resent her time with her teacher, surely. She probably got help on a school assignment."

"I guess. I don't know. I just know I couldn't stand that berk. Thinkin' himself so grand 'cause he'd a song on the radio. I gave him a miss whenever I could. A little of that smile of his went a long way."

McLaren flicked something from Booth's shirt before smoothing the wrinkles from the fabric. "Did Lorene like his music?"

"Could have done."

"He was quite good, from what I hear. A lot of people liked him."

"She's got a CD, I think. I don't really know."

"She doesn't play it a lot, then."

"Sometimes. I don't think she was crackers for him, like some of those birds. That fan club of his…not for her."

"Not a joiner of groups."

"She might've tried 'em out for a time, but she didn't stay. What a berk that president is."

"Mr. Unsworth, you mean?"

"Yeah. That's him. What a looney. Cookin' with flowers. He's another nerk who won't be missed much if someone tops him."

"You don't think Kent Harrison is missed?"

Booth shrugged. "Don't know, do I? He ain't missed by me, that's all I know. One less nerk in the world. They oughta hand a trophy to the bloke what topped him."

McLaren rotated his fist so that his pull on Booth's hair tightened. "You really mean that, Booth? A man's been murdered and you feel nothing for those who loved him?"

"Sorry."

"That's better. A little more compassion in the world is what's needed all around." McLaren's voice dropped in volume. "Where were you on the tenth of July last year? Oh, say, around half past eleven that night?" His lips were close to Booth's ear, giving the impression of intimacy.

"Me? You think *I* killed that bloke?"

"Just asking, Booth. Someone did. You obviously hated the man. You just said so."

"That don't mean I topped him."

"So, where were you that night?"

The shift in his eyes was so quick that McLaren might have missed it and the significance if he hadn't been staring at the teen.

Booth said, somewhat nervously, "Well, I was waitin' for Lorene, if you must know."

"Why? Where was this?"

"At the castle."

"Tutbury?"

"Yeah. At that olden days fair. Lorene wanted to go to it but I didn't fancy her bein' all that way from home at that hour of night, so I drove her."

"I assume you left together. When was that?"

"Don't know exactly."

"Give me an idea."

"When her teacher finished singin' his last set. We walked around a bit after that. We got somethin' to eat from one of them vendors and I bought Lorene a necklace. Then we left."

"You drive her straight home?"

"Yeah."

"And you...did you go straight home after dropping her off?"

"Yeah." Despite McLaren's fingertips still digging into Booth's shoulder, his answer came out more of a bark. "Yes. Straight up the A515 to my digs here in Buxton. I don't know when I got in. Didn't know I'd need a witness, did I?"

"So you saw no one who can substantiate your claim."

"My claim! Listen, this is the truth! That was the last time I seen that teacher. I didn't kill him and I came right home."

"And where is 'home', Booth?"

He gave an address on Holker Road. Appropriate, McLaren thought. Practically adjacent to the police station on Silverlands.

"You have a roommate?"

"Not who I'd like. Ow!" He winced as McLaren pulled Booth's head sharply to the right.

"Is that code for 'no, I don't'?"

"Yeah. Sorry. I'm just nervous. You know, you talkin' about me and her bein' there right before Harrison gets clobbered and all. I don't want her a part of that life if that's what happens to them."

"What do you mean?"

"Performers. Competition. Back bitin', fights for the spotlight."

"Not literally, surely."

"Don't know. I ain't one of them. And I don't want

Lorene to be one of them, either. I'm glad she's dropped that mob. Through spendin' her time with Pennell and his projects, too. Once was enough with that bloke. Another git."

McLaren released Booth abruptly, smiled, and patted his check. His whistle echoed against the brickwork as he passed through the alley archway.

****

McLaren sat in his car, the windows down, and debated about whom to see. Booth's information—and McLaren took it as information and not as time-passing gossip or bragging—brought up startling questions. The more McLaren considered the conversation, the more the questions nagged at him. Why did Booth resent people in his and Lorene's lives? Being in love had nothing to do with it; the reason went deeper. The boy portrayed the qualities of a loner. And a loner who had been profoundly hurt sometime early in life. Still, that did nothing to explain his animosity and suspicion of everyone around him. Why begrudge Lorene some time with Fay Larkin, if they were friends? And why keep Lorene's family at arm's length? Unless it was the other way round—Lorene's family had distanced themselves from Booth and Lorene, had dropped them for some reason. McLaren turned the key in the Peugeot's ignition. Time to kill two birds with a stone.

****

Despite Booth's comment that Lorene hadn't liked the Kent Harrison fan club enough to remain a member, McLaren wanted to get it from a more reliable source. A source whose point of view wasn't tinted with antagonism, anger, and jealousy. So, he prayed to the gods who had already blessed his day, consulted Aaron

Unsworth's scrawled note, and drove across town to Brown Edge Road to get one fan's slant on things.

The girl remembered Lorene and had been surprised when Lorene stopped coming. "After a few months, too. Not even a year. I was that sorry when it was plain she wasn't coming back. Odd, because she looked like she was having a good time. She'd join the discussions about Kent and his music, but she had so much more to contribute to the group. She was a walking encyclopedia of the medieval period. But maybe that was 'cause she was one of Kent's pupils. I guess she was just naturally interested in all of it."

Yes, Aaron had picked up her and the other member, and dropped off at their respective doorsteps.

The times matched what Aaron had told McLaren.

The second fan lived in Leek, Staffordshire, a market town a little over ten miles southwest of Buxton. His drive through traffic and along winding, mountainous roads turned into a blur of green, brown, and blue as he thought through the last few hours. An innuendo about Kent Harrison's devotion to Fay, Dena found, his own suspected involvement in her abduction… Just because the police let up on their interrogation and released his car didn't mean he was home free. They could just be giving him a long lead to implicate himself. He could be the mastermind behind the whole thing—for a reason as yet undetermined

He caught up with the other fan who confirmed the time, and added that Aaron had got into a slang-match with Lorene's boyfriend.

"You know the boyfriend's name?" McLaren asked as he strode down the front path with her.

"Booth. Don't know his last name. Don't know if I

ever heard it. He'd come to the club meetings with her-occasionally, thank God. I don't know what his problem is, but he sure is possessive. I felt sorry for Lorene, having to deal with that, but..." She shrugged, as if to say it was Lorene's life.

"Was the argument ugly? Did it last long? Did it become physical?"

Opening her car door, she shrugged. "I suspect it did, thought I didn't see it."

"Why do you think it came to blows?"

"The side of Aaron's face was red somewhat later. I saw it as we walked to his car. You know...under the outdoor lights. I thought at first it was just a shadow, but I could tell he was getting a black eye. His cheek looked bruised, too. I asked him what happened but he laughed it off, made a joke about his clumsiness. I guess they continued the fight elsewhere later on. It was just shouting when I was there. Booth got the rocket and stomped away. He probably found Lorene some place. I didn't see. I wasn't that interested. Anyway, I'm sorry I saw it all. It was ugly and frightening and uncalled for. Whatever their problem, they should have been able to talk about it in a civilized manner."

Interesting that Booth happened to forget that, McLaren thought as he returned to his car. But, then, if he were suspected of murder, would he admit—especially to an ex-copper—that he had a temper that would lend itself well to violence?

A phone call to Aaron confirmed that he ended up with a black eye and bruised cheek some time after that night. He denied Booth had done it; wouldn't specify how he got the marks, laughing and deriding his usual clumsiness.

McLaren rang off, tossing his mobile onto the car seat. Was it far fetched to link Booth to Aaron's battle scars? Farther fetched, still, to extend the link to Kent if Booth thought Aaron and Kent were monopolizing Lorene? McLaren rubbed his forehead, the questions and players dancing about inside his skull. Sighing, he made for the school.

Chapter Twenty-Four

During the drive to Grange Hall College McLaren reviewed the new information. People at the school might know of Lorene's penchant for Kent and might be able to confirm or deny Dave Morley's suspicions. Fay was the logical person to ask, and he'd also ask Trevor Pennell another question or two—without fear that he would erupt in anger over Dena.

McLaren asked Fay if she'd ever seen Lorene and Kent together that Sunday night. He stood again in her drama room aware of the time he took from her work. But her answer could affect his case.

"I didn't see them that night." Fay stared alternately at McLaren and the students in the hall. "I know Kent gave Lorene some personal time outside class, but that didn't mean anything. Not in the way you want it to mean."

"Miss Larkin, I don't *want* it to mean anything other than what it truly is. I'm trying to solve your fiancé's murder."

"I know what the loose tongues at Grange Hall College said. Kent was a handsome man and he often spent time with students—female and male. But nothing of a sexual nature went on between any of them. Least of all not Lorene Guard."

"You know this to be true? Or do you just want to believe it?"

"I know it's true. Kent wouldn't have anything to do with a child."

"But as to that Sunday night…"

"I wasn't at the Minstrels Court that day. I waited at his house. We were to have a late supper and then talk. I—" She broke off, averting her eyes from McLaren, and fussed with the items on her desk. Straightening the photo of her baby, she said, "He never came home. I heard a car stop, though."

"What time? Do you remember?"

"The police have asked me so often that I do remember. I probably won't ever forget. Around eleven o'clock."

"And Kent's last set ended at ten?"

"Half past nine, actually. I believe it came out during the trial that he left the castle close on to ten."

It wouldn't have taken Kent an hour to drive from Tutbury Castle to his home in Somerley. Had he and Lorene stopped somewhere for a tryst? Had he dropped her some place before returning home? If so, Booth did have reason to be jealous.

"I'd gone to the window to see if it was Kent," Fay explained. "It was Lorene. I saw her plainly in the light from the streetlamp. But I couldn't see the other person's face. I assumed it was Booth, her boyfriend, because they're inseparable, but I can't swear to it. It was a man, though, the other person. I could tell from the height and I heard him talk."

"Did you recognize the voice?"

Fay shook her head.

"Could it have been Dave Morley?"

"The police asked the same question. I never really considered it could've been Dave, but the more I think of it now..." She screwed up her mouth and frowned. "Of course, I wouldn't want to accuse an innocent person. And time has a way of coloring things. You believe you saw or heard something when you actually didn't. Because you've been thinking about a certain possibility."

Yes, McLaren silently agreed. He'd nearly been down that road himself.

"I've no more classes today. I have to go now." Fay stood up abruptly. "I've got to get home to the babysitter."

She picked up her tote bag, walked past him, and out the door.

McLaren lingered in the hallway for a moment, wondering whom he should see next when a young woman came down the hall. She passed him and entered the room. He decided to take a chance and followed. She glanced up, clearly surprised, as he approached the desk. "Hi. My name's Michael McLaren. I was told Fay Larkin teaches in this room. Are you she?"

"Oh, I'm sorry," the woman said. "You've just missed her. She's left school. I have this room at this hour."

"Just my luck." He put a tinge of exasperation into his voice and hoped it sounded authentic. "Guess this just isn't my day. I knew I should have rung, but the traffic out of London..." He grimaced, mentally praying the woman would make the correction assumption.

She did. "How frustrating for you. Is there anything I can do?"

He thanked her and said, "I don't know..." Best

not to appear too eager. Besides getting him more sympathy, it made him appear legitimate. He cleared his throat, as though reluctant to disclose his business. When the woman tilted her head and looked anxious, he said rather slowly, "It's about an investigation I'm conducting." He paused again, building more trust between then.

"I'd like to help, if I can," the redhead explained, her eyebrows lowered in concern.

"Well, perhaps you can." His smile flashed all the charm he could muster up. "As long as I'm here, it'd save me a bit of time and petrol. First off, did Miss Larkin take an extended holiday last year? Perhaps a leave of absence? Late spring or early summer, perhaps? I know it's an odd question," he said as the teacher stared at him, "but it might help with my investigation."

"As a matter of fact, she *was* gone. That's when I began my employment here. I was hired to fill in for her, then I was offered a permanent position after Fay returned."

"Do you know where Miss Larkin went?"

"Like a specific town or resort?"

"That would be fine, but even the general area."

"No. Sorry. I didn't even know her until she returned. I was new and it wasn't my place to ask my employer where a teacher was going."

"No, of course not," McLaren agreed before thanking her and tracking down Trevor.

He found the teacher walking toward the car park. Trevor admitted he'd been jealous of Kent's scholarship success, had needed money nearly to the point of desperation, that his wife had cancer and the outlook for recovery was bleak, but he swore he hadn't killed Kent. Trevor begrudgingly gave McLaren five minutes. "I suppose I had a motive for Kent's death, what with needing the money. I'm near retirement age, you know. We wanted to retire to a warmer climate— Cyprus, southern France, the Canaries... Didn't much matter." He drew in his bottom lip to stop its tremor. "Just so we were together. She hasn't that long to live." A tear coursed slowly down his cheek as he looked at McLaren.

McLaren let several seconds pass. "Where were you that Sunday night right after the Minstrels Court finished up?"

"You're accusing me of murder."

"I just want to know where you were. It gives me an idea."

"I'll tell you the idea you have. You have the idea of pinning me with Kent's murder. Well, it won't stick, McLaren, because I've got an alibi."

"Home with your wife?"

"I was meeting with Ellen Fairfield."

"The curator of Rawlton Hall?"

"Yes."

"At eleven o'clock at night?"

"It was a long meeting. We'd begun at eight and finished up at midnight."

"Must have been important."

"It was. I was helping Ellen plan an event like the Minstrels Court, except hers would emphasize Arthurian legends. It had to be different or she wouldn't draw the crowds to the Hall."

Nothing like starting your own festival if you couldn't wheedle your way into an existing one. The man must be desperate, but for fame or money? "So, who killed Kent?" McLaren asked, aware of Trevor's fidgeting. "Cyanogenetic glycoside was in his system. A poison found in hydrangea. A plant. Your brother is a passionate herbalist, Mr. Pennell. You, your brother, and Kent all frequent the same medieval re-enactments. Did you take a handful of Ron's dried hydrangea, slip into Kent's drink, for instance, slowly poisoning him so there would be one less competitor for the school scholarship funding?" He waited, aware of the traffic sound down the road, a rook calling from a tree.

"You know that's not true," Trevor said, anger coloring his tone.

"How do I? I don't know your motives."

"I have none. I didn't kill Kent, or slip anything into his food. You've got it all wrong."

"Then straighten me out. That's why I'm here."

"Ron had been helping Aaron with his natural foods cookbook. Ron taught him about herbs and spices. If you think someone slipped some poisonous plant into Kent's food or drink, don't overlook Aaron. He knows which plants are safe and which aren't. He's a chef, or didn't you know? Talk to him before you make up your mind that Ron or I had something to do with Kent's death."

Several students walked toward the car park, their voices light with laughter and talk of current films and music. McLaren asked if he could talk to them for a moment, and quickly caught up on Lorene's past and general school gossip. Every student agreed that Kent had been an outstanding teacher, giving of himself outside the scope of his job. Though that berk Fraser Unsworth was even beyond Mr. Harrison's powers, as one student phrased it. "But I mean, honestly, Fraser had no hope of ever being cool even if Mr. Harrison could give him private lessons for a *decade*. A born loser."

Others in the group may have agreed with the girl's assessment, but no one spoke to underscore the opinion. And as for Lorene, well, she'd missed the last few months before summer break—common knowledge among students and faculty. Prior to the time Kent was killed. A few girls had given Lorene a hard time, teasing her about sailing through Kent's class now that he and she were seeing each other, but Lorene had repeatedly denied it, saying Booth was her boyfriend, so why would she want an old man? But the rumor persisted even now, even to the winks and looks exchanged during McLaren's session with them. Lorene was last seen at the castle, talking to Kent. One eager girl echoed Booth Wragg's testimony of seeing Lorene get into Kent's car. Two statements, two different witnesses, given independently. Had they spent more time together than a teacher-student relationship should warrant?

He considered the result as he drove to Holker Road to check out Booth's alibi.

McLaren drove back to Buxton, hoping he could find someone now who could pinpoint Booth's arrival home. As he parked outside the block of flats in which Booth lived, a middle-aged man turned into the front garden and headed for the front door. McLaren got out of his car and jogged up to the man, calling him to please wait a moment. The man nodded when McLaren introduced himself and explained the reason for his question. Yes, he recalled that specific night due to

Kent Harrison's murder.

"Well, you would, wouldn't you?" he countered even-toned. "Even though it happened in Kirkfield instead of Buxton, it stays in your mind."

As to whether he remembered Booth Wragg being home or not, he was certain Booth had been, because the residence was a two up/two down. He and his wife had converted the building a few years ago and Booth was their first and only tenant. He was always aware of when Booth was home or away.

And on the night of the murder?

Definitely home. Later in the evening, from nine o'clock until he shut the music off around midnight. Yes, he knew personally Booth was there instead of leaving the music on and slipping out. He had knocked on Booth's door to ask him first if he wanted some leftover pizza—it never kept well for the following day, did it? That was around half past nine. Then, around half past ten, a mate of Booth's came over and stayed for about quarter of an hour—he remembered the door opening and closing. Besides, Booth had knocked on their door to ask if they had some paper towels he could borrow. A blare of music startled the man and his wife just as the evening television news had finished. It quickly subsided—"Probably just tuned the radio to a different station—"and they heard him walking around until the music and his pacing stopped near midnight. Yes, he'd swear to it in court, if he had to.

So why lie about being at the castle with Lorene if he was home by nine? Nothing more than an attempt to provide himself with an alibi, McLaren thought as he returned to his car. Or make himself appear the ladies' man. The blow to his ego had suffered enough if

Lorene had gone by herself to meet up with Kent. Booth didn't need to add to his mortification by admitting it to McLaren, who had physically humiliated him in the alley.

Chapter Twenty-Five

The interview room at Ashbourne police station could've been in most any of the Division's stations: a small room of brown-painted walls, three chairs, and a wooden table. A tape recorder deck of three cassette tapes took up part of the table; the microphone was fixed to the wall. Jamie began the interview, stating his name and rank, the attending constable's name and rank, the date and time, and the reason for the session. Ron Pennell sat in a chair facing Jamie and looked scared to death.

"I can't believe you were in this alone," Jamie said.

"Why not?" Ron tried to sound defiant but his voice broke. He studied the far wall and seemed not to hear Jamie's reply.

"Because I don't believe you have the strength to move an unconscious person from her car into yours. Nor shift her from your car into a basement room in a building. Someone helped you, or did it himself, and you're just the meal provider." He paused, giving Ron time to consider his answer. "You're adding to your own problem if you keep silent. Now, who partnered with you?"

"No one."

"We can check the mask, gloves and clothing we found for DNA. If there is another trace on it…" Jamie sat back in his chair. One of the tapes in the recorder squeaked momentarily as it passed over the recording head, sounding like a shriek or a rat. He exchanged glances with the constable at the other end of the table, knowing that they shared the same thought: Ron Pennell wouldn't keep silent much longer. For all his good intensions, his fear was too great. He had never experienced this and, for the average person, the mysteries of Police Power were frightening enough. Never mind being involved in a kidnapping case.

Jamie doodled in his notebook, as though he had nothing but time before him. He cleared his throat and stated for the benefit of the recording that Mr. Pennell was still thinking.

Ron grabbed the edge of the table and looked at Jamie. He leaned forward, as though sharing a secret. His words were barely above a whisper and he cleared his throat and started again, this time speaking slower and with greater volume. "We weren't going to kill her. You can tell that because we were feeding her."

"Who is *we*, Mr. Pennell?"

"Clark MacKay and I." He lowered his head and brought his hands to his lap. Staring at his clenched fingers, he said more quietly, "We just wanted her out of the way for a few days. While that ex-police detective ran around talking to people. We hadn't planned to kidnap Dena. It was a spur of the moment idea."

"If you were concerned with Mr. McLaren's questioning of people, why kidnap Dena?"

"She'd spoken to me at the Minstrels Court. She said she was asking questions about Kent Harrison for a friend of hers who was interested in reviewing the case. We thought she was really an undercover officer investigating people from the original case. Clark didn't want the case reinstated because he feared Kent's dirty laundry would be aired, that it would tarnish his image, and the events Clark had planned would fall through. Clark had a lot of money riding on Kent, even a year after the murder, and he feared he would lose all that if the police probed again into Kent's life. There's usually some scandal not too deep if you dig for it. I got frightened and told Clark that evening. We didn't know what to do. When that ex-detective talked to Clark we really thought things from Kent's not-too-pristine past would come to light and destroy the plans. That's when Clark got the idea of kidnapping Dena. We thought that if she were out of the picture, the questions might stop. We thought she was the chief investigator." He'd spoken in a nearly non-stop gush of breath. When he finished, he sat back, his gaze still on Jamie, and waited.

"How did you abduct her? From her car?"

Ron nodded, his face flushing with color. "Clark followed her that day. We were near to panic by then. He figured the only way to stop her asking questions and dredging up Kent's murder was to abduct her. So when she stopped in that lay-by, he figured it was the best place and time to grab her. She had just finished talking on her mobile, so she wasn't aware Clark walked up to her. That's when he hit her on the back of the head and carried her to his car."

Clark had picked a good spot for the abduction, Jamie agreed. Secluded from the A515 by a stand of trees, neither he nor Dena would attract any unusual attention. Jamie sat up and asked where they had kept her.

"Two places, actually. The first night in a basement room of Rawlton Hall."

"The manor house?" Jamie's eyebrows raised in astonishment. "Why such a public place? Weren't you concerned you'd be found out?"

"It was the only place we could think of. We waited until closing time and everyone had gone. I had borrowed a key from Ellen Fairfield about six months ago. She thought nothing of it. I mean, if a painting or silver service was stolen it'd point to me." He traced his thumb across his palm. "I go there some evenings because I'm working on a large project. Ellen wants the gardens redesigned and I needed to consult the historical drawings and books to be certain my ideas were accurate for the period. Besides, they had more space than I have, so I could make scaled sets and then pop outside to see the actual gardens, see if it would work with the house architecture." He wedged his fingers beneath his thighs and continued in a monotone. "We carried Dena into the basement room and left some food for her. We figured she'd be well hidden because no one goes into that room any more. The staff member who had it as an office retired and most of the furniture was moved out. Ellen had decided not to replace the person." He paused, his eyes large and bright with anxiety.

"Did Ellen know about any of this, either the kidnapping or how you used the basement room?"

Ron shook his head, protesting her guilt. "She has no reason to go down there. I worked with her for two years until quite recently when I set up my own business. I felt the odds favored Ellen's continued neglect of the basement, so we assumed Dena would be safe there for a day or two. I didn't want to keep her too long in such a public spot, though. Anyone could've found her there."

"So you moved her."

"Yes. Late at night. We put two crushed sleeping tablets in her evening meal."

"Where did you put her?"

"Where you found her." Ron's voice was barely audible. "My friend's house in Ashbourne."

Jamie read the address for the tape recording. "Why there and not your own house or Tutbury castle?"

"I couldn't lodge her because I was frightened my wife would find her. By the time we'd shifted Dena to the house we were scared. It had seemed a good idea at the beginning, but the longer we had her, the more frightened we became. I asked Clark how we were going to let her go. I knew she couldn't identify either of us because we moved her only when she was out cold, and every time we brought her food we'd wear that costume. We never spoke to her, either. That way she couldn't ID us by our voices." He paused, moving his tongue over his lips. "That's why we dressed up, so she wouldn't know who we were. I mean, you don't take all those precautions if you're going to kill someone, for Christ's sake! We were going to let her go!"

Jamie exhaled loudly. For all of their impulsiveness, they seemed to have thought the plan through very well. "And you chose your friend's house because…"

"They're out of town. Sarah *and* Steve. I'm house sitting. Well, to a degree. I know what I told you, but I really was keeping tabs on the house. Water the plants, feed the canary…" Ron grimaced, as though expecting Jamie or the other constable to rush from the room to arrest Clark. Instead, they both sat there in silence. The tape squeaked again. "No one knows Clark or me in that neighborhood. I thought that in case a neighbor did connect us with Dena's kidnapping we couldn't be identified since the neighbor wouldn't know our names."

"And you did all this because you didn't want Dena to reinvestigate Kent Harrison's murder and jeopardize the success of the forthcoming fete." Jamie leaned forward so that he nearly touched Ron. "Did you want to shut her up because you or Clark had killed Kent? Maybe your brother was connected to it, too. You wanted to protect Trevor."

Ron's denials still rang in Jamie's ears as he left the room.

McLaren leaned his head back and considered possible suspects. Aaron, one of Kent Harrison's neighbors, might have been slipping hydrangea buds to Kent, gradually poisoning him for weeks, but Kent hadn't died from plant poisoning. Aaron had been dealing with his wife who'd left him. And there was the sticky question of motive. Aaron had no reason for killing Kent, none that McLaren had been able to discover. Trevor, however, did fit nicely into the murderer role. With his wife dying of cancer, he wanted to win the school scholarship for the cash. It could help with medical expenses.

And Ron had been at the Minstrels Court that Sunday night. The event had ended at eleven o'clock. Ron had stayed till closing time, making sales, talking to people, and closing up his booth. He finally left at half past eleven, seen by the security guard in the car park and by Clark MacKay as he locked up the castle. Ron couldn't have driven from Tutbury Castle to Kirkfield and killed Kent, even if he conveniently met him in the forest so he wouldn't have to transport his body. He hadn't the time. Not even if the witnesses were wrong and had him leaving the castle an hour earlier.

McLaren made a note to check with Ellen Fairfield about the lengthy meeting.

So, he thought, sitting in his car, he was at a dead end. What to do?

He rubbed his forehead, his mind dizzy with the day's scenes. One in particular nagged him, shimmered more than the rest. He'd been at the school. He'd spoken with a group of students who still remembered Kent's kindness...

McLaren sat up, his mind on fire. He'd been going about it all wrong, concentrating on jealousy and anger. First class berk! How many times had he heard that Kent helped everyone? If Kent had *not* helped someone, and that someone had not only expected and counted on help but had also been angry enough...

McLaren rang up Cheryl Kerrigan, the Home Office forensic pathologist who worked periodically for the Derbyshire Constabulary. As he waited through the 'hold' music, he saw the elements of the case fitting together in his mind. And it all hinged on the victim. Kent Harrison and his time with Lorene—a troubled student who sought his counsel. Kent, who'd advised her on her pregnancy. For that's why she left school before finishing the term, McLaren believed. And that pregnancy resulted in a child's birth and the adoption of that child by Fay Larkin. Kent Harrison, the great helper, the solution provider of everyone's problems. Did McLaren see or just imagine the baby having the same shaped nose as Lorene's?

The music cut off abruptly and Cheryl's voice kicked him back to his present question. "What can I help you with, Mike? Another case?"

He heard the hint of interest in her voice, imagined her leaning forward in her desk chair, the rush of requests momentarily forgotten. "No, still the same one," he said, amused that Cheryl would think he'd cleared up the Harrison murder so quickly. "I'd like the details of the postmortem, if you've got a moment."

"Asphyxiation."

"Through strangulation."

"Yes. I thought I told you."

"Just making certain." He was close to finishing the case and didn't want to make a stupid mistake.

"Right. He sustained a blow to the head, probably to render him unconscious, and had enough cyanogenetic glycoside in his body to be fatal in another few hours."

"But it didn't come to that," McLaren supplied, recalling his notes. "He was strangled with a wire." It was easy to assume it was from a guitar, considering the music connections, but there were other kinds of wire. He wasn't going to assume.

"It wasn't recovered, Mike, but it left traditional marks around the neck, a fairly deep cut into the skin that could only have been made by a wire. Anything else?"

"No, that's all. Thanks, Cheryl."

"Awfully short call this time. Does this bode well

for you?"

"You'll no doubt hear one way or the other. Thanks." He closed the phone, cutting off her goodbye. Tossing the phone onto the passenger seat, he sank back into the upholstery. The landscape rocked wildly. More than that, Kent's face peered at him. If Kent had died by strangulation with a wire, could it have been a wire guitar string? Fay had mentioned that someone had cut Kent's guitar strings. Or, to be precise, four of them. Twelve, ten, eight and seven. McLaren picked up his notebook and wrote down the string numbers. Why not cut all the strings, if the person had set out to vandalize Kent's instrument? The lower two strings, he could understand, snipping them in a hurry. But only one of the two E's had been cut. The vandal had skipped the eleventh string to cut the lower string in the next pair, one of the A's. Yet, strings eight and seven were both cut. Why cut both D's and not both A's and E's? McLaren stared again at the paper, writing and rewriting the string names in a variety of doodles while he thought. He nearly stopped breathing when one of the scribbles seemed to jump from the page. D-E-A-D. The guitar strings hadn't been cut as an act of vandalism; they'd been cut as a warning. They screamed of hatred and of premeditation.

McLaren turned his key in the ignition and roared out of the car park. Only one person he could think of who knew about guitar strings: Dave Morley.

But Jamie's phone call altered McLaren's plans.

"Jamie. What's going on?"

"More than I'd like. Ellen Fairfield's in hospital."

"Anything serious?"

"I haven't seen her. I'm still at the station. One of

the constables responded to the 999 call and I learned from him that she was attacked."

McLaren nearly choked on the word. "You're kidding!"

"I'd just spoken to her several hours ago. Maybe if I'd arrived later…"

"Where did this happen? Anyone see it?"

Jamie relayed the information, scanty as it was. The attack occurred in the car park at Rawlton Hall as she left for the day. A man hit her but was scared away by the gardener before he could do anything else…if he intended to. No, the gardener didn't hear a thing, he merely came out of the storage shed after putting away his tools. No, he didn't see the bloke's face but he was dressed in a denim jacket, jeans and a cloth cap, if that helps. Yes, he put in the emergency call. No, Ellen didn't get a good description, either. Yes, she's all right but for a few scrapes and a very sore head where it met the weapon, but she's being kept overnight at Uttoxeter Hospital for observation.

"Do you think the bloke wanted her mobile or handbag?" McLaren suggested it more from routine than something he believed.

"How should I know?"

"Isn't it odd that someone we're interviewing in this case is now attacked?"

"It could be a simple assault. They're common enough. But I do agree it bears looking into. And, off the record, Mike, I can't believe it's a coincidence, even if it occurred at closing time and the place was practically empty."

McLaren thought back to the Hall and grounds. The storage shed sat hundreds of yards from the main building, parenthesized by a handful of arborvitae. A guard's booth at the entrance to the car park served as both ticket seller and watchman location. Besides sporadic clumps of yews and boxwood, nothing else could be effective cover for an attacker bent on surprise. The man had to have hidden behind Ellen's car.

"Sounds very plausible. Anyway, I have to get back to the interview room. Clark MacKay's just arrived."

"Is Ellen capable of receiving visitors?"

"I wouldn't know, but I wouldn't think so. If it's only a simple blow to the head it wouldn't require police at the doors or screened entry."

"Did the constables find anything at the scene that might give a lead to the attacker's identity?"

"I haven't heard. I've been conversing with Ron."

"Sure. Have a good time with Clark. I assume he's mixed up in all this."

"I wouldn't be talking to him here if he weren't."

McLaren rang off and headed for the hospital in Derby.

****

Uttoxeter Hospital, resplendent with its glass entryway, sat between a spaghetti-pile of roads and among trees. The sun hovered at the top of the leafy mass, casting blue shadows that angled eastward. McLaren parked near the emergency entrance, checked his watch, and entered.

A nurse in the emergency room consulted her computer, said Ellen Fairfield would be kept overnight for observation, and directed McLaren to a room on another floor. "You *are* a family member, aren't you?"

she asked as he turned.

"Pardon?"

"Visitation by close family members only."

He hesitated, his mind racing.

"Is your name on our list?" The nurse leaned closer to the computer screen. "Approved names only. Sorry."

McLaren nodded, and said he'd write Ellen a get well note.

He returned to his car, donned his baseball cap and a long sleeved shirt, and walked in the main entrance. He bought a magazine on British history, a pack of chewing gum, and a box of chocolates in one of the gift shops. He popped a stick of gum into his mouth, began chewing, then took the lift up.

The ward hummed with hospital staff, conversations, and visitors. McLaren considered faking a delivery slip but when he located her room he shoved his mobile into his pocket. No police constable stood guard. He wouldn't be challenged.

McLaren stopped outside the room, staring at the magazine and chocolates, and wondered if it was a good idea after all. Ellen's injuries evidently didn't demand the emergency or intensive care rooms. Just overnight obs in an undistinguished room, as the nurse said. But would he be bothering her recuperation?

He knocked on the door. An emphatic "Come in" sounded, and he entered. No visitors or police officers gathered around her. She was alone, her head bandaged, and reading a book, but she set it down on seeing him.

"Mr. McLaren?"

"I just heard you were here." He walked up to her bed and handed her the chocolates and magazine. "I hope your stay isn't long."

She thanked him for the gifts, laying them beside her on the bed. "I kept insisting I was fine, but they wouldn't let me leave." Her hand touched the gauze pad taped to her forehead. "Something about making certain I had no concussion. I wasn't hit that hard, but I guess a rock can do more damage than one suspects, never mind the headache. I have the impression my assailant started to grab my neck, but I wouldn't swear to it. Anyway, I'm not dwelling on my impression or the cut on my head. The nightmares will be bad enough." She wriggled, sitting up straighter. "I expect I look worse than I am. At least the scrapes from the fall onto the gravel are painful." She twisted her arm and glanced at the red cuts.

"Head injuries are nothing to take lightly. What's overnight if it will save you grief later?"

"I suppose so." She sank into her pillow and pulled the sheet up. "Though this forced relaxation isn't my idea of time well spent. I've a ton of work to do at the Hall. I'm up to my ears in planning an event, and here I sit." She gestured at the novel she'd been reading and grimaced.

"Is the event something new, or next year's version of a current program?"

"Oh, it's new. I've been planning it for more than a year. I hope to give Clark MacKay's Minstrels Court a little competition with my own group of musicians and historical actors. Reenactments are popular, but I'm going to give people the chance to play-act along with the professionals. They won't get to do that very often."

"Did Kent ever appear in your venues? Perhaps Dave was angry that Kent had gone solo at the Hall and left him at Tutbury."

She shook her head and assured him that she had done nothing other than offer a bigger venue to Kent Harrison. "I've got publicity connections that Clark MacKay can only wish for," Ellen said, giving a faint smile as if she imagined her victory.

But the triumph had never materialized, for Kent had repeatedly, unwaveringly refused her job offers. He wouldn't betray Clark's kindness and trust. Clark had given Kent his first professional chance, offering him a spot at the Minstrels Court when the rest of his singing buddies were holding down their weekend gig at the pub. He had confidence that Kent was destined for stardom and he felt compelled to help the singer on his way.

"Do you have someone as good as Kent? Authentic music can make or break these affairs."

"There are more musicians of this type and excellent quality than you'd expect. You just have to know how to put out the call." She punched up her pillow and sank back on it. "You also have to know how to refuse a person. The people who think they can perform…" She shuddered, as if recalling a less than melodious audition. "I understand the lure of the spotlight, but trying out before they're ready, not to mention not realizing they have no talent, wastes their time and builds up hopes that can't be met. I'm sorry to turn anyone away, but honestly, the people who try out!"

"I guess we all have dreams, Ms. Fairfield."

"Granted, but how many times do you have to be told no before you abandon that pursuit? I feel like I'm robbing them of their hope."

McLaren said most people take audition rejection

well. "Sorry to change the subject, but about the attempted robbery…do the police have a suspicion who it was? Do you?"

"I haven't a clue. I wasn't very vigilant, but this sort of thing has never happened before. The folks who visit the Hall aren't normally…"

"That energetic?"

She laughed and said she would've described them as mean.

"Have you any idea why you were attacked? I assume this hasn't happened before to anyone there."

"I figured it was just a crime of opportunity. He was at the Hall, he saw me, and realized no one was around, and he hoped to grab my handbag and mobile. What else could it be?"

If my girl friend hadn't been kidnapped, I'd think the same as you, he mused. There's comfort if such things aren't personal. He nodded, removed his chewing gum and wrapped it in a facial tissue before tossing it into the trash bin.

"Where were you Tuesday afternoon?"

Ellen opened her mouth, looking puzzled, then said she'd been at the Hall.

"All day?"

"I believe I had a meeting with a potential entertainer, if it's any of your business."

"Did you meet at the Hall?"

"Honestly, I don't know why you need to know. It's my business and has nothing at all to do with Kent or my attack."

But had it something to do with his attack at Beresford Dale, he wondered, studying the woman's face. She seemed calm enough and didn't avoid his gaze. He cleared his throat and nodded. "So the police are investigating."

"They probably won't find him. I didn't see his car or number plate."

"And coming from behind, as he did, you didn't see him. Was there anything about him—not his appearance, obviously—that you recall? A smell like aftershave, or his voice?" Tattoos were wonderful identification. If the berk had one on his arm and wore a short-sleeved shirt…

Ellen took a sip of water and apologized that nothing stuck in her mind. "Maybe I'll think of something later."

"Just a consideration. Don't force anything. Do you know the attacker used a rock?"

"That's what the police said. I guess they found it where he dropped it."

"It would stick out on the gravel, yes. So, chummy didn't get your handbag or mobile, then. I heard that your gardener scared him off."

"I was lucky he was working late. We're redoing the garden, and I think he was preparing the roses for transplanting."

"Who's designing it?"

"Ron Pennell. He's quite good. He's into herbal remedies, as well."

McLaren hadn't the heart to tell her some other designer would have to take over Ron's job. He wished her speedy recovery, and left the room wondering if Ellen's assault had anything to do with his investigation. Or, perhaps more perplexing, who would be so desperate as to risk being seen during a daylight robbery.

Chapter Twenty-Six

Clark MacKay thought at first to string the police along, making a joke of Dena's detention, but as he sat in the interview room at the police station he came up with a better plan: tell the truth.

He was spared the humiliation of being handcuffed in front of his staff, the police allowing him to walk—escorted—to the police car. And during the ride to the station he still couldn't envision anything more than a an hour gone from his day and the explanation of the abduction. He would be financially slapped on the wrist and released with a warning. But the handcuffs sobered him. The entry through the sally port, the walk past the bank of lockers holding prisoners' personal effects, the CCTV monitors displaying every second in the cells and exercise yard, and the booking process killed the humor as surely as if the listener had known the joke's punch line. Clark's embarrassment manifested the longer he talked and the explanation, even to his ears, sounded ludicrous if not serious.

When the arresting officer barked, "Well?" Clark realized he hadn't heard the question. He had been thinking of Ron, wondering if he were being interviewed or already sat in a cell. Either mental image disturbed him, and he glanced at each officer as if trying to discern the men's impressions. But he needn't have bothered. The entire arrest process explained his situation: serious.

Clark echoed Ron's account of Dena's capture and confinement, and added an explanation for it all. The narrative emerged slowly, in broken sentences and red-faced grimaces, yet ended as a rush of relief and spiritual cleansing. He stared at Jamie, willing an acceptance to the truth and an end to the ordeal. "I realize I committed a crime when I kidnapped her." Clark's voice threatened to break again. "But at the time all I thought of was the money I'd sunk into the commemorative festival for Kent. It'd be undone if the media learned Kent had got a student pregnant a few years ago and was currently having an affair with another. I'd be financially ruined. I had to stop Dena from talking and reopening the case."

"What has Ron to do with this?" Jamie asked, tapping his pen on the pad of paper in front of him. "Did he kill Kent Harrison?"

"No!"

"You concocted Dena's kidnapping scheme, thinking you could at least keep her quiet for a few days before you murdered her."

Clark's face blanched and he sat rigidly in his chair, his fingers bloodless from their grip on the edges of the seat. He stared at Jamie, trying to think. A conversation in the hall outside the interview room filtered through the closed door, and Clark shifted his gaze to the door, expecting more officers to come in. But the voices faded, a door closed, and Clark looked again at Jamie. "No."

"Then please tell me. I'd like to understand this."

"Ron and I got frightened when she began asking questions. She talked to Ron at the Minstrels Court and had mentioned she was conducting preliminary interviews for a friend. Ron and I assumed that the friend was a police detective. Who else would be dredging up an old murder case? From Trevor, Ron was aware of the talk at the College, how jealous Trevor was of Kent always winning the school scholarship. Ron and I figured it wouldn't be long before the police would think he had killed Kent, or helped Trevor kill Kent, since they're brothers. Ron's real close to Trevor, would do most anything for him."

"Including murder."

"As I said, that's how the police reasoning seemed to us, Ron killing or assisting in Kent's murder to assure Trevor winning the scholarship the following year." He paused and brought his hands to his lap, where he folded his fingers and sagged back into the chair. "I realize that I committed a grave crime when I kidnapped Dena and held her captive, but I was going to release her."

"That doesn't negate the seriousness of the kidnapping."

Clark nodded. "The whole thing was my idea, officer. Ron hadn't anything to do with it. I'd be grateful if you'd let him go and just punish me."

"Unfortunately, Ron's an accomplice, Mr. MacKay. It may be after the fact, but he participated in the incident."

"Yes, I understand." He took a deep breath. "So, what happens now? After sitting in jail, I mean."

McLaren detoured on his trip to Rawlton Hall to the music shop. Although he was anxious to poke around the grounds and car park, he reasoned he should talk to Dave. After all, Dave might be getting off work soon. The Hall would always be there.

He imagined Dave Morley sitting in jail, perhaps warbling a bluesy type of song about being on a chain gang. The mental image made McLaren smile. He was getting close to the end of the case. Dena had been rescued. The sunset spread across the sky in purples and gold. He pushed a cassette tape into his tape recorder and soon was singing "The Parting Glass" at the top of his voice.

Dave Morley probably would have been happier to see anyone but McLaren, but answered his questions without prodding. Anything to get the man out of the shop.

"I didn't cut the strings on Kent's guitar," Dave said, clearly annoyed. He stood, feet slightly apart and arms folded across his chest, facing McLaren. His jaw tightened. "That is an absurd accusation. Kent and I were singing partners. How often do I have to tell you? Why would I sabotage my future by hobbling Kent, in any form? Just because you think Kent was strangled with a guitar string, and I happened to be a guitarist and a clerk in a music shop, you're trying to pin this on me." He took a step closer to McLaren and pointed his index finger at him. "Circumstantial, at best. You're grasping at straws. Ellen Fairfield plays guitar, if you're so keen on that angle. So do dozens of other people who knew Kent. Probably a good percentage who're members of his fan club. Focus on one of them 'cause I'm telling you I didn't touch Kent."

"Maybe *you're* grasping at straws, Morley. You're scared because you killed Kent, and you're naming anyone you can think of to steer me away from you."

"Ellen Fairfield is a logical suspect, if you'd take a

minute to think."

"Because she plays guitar," McLaren snorted.

"Because she was angry Kent wouldn't leave Tutbury Castle and sing at Rawlton—her Hall." Dave shook his head and eyed McLaren with obvious scorn. "If you appeared at these functions you'd know the rivalry between the curators. It's a competitive business. And a satisfying one if you get popular acts and events that bring in the paying public. Many a job hinges on ticket sales. So I think it would benefit you to ask Ellen about any quarrel with Kent. The female of the species is deadlier than the male."

McLaren tried to picture Ellen throwing a wire around Kent's neck and strangling him. Ellen was a petite woman; Kent had perhaps six inches on her in height, plus several more stone in weight. McLaren doubted that Ellen could have strangled Kent, even in a surprise attack. "Do you mind telling me where you were that night?"

Dave sighed, as though resigned to going over it all again. "I rang Kent at his home phone and at his mobile numbers. I couldn't raise him. Surely you can check all this through phone records."

"Even if cellular towers show that you roamed around, phoning from your mobile, that doesn't establish your alibi. You could have killed Kent before all this phoning business started."

"And knowing that Kent was safely out of the way, I kept ringing his phones in a supposed state of anxiety, trying to find him and establishing that he was alive. What crap!"

"If you don't like that, offer me a better one."

Dave opened his mouth, started to say something,

then stopped.

"Yes, Mr. Morley? I'm sorry, but I didn't quite hear what you said."

Dave watched one of the shop clerks hand a guitar to a customer, then looked again at McLaren. "I was with Clark MacKay and Sheri Harrison. At the castle. We were planning a new event."

McLaren frowned and his voice was tinged with frustration. "Why didn't you say this before?"

"I didn't want to involve her."

"Involve her?" McLaren's right eyebrow mirrored his surprise. He knew about the meeting between Clark and Sheri. Other castle staff had corroborated it. What was there to involve Sheri?

"Yes." Dave's voice lowered so no one else could hear. "I went back with her after the meeting, to her house. I spent the night with her."

****

He substantiated Dave's alibi with two of Sheri's neighbors. One had arrived home at the same time and had seen them go into Sheri's house. The other neighbor had seen Dave leave early Monday morning. Which left the possibility of Dave killing Kent before arriving at Sheri's or sneaking out during the night to kill Kent. But that seemed far-fetched. Why risk Sheri noticing Dave's absence or someone seeing you leave? McLaren couldn't see an amateur having the nerve to do that. Dave would have killed Kent before bedding down with Sheri, and there hadn't been time for that. They had left the meeting and driven straight to Sheri's. McLaren had to look elsewhere for the killer—guitarist or not.

He sat in his car outside Sheri's house, tired to the

bone from his day. The sun seemed to have raced westward and now hovered near the horizon, leaving reminders of its summery glory in the fiery reds, crimsons and violets clothing the clouds. The canvas behind him stretched into the indigo-hued heaven, intensifying the white and gold edges. Despite the set back to his investigation, McLaren sighed. All in all, a satisfactory day.

His mobile rang and he begrudgingly emerged from the sunset's trance. "McLaren," he answered, his gaze still on the mottled clouds.

"Michael?"

The voice brought him fully awake and he sat upright. "Dena! Anything wrong?" Perhaps not the most romantic way to reply, but considering her recent experience, it seemed the most logical. "You need something?"

"Yes," she said, the laughter in her voice. "You. When are you getting to Jamie's? You said after teatime. Well, it's been and gone."

"Oh?" He checked the time on his watch. Nearly eight. He started the engine and eased away from the curb. "I'm just coming now. Sorry, but I got more involved than I thought. I'll be right there."

"Fine. Where are you? Not that it matters, but we'll put on the kettle for you."

Where was he? He panicked for a moment. He'd lost his bearings while watching the clouds change colors. Glancing at the houses on the street he said, "Oh. Ashbourne. Just wrapping things up. I'll be—"

"Yeah. Right here."

"Uh, Dena? Nothing's wrong, is there?" He felt a fool for asking, but the kidnapping was fresh in his mind. "You'd tell me if you were scared...or anything."

A lifetime crawled by before she answered. "I'm jittery. I won't lie about that. But Paula's been here constantly. Sitting beside my bed or just in the next room. And I'm tired. But on the whole, I'm fine. I'll be better when I see you." She hesitated, as though wondering what else to say. "You'll be here soon, then." Her voice slid over the phone and she rang off.

He turned up the volume on the cassette tape, feeling he would implode in happiness. Dena was waiting for him at Jamie's, and soon he'd move her to his house, where it would feel natural and right for her to be. He could imagine her standing by his front window or sitting on the swing in the garden, looking for his arrival. Or in his kitchen, getting the meal ready. Or stretched out in bed, drowsy from a nap, her hair in disarray, yet not caring because she looked at him with love in her eyes. He turned onto the A515 and sped northward, anxious to be with her. To protect and love her, even if their time was short. As he turned onto the A6 outside of Buxton, a new song began. His singing stopped abruptly and the vision of Dena changed. He didn't need the lyrics of "Marie's Wedding" to put the idea into his head. He'd thought of that long ago.

****

Rawlton Hall appeared hardly more than a silhouette against the fading evening sky by the time McLaren eased over the brick wall and dropped to the ground. The impact barely made a sound and he glanced at the dark shape before him, half expecting it to jump in fright. He crouched at the base, hardly daring to breathe, and glanced around. From his low angle, the turrets seemed to scrape the clouds that crawled out of the west, their bellies dark and holding the scent of rain. A shaft of moonlight spilled onto the crenellation and down the wall, and threw back pinpricks of light from the leaded window.

McLaren drew in a breath, trying to still his racing heart, and half stood. The sounds of crickets and owls remained unchanged, as did the splash of the brook. He glanced at the Hall, waiting to be bathed in spotlight glare or attacked by dogs. But the night remained unchanged. Nothing seemed upset by his presence. He snapped on his torch and made his way to the car park.

Other than two estate vehicles at the far corner, it was devoid of cars. No watchman appeared from the booth near the main road; no dots of torchlight marked the grounds. McLaren walked slowly as he swept his torch beam across the rock-strewn surface. Time crawled with him, having no presence other than his breathing and the sporadic calls of night birds. A breeze played across the grass and wound through the trees, bringing a drop in air temperature and the pending rain scent closer. He glanced at the sky as thunder rumbled in the west, then pushed on.

He'd covered the bulk of the area when a car slowed on the road. The headlight beams flicked to high as the car stopped on the verge. The purr of the idling engine bore into McLaren's ears and he ducked behind the booth and turned off his torch. The motor stopped, a car door slammed, and a figure stepped across the stream of light, shutting it off momentarily. As the shape moved onto the verge the footsteps dulled. A muffled "Damn" floated over to McLaren, followed by the crunch of disturbed gravel.

McLaren crouched behind the booth, his palms

against the wood surface, his stare on the moving shape before him. The form paused at the entrance to the car park and stopped for what seemed like an eternity. Waiting for his eyes to adjust to the darkness, McLaren wondered? The gravel crunched again, moving toward the other end of the lot, coming toward him. The sound continued until the figure stopped at the point closest to the Hall. Moments later, a bright light snapped on, directed at McLaren; he flattened himself on the ground. The light holder seemed not to notice him, for the beam immediately shifted downward and began sweeping sideways in meter-wide arcs.

The examination of the car park lasted for nearly a half hour. McLaren shifted his position several times to keep out of the searcher's view, for that's what the person obviously was doing. Looking for something. But what? Or was it just nerves, perhaps returning to the scene of the assault to find something that might have been left behind? He could think of no other explanation that fitted this midnight visit.

The figure finished his hunt and retraced his steps, but more haphazard this time. He hurried, the light flitting over patches of gravel that looked newly disturbed. When he'd finished with the lot, he walked around the perimeter, venturing onto the lawn and periodically probing the grass. Several times he would straighten and throw something toward the Hall, a twig or stone or coin, McLaren thought. Once the figure even pried something from the soil, but dropped it with an angry "Hell."

He stood at the patch the torchlight playing over the expanse of gravel in random bobs and jerks. It disappeared behind some trees, focused on the roots and soil around the trunks, then emerged to shine again at waist-level as it pointed at the ticket booth.

The footsteps moved faster this time, the crunch of gravel firm and headed toward McLaren.

He kept the booth between them, creeping as quickly as he could to the opposite wall as he corkscrewed around. The figure evidently didn't hear, his light and gaze on the ground. When the light suddenly snapped off and only the rumble of thunder sounded, McLaren froze. Should he remain there or move? What was the person doing?

Despite the warmth of the night, perspiration soaked McLaren's shirt. His pulse throbbed in his throat. He considered tiptoeing around the booth's corner and jumping the man, but if he mistook the man's position, coming face-on, and the man saw him…

The gravel shifted and the steps turned the way they'd come. McLaren stepped back as the light played into the lot. When the figure cleared the booth, McLaren lunged forward.

His fingers reached for the man's clothing as he found himself falling. The torches crashed to the ground, and McLaren and his adversary were plunged into darkness. Arms and legs thrashed as both men fought for control. McLaren grabbed a wrist but felt it turn and slip from his grasp. His palm pushed against the ground to keep him upright, but he crumpled as a shoe kicked his side. He fell in a rush of pain and blackness.

He shook his head desperate to remain conscious, aware of the footsteps that now ran to the road. The light bounced, marking his assailant's journey. It cut off as it reached the car, and for an instant the headlights revealed jeans and the lower portion of a yellow T-shirt. The door slammed, the engine revved, and tires screeched as they reclaimed the tarmac. The silence after the car's retreat was nearly deafening.

McLaren got to his knees, his right hand on his ribs, and stared at the road. Nothing but the stench of exhaust fumes remained to show the car's existence.

This is twice I've been attacked, he realized, feeling his heart thudding in his throat. Granted this meeting was coincidental, but the Beresford Dale encounter was planned. I was followed, but by whom? I'd spoken with all the key players in the case by that time, but I can eliminate those who hold steady working hours. But Booth, Fraser, and Ron come and go as they please. Unless Ellen, Clark, and Sheri, who obviously had flexible hours, and weren't chained to their offices, added the side trip to their workday. Man or woman could've rigged the wire at the river. That took no strength. But the wire that strangled Kent…

Now he'd been tripped by a wire, the intent clearly to kill him. He exhaled heavily, not feeling as encouraged as he had minutes ago. He fingered his scalp. No broken skin. He tested his side, and stood up. Nothing seemed to be broken, but he flexed his muscles and tested his back. When nothing screamed at him, he walked to where the torch lay and he picked it up.

Something winked at his feet. He flicked the torchlight several times, making certain the glint in the gravel was other than a piece of cellophane or metal pull tab. The object was a shiny solid about thirty-five millimeters long. He turned it over with the tip of his pen. A Fender heavy flat pick stared back at him, its tortoise-shell coloring bright under the light.

He pushed it onto a page from his notebook and stared at the hole in the pick's center. Kent Harrison hadn't performed at Rawlton Hall, according to everyone he'd talked to. Ellen had been pursuing him, but had he played here? McLaren straightened up, folded it in the sheet of paper, and slipped it into his jeans pocket. It wouldn't be here one year after Kent's death. Besides, it was pristine; no gravel, cars or shoes had scuffed it. And it was far enough away from his scuffle, so his assailant wouldn't have just dropped it.

He frowned, wondering if the pick actually meant something. Maybe guitar picks weren't that unusual. Those punched with holes might be somewhat more rare. But one person of his acquaintance narrowed the suspect list. He grabbed his mobile and jogged back to his car as the clouds ripped apart.

****

McLaren hadn't slept much that night. Sunrise Thursday morning found him awake and dressed and out of the house. Not that the morning was much different from most others, but the knowledge that Dena was at Jamie's, that she could have been with McLaren, made the house walls press in on him until he was near to panic. Now that she was so close, he felt more alone than ever, more aware that he wanted her to share his life. He wanted to drive to Jamie's to look in on her, but he knew she would still be asleep. Might be asleep for most of the day. So he swallowed his impatience and heartache with his coffee and hurried from the house.

He breakfasted at an umbrella table in the outdoor eating section of the hotel in Castleton, a village lying minutes from McLaren's village of Somerley and centuries from the present. Castleton held on to its ancient heritage and landscape with a fierceness any old Highland chief would have admired. Nestled in a valley in the High Peak district, it sometimes enjoyed and endured seclusion when wintry storms howled through the deep gorge of The Winnats mountain pass, cutting them off from the rest of the dale. Yet even in winter's worst offering the village had company. The ruined keep of Peveril Castle towered over them, high on its nearly inaccessible hill, whispering of its glory days in the late 1100s. All in all, McLaren thought, scanning the horizon from the hotel courtyard, a serene, attractive place to live.

He had deduced part of the case before falling asleep last night, and had put together the rest of the pieces while breakfasting. The jigsaw puzzle of people and motives seemed clearer with each passing moment. Sitting back in the chair, he allowed himself a minute to think through it again, wanting to make certain the pieces fit together. Both Fay Larkin's and Kent Harrison's extended absences from their jobs coincided with Lorene's abandonment of her school studies. Because, McLaren reasoned, the two adults were with Lorene as she gave birth to a baby girl. Without the support of her family, Lorene had turned to her favorite teacher for advice, and he and Fay had become surrogate parents, being by her side for the birth. Booth hadn't stated it in so many words, but why lie about it? If Lorene had become pregnant outside the blessing of marriage, her parents may well have turned their backs to her. So, helpful Kent Harrison steps in and picks Lorene up at Tutbury Castle at night. Kent and Fay, who were going to be married, saw Fay's predicament as a blessing. Adopt the baby, thereby making them a family and relieving Lorene of the embarrassment of an obvious pregnancy, as well as alleviating the burden of a child.

He stirred his coffee, smiling at the way life worked out at times. Yet, even if Kent had solved Lorene's pregnancy problem, as well as his and Fay's desire to create their own family, one answer remained unsolved. Who had killed Kent?

McLaren exhaled slowly, oblivious to the warmth of the sunlight already heating the stone walls of the hotel. A rook called noisily from a tree bough and turned its head, as if eyeing McLaren's half finished piece of toast.

Dawdling over coffee wasn't an option this morning, but he did order a second cup, needing to go over motives and alibis of the key players. Of the people associated with Kent, however tenuously, Clark, Sheri and Dave appeared to have alibis. The remaining suspects could have been anywhere, doing anything. And as for motive... McLaren nearly threw the coffee cup in his frustration. Everyone seemed to be angry or jealous of everyone else. Especially at Kent. But why that had been, McLaren still couldn't fathom. Kent Harrison had been an uncommonly caring person who helped anyone who asked. Why kill someone like that? The answer hit McLaren as he reached for the cup. He had started down this trail yesterday, but had been sidetracked. Standing, he threw a couple of pound coins onto the table and strode toward his car. He hit the B6061 on his way to Kirkfield, cursing his blindness. Just because someone had asked Kent for help didn't mean Kent had complied. There was one person then, and still was, frantic for musical help.

Chapter Twenty-Seven

If Kent had refused to help someone, McLaren reasoned as he drove toward Somerley, and that someone had become angry, especially when seeing Kent helping others...

McLaren leaned forward, nearly hugging the steering wheel. That one person ignored by Kent, perhaps had been so desperate that his rage had led to murder.

That rage still percolated a year later, focused on Ellen Fairfield. The curator could've given a boost through employment, but evidently hadn't. Yes, it made sense when viewed from this angle.

The village stirred in the early morning light—people leaving for work, shopkeepers sweeping the pavements in front of their stores, aromas of freshly baked bread and fried breakfasts perfuming the air. McLaren turned his car onto Dena's road and moments later parked opposite Kent's neighbor's house. Aaron Unsworth and his son, Fraser, lingered by their car, talking about the Minstrels Court.

A man across the street straightened up from weeding his perennial border. McLaren jogged up to him and introduced himself. "Sorry to bother you so early, but if you could give me thirty seconds, I'd be grateful."

The neighbor nodded and dusted his garden gloves

on his jeans.

"Do you know Fraser Unsworth?"

"Certainly. That's him talking with his dad." The man nodded toward the teenager. "Do you want to be introduced?"

"No, that's not necessary. I meant do you know his guitar playing, if you know how good he is."

"I've just heard him now and then. If you're thinking of asking him to perform somewhere, I have to tell you in all honesty he's not ready. Never will be, if I'm any judge. He's very bad, despite his practicing. I guess some people have musical abilities and some don't no matter how hard they try."

"Fraser has been trying."

"For years. Fraser asked a semi-pro musician who used to live here, for lessons. Music lessons, stage performance lessons, repertoire help." The man shook his head and grimaced.

"The lessons didn't help?"

"He never got the lessons. At least, not from Kent. I never saw Kent over here."

McLaren thanked him and walked back to his car. Despite the heat that was already building, McLaren kept the car windows closed and rang his house. He hated to wake Dena, but he needed to talk to her. Jamie's wife Paula answered with a cheery good morning.

"Morning, Paula. It's Mike."

"I figured it would be. I didn't even have to glance at the caller ID. You want to talk to Dena, I assume. Jamie's already at the station."

"Only if she's awake," he said hurriedly. "I know she needs her sleep—"

"Believe it or not, she's right here. We're having a cuppa and a nice girl chat. One minute."

A muted word reached McLaren's ears as he heard the phone receiver being handled. Then Dena's voice greeted him.

"Sorry to wake you," McLaren said, feeling guilty.

"You didn't. I've been up and showered for half an hour. I'm about to have my second cup of tea, so this *is* progress. Did you want to tell me you love me?" The smile came over the phone.

"Constantly." He tried not to think of Dena dressed in one of Paula's nightgowns, her hair uncombed, her eyes bright with sunlight—looking defenseless and desirable at the same time. Watching Aaron and Fraser, he said, "I realize you didn't spend every moment of every day staring at your neighbors—"

"But…"

"…but what's your opinion of Fraser Unsworth's guitar playing?"

"If you mean can he turn pro, catapult to stardom on 'Britain's Got Talent' or land a paying gig in a pub…no. At least not within the next decade."

"As bad as all that?"

"Awful. I don't really know about his singing ability. That seems to be whatever the current fad dictates."

McLaren nodded. Some of the rock bands he'd been subjected to were comprised of guys who sounded as if they were shouting instead of singing. Perhaps 'rage' was in. "How about if he took voice lessons?"

"I think you have to have a good base, don't you? Like pleasing tone or ability to carry a melody?"

"And you know for certain Fraser doesn't possess

this."

"Well, I've heard him a few times when he practiced outside. Unless he was imitating something other than a singer."

"I get the idea. How about his musicianship? Any hope that he could turn into an instrumentalist or a backup guitarist for some singer?"

"Not unless he's improved since the last time I heard him."

"When was that?"

"Last month."

"Ouch."

"Precisely."

"Could Kent have helped him, do you think? Better yet, *did* Kent help him?"

"With guitar lessons?"

"That, yes, and anything else—tips on getting into the music business, stage presence, maybe a name to contact."

"You're joking."

"Am not. Do you know?"

"As you said, Michael, not that I spend every moment of every day staring at the residents on my street, but in all the years Fraser's been thumping away on his guitar, I've never seen Kent over there. If Fraser's taking lessons, it's at Kent's house or somewhere else."

"Don't you think that's odd?"

"What? That Fraser wants to get into music?"

"No. That Kent wouldn't help him. The chap's known for his benevolence. He helps everyone he meets, if I'm to believe what I've heard."

"He did."

"So why didn't he help Fraser?"

"You're the detective, Michael. You find out. But it *is* odd, now that you bring it up. Kent was the kind of person who'd give you the shirt off his back if that's what you needed. I don't understand either why he ignored Fraser."

Dave Morley practically repeated Dena's statement verbatim. He'd never seen Fraser Unsworth taking lessons at the shop, nor had he ever heard Kent mention giving lessons to Fraser. "Not that we talked about every thing in our private lives," Dave explained over the phone, "but Kent spoke of other students of his. Outside school, that is. He had given guitar lessons to a number of people, and I never heard Fraser's name come up. You'd think if he was anywhere near performance level, Kent would've given him a few minutes to sing during our gigs."

After ringing off, McLaren called Dena again. She sounded amused to talk to him so soon but listened thoughtfully to his question.

"You said Kent gave of himself to anyone—well, just about anyone—who asked."

"Yes. It was well known."

"And you said he'd give the shirt off his back."

"I meant it figuratively, Michael. But he *did* give whatever he had, if he could spare it or not."

McLaren's breath caught in his throat. He asked rather sharply, "Like what? Do you know any specific thing?"

"This is important, isn't it?"

"Yes."

"Well, I remember once or twice seeing Kent give money to Fraser's friend. Just a pound or two. He'd do that periodically, give a bit of money to someone. And one time he drove somewhere with some bloke. I don't know if he took him to a shop or the bus depot or where. I'd heard them talking in Kent's front garden."

"Anything else?"

"Just something of no consequence."

"What?"

"Last spring—last year, not this year—"

"Months before Kent was murdered."

"Just that last spring Fraser wanted to try out for a music group at school. He wanted desperately to get into the group, to make a good impression with the judging committee. Kent gave Fraser a new guitar capo and guitar strap, and a box of flat picks."

"Do you know what kind?"

"Of picks?"

"Yes. And capo."

"You're serious."

"Please, Dena."

"I should think flat picks that he used. Fender heavies with holes punched in them."

"You know this?" He couldn't keep the astonishment from his voice.

"Yes. He constantly lost them. I'd find them on the pavement outside his house and he'd joke about keeping a supply in his car."

And he threw them out to the crowd as souvenirs, McLaren recalled. "You wouldn't know about the capo, by chance."

"Fraser stopped Kent as he came home one day from school. Kent had just got out of his car and they talked on the pavement. Kent opened his guitar case and handed Fraser a capo. One of his own. One of those made of the thick, heavy elastic and grommets near the ends to tighten it."

****

Jamie arrived in a police car devoid of flashing blue lights or screeching siren. In fact, he rolled up behind McLaren's car so smoothly and silently that his tap on McLaren's car window was the first McLaren knew of Jamie's arrival. McLaren reiterated his case findings to Jamie, running over his reasoning in case he had overlooked anything. Jamie listened without interrupting, mentally sliding the puzzle pieces together as McLaren talked. At the end of the explanation Jamie nodded toward Fraser, who sat on his front porch strumming his guitar. "You do the talking. It's your case."

The boy looked up as McLaren and Jamie came up the walk. He appeared to be sixteen or seventeen, with brown eyes and short, brown hair combed back behind his ears. His arms were free of tattoos prevalent in the current society, but the fingernails of his right hand were long. For finger picking, McLaren thought as he halted a few feet from the teen. Fraser stopped playing and set the guitar to his right side before he asked what they wanted.

"Some help on a case I'm investigating," McLaren said as Jamie stood at ease a few feet to Fraser's left. "This is Police Detective Kydd and I'm Michael McLaren." He let their names and their significance sink in before he continued. "I understand you knew Kent Harrison, your former neighbor. Is that correct?"

Fraser slowly got to his feet. "Yes. I knew him. Nice man." He glanced toward the street. "What's this about?"

"You've got a girlfriend."

"Yeah." His voice quivered. "Something happen to Constance?" He eyed Jamie, then glanced at the police car. "You're police. Is that why you're here, because she's hurt?"

"Your father mentioned her when I was last here."

"Oh, yes? I don't remember."

"You were in the back room, tuning your guitar. Your father said you were practicing for something and implied it was something for her." He gave Fraser a moment to absorb what he was saying. "You got a capo and some guitar picks from Kent."

"Yeah. Like I said, he was a nice guy. He'd give you anything."

"But he wouldn't give you lessons. Or advice." McLaren stepped toward Fraser. "May I see that capo?"

"Are you kidding? You want to see my guitar capo? You're nuts!"

"Is this it?" McLaren reached down and picked up the capo. He held it out so Jamie could see it. It was a small, palm-sized tool that clamped around the neck of a guitar to raise the pitch of the strings. A steel bar, about three inches long, was padded in a cylinder of hard rubber. To secure the bar to the guitar neck the guitarist stretched two heavy lengths of elastic around the back of the neck and fastened them to the tip of the metal bar, slipping the tip into one of the holes. "It's seen some hard use, Fraser. The elastic is frayed." He tapped on the ends of the two lengths of elastic. The tape that deterred the fraying was missing from one piece; the other piece of tape was at an angle, nearly ready to fall off. Several small holes were spaced near two pieces' ends and grommeted, like holes in a belt. A grommet was missing from the end of the badly frayed length of elastic. "When did you lose the first grommet?"

Fraser stepped off the porch, disbelief in his eyes. "What the bloody hell does it matter? It's an old capo; it's worn out. How the hell do I know when the grommet popped out? You're insane, mate."

"I think you lost it at the boulder the night Kent Harrison died. I think you killed him, drove his body as near as you could get to the wood, carried him to the boulder and dumped him."

"You're daft. Anyway, even if I did that, why would I have a capo with me? Doesn't make sense."

"It does if you had it and your flat picks with you because you were trying to get Kent to give you a lesson. It does if you had them in your pocket, ready to serenade your girlfriend whenever the occasion arose, or in case you get a chance to try a friend's guitar. I carry mine with me." He plunged his hand into his trousers pocket and withdrew an elastic capo and a few flat picks. "Not that unusual, Fraser. Especially if you live for music and a chance to prove yourself."

Fraser darted to his right, between McLaren and a boxwood shrub, and disappeared around the side of the house. McLaren yelled to Jamie, who dashed in the opposite direction. McLaren skirted the house, plunged through the perennial beds and between bushes, then burst into the back garden. Fraser wasn't there.

McLaren yelled to Jamie, asking if he had seen Fraser. Jamie rushed into the garden. "No. He couldn't have got past me. He must be back here."

They approached the tool shed from opposite sides, motioning to each other that Jamie would go ahead to check the back of the shed and McLaren would try the door.

McLaren positioned himself at a right angle to the front corner of the building so he could see both Jamie and the shed's door. Jamie moved as silently as a falcon plunging after its prey, a mere shadow floating over the land. He eased his head around the corner, his body angled out of sight. McLaren waited, watching Jamie's taut body, ready to rush forward to tackle Fraser. Jamie stood upright suddenly and eyed McLaren, shaking his head before he crept to the opposite front corner of the shed.

Seeing that Jamie was placed strategically, McLaren inched to the building's front. Standing with his back to the façade and to the side of the door, he extended his right arm. The pounding echoed off the back of the Unsworths' house, startling the sparrows from the trees. No one opened the shed door. McLaren pounded again, calling to Fraser to come out. Still the door remained shut.

Jamie sneaked around the back and circled to the spot McLaren had vacated. From this angle several yards away he had an unobstructed view of the door. McLaren grabbed the latch and eased the door open.

The shed's interior held only gardening tools, a few terra cotta flowerpots, and bags of fertilizer. Jamie could see the back and side walls. The door took up most of the front wall dimension, and the length that was left couldn't conceal anyone. Fraser wasn't there.

Walking up to Jamie, McLaren nodded toward the house. "Unless he crashed through the hedges or scaled the wall, he's inside."

Jamie eyed the dense row of boxwood. No one

could get through that mass of branches. And the brick wall, besides being slick with moss and mold, rose over their heads, serving its purpose of keeping out people. Nodding, Jamie said, "Fraser's too short to get over the wall. Besides, there are no scuffmarks on the bricks. Shall we see if he's at home?"

The house showed no sign of life; no music or conversation flowed from the open windows, no figure showed itself. Only the back door, swinging slowly open in the breeze, hinted at recent activity.

McLaren reached the door first, but waited for Jamie. They entered slowly, peering cautiously into every gaping doorway before easing into the room. The back door opened onto a sun porch that, in turn, flowed into the kitchen. Jamie opened the pantry door, expecting Fraser to leap out, but met nothing more surprising than a half dozen aprons hanging on the back of the door.

They inched down the hallway, walking on the balls of their feet, trying to make no sound to alert Fraser of their location. The dining room and front lounge also harbored no one.

The faint sound of a window opening came from a back bedroom, and the men eased ahead. Stopping at the room's door, they peeked inside. Fraser stood by the open window, pointing a knife to his girlfriend's throat.

Chapter Twenty-Eight

"You come any closer, I'll kill her. I swear I will!" Fraser's panic filled the room. He moved the knife so that the tip of the blade touched Constance's throat. She let out a cry and closed her eyes.

"Fraser, please don't hurt her." McLaren inched through the doorway. "Nothing is worth hurting an innocent person."

Fraser backed up, pulling Constance with him, until his calves touched the wall below the window. His left arm wrapped around her shoulders, hugging her to his chest; his left hand held the knife firmly against her throat. He fumbled for the edge of the window with his right hand and half sat on the sill.

Silent as a wraith, Jamie eased from the hallway, out the back door. McLaren saw him moments later inching up to the left side of the window, embracing the wall and the obscurity it gave.

Fraser's right hand gripped the side of the window frame, balancing his body as he slid his hip onto the sill. The lower edge of the double hung window hit the teenager across his shoulders and he bent his torso slightly in readiness for his exit. In this position, Fraser's back presented itself fully to Jamie and he moved to within an arm's distance of the boy.

Seeing Jamie's shoulder behind Fraser's back, McLaren stepped farther into the room. He stood several feet from Constance, close enough to see the wet tear tracks on her cheek and the red patch of skin where the knife point pressed against her skin. The girl's eyes shone with tears and fright, and she stared at McLaren, silently pleading for help. "Stay right where you are."

McLaren held out his arms, slowly rotating his wrists so Fraser could see his hands. "I'm not armed, if that's what you're worried about. I don't have anything concealed, either." He took a small step forward. "You can check me if you want." His right hand grabbed the bottom of his shirt, ready to pull it up.

Fraser's grip of Constance's shoulders tightened. "I warned you," he barked, his voice quavering. "Don't come any closer. I don't want to hurt her, but I will if I have to."

"You'd hurt her just to get away from me?"

"That's what I said."

Constance turned her head from Fraser, her sobs nearly choking her.

Fraser pressed the knife blade flat against her throat, blanching the skin and magnifying his threat in the single action. He glared at McLaren as he yelled for Constance to shut up.

"I thought you love her."

"I do. More than my life, more than you can possibly understand."

"If you love her, why would you want to hurt her?"

"Because…" Fraser screwed up his eyes, blinking away the tears that were already trailing down his cheeks. His voice quavered, but his grip on Constance and the knife remained firm.

"Because?"

"We made a pact."

The answer startled McLaren, and for a second he couldn't think.

"We were going to be married." He shifted his eyes to meet Constance's gaze, and his voice softened. "I love her. We swore we'd go through life together as husband and wife." His bottom lip quivered and he wiped the tears from his cheeks with his free hand.

"Then if you love her, let her go."

"I don't want to live without her. It's that simple."

"Is it?" He nodded at Constance. "Is life and death and love so simple? If you love her as passionately as you claim, wouldn't you want her to live? To go on remembering and loving you?"

Fraser brought his arm up to his face and drew it beneath his nose.

"You know, Fraser, to live in someone's heart like that, like Constance would do, is an incredible thing. How many people are loved so deeply, for decades, like that? You have an uncommon love if your feelings for each other are that strong. Don't throw it away, Fraser. On either of you. Love and life are too precious to destroy either so wantonly."

Fraser blotted his teary eyes on the back of his hand and sniffed. Constance murmured that she loved him and wanted to become a family with him. The boy pressed his lips together, his throat quivering.

"We can talk about this, you know." McLaren's voice was low and smooth, barely audible above the crying. "This isn't the only way out of your difficulty, Fraser. Please let Constance go and we'll talk." He had inched forward, barely perceptible, while he talked, keeping the teenager's focus on his speech. As he finished, he stopped. He could grab Constance if he wished.

Fraser bent forward, easing his shoulders out the window. His left hand slid down Constance's left arm to grip her wrist. The knife pointed at her midriff. "Yeah, we'll talk. You'll talk and I'll be inside a jail cell. No dice, mate. I'm not stupid. Now, back up." He pulled Constance after him as he ducked his head to clear the window frame.

McLaren lunged for Constance's arm. His fingers had barely closed around her wrist, pulling her aside, before he realized he'd been stabbed.

Fraser's startled yell drowned out Constance's scream. She leaned against McLaren, sobbing onto his shoulder. She seemed oblivious to the soothing caresses against her hair—and to McLaren's right hand pressed against his side, trying to stem the flow of his blood.

****

Late that afternoon, after he had been treated and released from hospital, he lay on the sofa in his front room, propped up by pillows and comforted by tea, soup, and Dena's kisses. But, by the anxiety shining in her eyes, she needed comforting, too, so Jamie again repeated the doctor's assurance that the knife had missed vital organs, that McLaren would be very sore for a week or two, and that he would fully recover with no ill effects.

During the telling Dena scrutinized Jamie's face with the intensity of a defense attorney questioning a suspect. But third time was the charm, evidently, and she gave Jamie a small smile, thanking him as she made room for herself on the sofa.

"Constance is all right," Jamie added, not sure if

Dena heard him now that she held McLaren's hand. "And Fraser's enjoying a restful stay in one of the Force's best cells, so all's well, as they say."

McLaren grimaced and grabbed his side as he struggled to sit straighter. "Did I thank you for your help?"

"Yeah, you did, but you can say it again." Jamie swallowed the last of his coffee and grinned. "I'm glad you're still around to ask."

"Me, too." Dena brought McLaren's hand to her lips and kissed it. "I'm sorry, Michael, for messing up your investigation. I thought I would be a help, but I just succeeded in causing problems."

McLaren opened his mouth, ready to vent his frustration and fear, to voice his earlier thoughts. He had been ready to scold her, to yell that he never wanted to go through that again, that he couldn't function if he had to worry about her every time he worked a case. But seeing her eyes, the concern painted across her features, and hearing the regret in her voice stopped his words. Of course she was sorry. Besides, hadn't she suffered more than he had?

He kissed her cheek, murmuring it was the most interesting case he'd worked on in years.

"And here I thought it all had to do with the Minstrels Court," she said.

"At least the event isn't tainted by the memory of Kent's murder. They'll have a dedication to him each year—something like naming one of the musical evenings after him."

"That's super. The fete's too nice to live under a cloud like that. A lot to learn and many nice things to look at."

"Too bad Fraser couldn't be part of the performances," Jamie said. "I realize he wasn't quite ready to perform, but attacking a potential employer with a rock is no way to gain a job. Did the guitar pick in the car park point you to him, Mike?"

"That clinched it, but I had suspicions from talking to him, Dave, and Ellen. Then seeing Fraser's demeanor when he asked Dave for help prodded me to consider him more seriously."

"So Fraser killed Kent Harrison, then," Dena said.

McLaren nodded, still amazed at the story. "He was consumed with jealousy. Kent helped everyone under the sun but wouldn't help Fraser."

"Why not? Did Fraser say?"

"It all stemmed from Fraser's get-rich-scheme, if you want to label it that way. He wanted to impress his girlfriend. She loved music so he thought the quickest and surest way to her heart was to become a musician. He had wanted lessons from Kent, but when that didn't materialize, he thought he could short circuit his lack of talent and the years of hard work and study by getting into the business via Kent's professional associates. Kent wasn't impressed with Fraser's idea and told him so. Fraser, seeing only the people Kent had helped and Constance just out of reach, exploded in anger and jealousy. Why was he any different from the dozens Kent had helped? But Kent refused to compromise his integrity and wouldn't get Fraser an audition with a music producer he knew in Manchester."

"No easy road to stardom for Fraser, then."

"No. Just years of hard work. Which he didn't want to put in. That's when Fraser plotted Kent's murder."

"How did Fraser get Kent's body to the boulder?

His car was parked in the dirt track near the wood."

"Kent drove the car to the area, planning to meet Fraser there for a talk."

"Odd place for a talk. Why not at his home?"

"Fraser told Kent he wanted to ask his opinion about an outdoor pageant he and a few friends wanted to put on. They were going to hold it at night and Fraser needed Kent to see the area as it would be, with the lighting. I don't believe Kent thought it suspicious or odd, for he obviously met Fraser there."

"How did the car get back to Kent's driveway?"

"A friend of Fraser's drove it back after Fraser killed Kent and dumped his body in the wood. The police found several strands of hair from an unknown person in Kent's car, but couldn't match it to anyone. Fraser walked slightly behind Kent as they entered the wood so he easily coshed Kent with a rock, knocking him out and easily strangling him. He used a rock on Ellen Fairfield, too. I don't know if he was going to kill her or if he was merely venting his anger. But that rock attack seemed like a prelude to murder and reminded me of Kent's assault. It was just too coincidental."

"That's why Fraser had no marks on his arms, then," Dena said. "Kent didn't have time to hit back in defense. Poor Fraser. He should've left well enough alone."

"He compounded the problem by lying about his dad's return home that Sunday night. He said he stayed up and talked to Aaron about his mother leaving them. Aaron had told me he'd gone straight to bed. If Aaron told me the truth, he wouldn't know Fraser wasn't home."

"He was probably killing Kent at that moment."

Dena shuddered and lowered her head. "But what about the hydrangea in Kent's stomach? Were two people trying to kill him?"

"Fraser stole some of the hydrangea buds from his dad. Aaron was writing that natural foods cookbook, if you remember. He had a lot of different plants, spices and herbs in the house so he could experiment with his original recipes. I don't think he even missed the buds when Fraser took them."

"He probably took a little bit at a time so he wouldn't be found out."

"But it was too slow for Fraser. He was impatient. His anger dictated he kill Kent immediately."

Dena trembled and squeezed McLaren's hand. "The poor, dear man. I'm sorry it ended that way."

"I wouldn't have been if Jamie hadn't been around to help."

"Speaking of which…" Jamie set down his coffee mug, grabbed his car key, and stood up. He looked at his friend, a faint smile at the corners of his lips. "Get some rest, Mike. You'll need it because, knowing you, you'll be neck-deep into helping someone else tomorrow."

Author's Notes

Tutbury Castle is real, of course, and is home to many activities throughout the year, thanks to castle curator Leslie Smith's hard work.

Since story, as well as murder, is all about conflict, I set up conflict between two grand structures and their curators.

Rawlton Hall does not exist except in my mind. I have patterned it after many such places I've visited.

"The Swans' Song" is my creation. I wrote the lyrics based on traditional verses from "The Bird Song," a folk song contained in the classic collection of Child Ballads. Hopefully folk purists won't be upset, but someone had to write the original bird song in the first place. I've just added to the history.

Last Seen has a companion song. "The Swans' Song" is available on a single-song CD recording. This contemporary-style folk song, arranged and performed by Bryan Toben and Lola Hennicke Toben, is available through the author's website:

http://www.johiestand.com/lastseen.html

McLaren has his own website. Log on to learn about quirky British customs, interesting places to visit in the UK, cooking recipes, music anecdotes, and a calendar of appearances by the author:

http://www.mclaren-mysteries.com

I apologize for any mistakes that may have crept into the story, but they are solely mine.

~*Jo A. Hiestand*
St Louis, MO

Acknowledgments

Accolades to Leslie Smith, Curator of Tutbury Castle, for supplying information and inspiration, and for enthusiastically answering my endless questions about the castle's layout, history, and events.

Also to Charlotte Pietrzak, Tutbury Castle, for supplying visual help and answers.

Thanks to Dr. Gareth Williams, of the British Museum, for help in hunting down Tutbury Castle maps.

A doff of my hat to Dr. Ruth Anker for aiding me in dispatching our victim.

My deepest gratitude and friendship, as always, to Detective-Sergeant Robert Church, Derbyshire Constabulary, and Detective-Superintendent David Doxey, Derbyshire Constabulary (ret.), for unlimited, untiring expert help in detection, proper procedure, and forensics.

And accolades to Paul Hornung, St. Louis-area police officer, who returned the new and improved manuscript amid an arrest.

This book could not have been written without any of these professionals' help, to whom I most sincerely thank in a most inadequate manner.

Thanks also to Cindy and Lori of The Wild Rose Press, Inc., who believed in McLaren and gave him another appearance.

A word about the author...

Books, scouting, and music filled Jo A. Hiestand's childhood. She explored the joys of the outdoors through Girl Scout camping trips and summers as a canoeing instructor and camp counselor. Brought up on classical, big band, and baroque music, she was groomed as a concert pianist until forsaking the piano for the harpsichord. She plays a Martin guitar and has sung in a semi-professional folkgroup in the US and as a soloist in England.

This mixture formed the foundation for her writing. A true Anglophile, Jo wanted to create a mystery series that featured a British police detective who left the Force over an injustice and now investigates cold cases on his own. The result is the McLaren Mysteries.

Jo's insistence on accuracy—from police methods to location layouts—has driven her innumerable times to Derbyshire. These explorations and conferences with police friends provide the detail filling the books.

In 1999 Jo returned to Webster University to major in English. She graduated in 2001 with a BA degree and departmental honors.

She has combined her love of writing, board games, and music to co-invent a mystery-solving game, *P.I.R.A.T.E.S.*, which uses maps, graphics, song lyrics, and other clues to lead players to the lost treasure.

Jo founded the Greater St. Louis Chapter of Sisters in Crime, serving as its first president. She is also a member of Mystery Writers of America. Besides her love of mysteries and music, she enjoys photography, reading, change ringing, and her backyard wildlife.

Her cat Tennyson shares her St. Louis home.

http://www.johiestand.com

Thank you for purchasing
this publication of The Wild Rose Press, Inc.

If you enjoyed the story, we would appreciate your
letting others know by leaving a review.

For other wonderful stories,
please visit our on-line bookstore at
www.thewildrosepress.com.

For questions or more information
contact us at
info@thewildrosepress.com.

The Wild Rose Press, Inc.
www.thewildrosepress.com

Stay current with The Wild Rose Press, Inc.

Like us on Facebook

https://www.facebook.com/TheWildRosePress

And Follow us on Twitter
https://twitter.com/WildRosePress